For Claire, the first to get excited

A Perilous Margin

Alison Theresa

Wernbrook Publishing, London

2016

Published by Wernbrook Publishing

First Edition First Printing, 2016

ISBN 978-1-5262-0249-9

www.alisontheresa.wordpress.com

"We are on a perilous margin when we begin to look passively at our future selves."

George Eliot

Middlemarch

Acknowledgements

Thank you to Robert Murphy, Michelle Fielding and Dot Wright for reading and commenting on very early chapters.

Thank you to Claire Dodds-Eden for reading an early draft and making it all seem real and possible.

Thank you to Celine Kelly from the Writers' Workshop for providing invaluable advice.

Thank you to Beth Gibson, Brendan Gibson, Dot Wright and Judith Witheridge for reading, and rereading, the final draft and giving useful, funny and encouraging comments.

1983

PROLOGUE

It was a relief to have reached closing night. Caroline stood in the dark on the front step, her sixth cigarette of the evening balanced between two fingers and her coat buttoned to the neck. It was the winter solstice and Sydney had plunged into an uncharacteristic cold snap. She wished she had gloves.

A burst of laughter from inside the gallery reached her and she knew she had to go back in, one final time. She stubbed out her cigarette, the last of the smoke curling around her tongue.

Inside, Lawrence and his few closest friends were lounging on the floor. Caroline hesitated outside the seemingly closed circle. She could see two bottles of red wine and a bottle of whiskey sitting within the group, the dark glass of the bottles hiding the remaining liquid. Lawrence had hardly drunk in months while he was putting together the exhibition and she could hear his now heavy tongue pushing itself around his mouth, attempting to make words. The larks of his friends sounded cruel in the circumstances, although they too were deranged with drink.

Caroline saw Bridget reach a hand towards Lawrence, as though to pull words more articulately from his mouth, her fingers hovering just inches from his lips which were stretched in a pained smile. He cackled suddenly, loudly, his teeth bright in the half-light, and Bridget shrieked. Her beauty, eye-catching in most situations, was overwhelming in the dimmed light and Caroline tried to ignore the pull of jealousy as the woman's long fingers rested against Lawrence's arm.

She decided to leave them to their games. Her exhaustion was more than physical and she was unsure what to do. She just needed to not be here anymore, to not be worrying about Lawrence and how he might be feeling.

Her three sculptures had attracted the most attention, although they had sat outside the glare of the spotlights which shone on Lawrence's paintings. Visitors had approached with wide smiles and warm handshakes to congratulate her and she had smiled her thanks. It was difficult to appreciate her own success, however, while Lawrence skulked uninterrupted through the gallery. Even his friends had struggled to find positive comments to make about his strange, muddled paintings.

But now it was over, and it was time for it to feel over. She wondered if there was anything left that needed packing up.

A sudden, yelping sound called her attention back to the group. Lawrence was lying like a cockroach on his back, his head twisting this way and that while Bridget crouched over him in mimicry of an exorcism. The howls of laughter spurred him on, his movements became more violent, distressed, genuine. Bridget began backing away, her knees shuffling over the wooden floor, the drunken expression on her face unable to react to the situation. Penny had already stopped laughing and reached a hand over, her palm soft against Lawrence's cheek and her head dipping towards his ear. Caroline could see her lips, stained red from the wine, moving, but the words were inaudible. A few moments passed before he stopped writhing, though his chest continued heaving as his friends looked at each other nervously.

Penny caught Caroline's eye. "You should probably take him home," she said. The directive would have been out of place coming from someone else but Penny was practically family and Caroline nodded.

It took over an hour to get him back to their one-bedroom flat in Ashfield. Caroline, expecting their late return, had left the lamp on over the desk, and the soft light as she opened the door welcomed them home. The walls of their flat were a mottled grey, the curtains an almost see-through beige, and the combined effect was comforting, if colourless.

She manoeuvred Lawrence into the room and was relieved that his brain began functioning again with the familiar surroundings. He dropped his head onto her shoulder and mumbled something, planting a wet kiss at the base of her neck before extracting his arm from her grasp. The bathroom door slid shut behind him with a thud.

She began to feel drunk. The heavy responsibility for another person had kept her focused on the journey home.

Now, the room spun slowly. She let her bag drop to the floor and sat at the desk, her head in her hands. The sound of Lawrence retching made her temples throb.

The bathroom door opened behind her and a loud thump told her that Lawrence's shoulder had made contact with it. His steps stumbled through to their bedroom, and she heard the creak of the bedsprings. She thought about going in and lying next to him. She imagined the stench of alcohol and vomit, and it made her nauseous. The glow from the lamp warmed the faded green of the couch beside the desk, and she pulled herself onto it. It was too short so she tucked her legs up. She knew that she would wake up cold and stiff, but it would be nothing compared to how Lawrence would feel, failure blooming painfully from the midst of a hangover.

As her body relaxed into the couch she had time to smile slightly through her liquored exhaustion. The guilt that her work had received more praise than Lawrence's faded away and she thought uninterrupted about her sculptures. A calm spread through her as she remembered their creation: the days and weeks and months of painstaking, frustrating work, culminating at last in satisfaction. Two were figures, one was abstract, all of them called to mind the tension she felt about being herself. Somehow, creating a physical representation of that tension had made her face it in a way she never had before and had been a way to see herself clearly for the first time. Sleep crept over her and she enjoyed a private moment of pure satisfaction.

2013

ONE

Andie unpinned the name badge from the front of her shirt and dropped it into her bag, ready for the next day. The security man, chatting to his girlfriend via the bluetooth piece in his ear, waved her out of the store while he did one last sweep between the racks of fashionably ragged clothes. Andie stood on the footpath outside, clutching the store keys in her hand. She didn't like using this exit but they had to at the end of the night. It led them out to a narrow, suburban street which, although only a block from the main road, felt desolate. At this time of night there were few cars and no pedestrians, and the towering blocks of flats created a solid darkness despite the streetlights.

Andie's phone vibrated against her keys in her bag but she ignored it; it was probably George telling her to hurry up. At ten minutes past eleven she was running slightly late but not enough for a phone call, surely. The security guard emerged and stood behind her as she turned the lock on the door. It slid greasily into place.

"See you tomorrow," she said and he waved, nodding enthusiastically but speaking only to his girlfriend on the phone.

The pub where she was meeting George was a couple of

blocks away on the main street. It was a pub she had history in and generally tried to avoid, and she wished George had suggested meeting somewhere else. She was, however, looking forward to a cold glass of cider and a comfortable chair and, keeping her mind on that, she marched uphill, undistracted by the revellers around her.

King Street was busy with its normal Friday night crowds: a mixture of university students in mismatched clothes and the older generation – real adults, in Andie's mind – who were wearing suits and had probably come from the city for the slightly different nightlife on offer.

Two bouncers were guarding the door to the pub, their black shirts stretched across the muscles running over their chests and arms. They weren't tall but their bulk gave the impression of height. They waved her through without checking her ID and she tried to be pleased that she looked unquestionably old enough to enter.

George was sitting on the top floor at a table for two, staring at his phone, one hand wrapped around the beer in front of him. It was a student pub and Andie, although a student, felt vaguely uncomfortable at twenty-seven years old. Most students who came here were barely twenty-one. She fought her way to the front of the bar and ordered a cider from a barman with a baby face and blonde hair. She couldn't help glancing cautiously at the crowd before she joined George at his table.

"Sorry I'm late," she said. "Long shift." They raised their glasses to say cheers and Andie drank quickly. It was the first day that felt like spring was pushing its way into the city and she was grateful for the cool, light drink after feeling hot all day.

"Oh well, it's over now," George said, leaning forward. "What are you up to tomorrow?"

The DJ was remixing Michael Jackson's Billie Jean with the Rolling Stones' You Can't Always Get What You Want, creating an unexpectedly catchy dance beat. No one was dancing, however, as the streetlights shining through the windows ruined the anonymity of the dancefloor.

"It's Saturday," Andie had to half-shout over the music. "That means studying and work again at five." She took another drink.

"The semester has barely started, how on earth do you have so much studying to do?"

"A communication degree is different to most Arts degrees, you know," Andie said, leaning even further forward as the noise surged. In front of them was a pool table where a dozen young men seemed to have created their own drinking game.

"Oh come off it! You're only taking two courses at the moment! Is that even allowed?"

"I know!' She clutched her head in her hands. "I got a letter from Centrelink telling me to confirm that I'm a full-time student!"

"Pick up another course, you lazy girl!" George laughed loudly.

"But I hate them all!"

She had already told him this. She had chosen to do a Media and Communications degree because it seemed like a faintly creative choice which would help her to get a well-paid job afterwards. But she had been struggling for two years to complete the courses necessary to finish the degree, preferring to take other Arts courses – sociology, philosophy, art history – which were open to her but would not directly contribute to her degree.

"Do another Arts subject, who cares if it takes you a decade to get a degree at least you won't lose your benefits!"

She nodded. He was always right. "I will. I went to a tutorial during the week to test out a new class. I'll probably sign up." She could already see the bottom of her glass. "Can we go somewhere else?" She asked as George finished his drink as well.

"Really?" He said, staring at her incredulously. "It's been two years Andie! And it's the best pub on King Street!'

"And I've avoided him successfully for two years, I don't want to stop now. Come on, he always used to come here. Please?"

"Fine!" George stood up so quickly that his knees set the table wobbling and their empty glasses clattered over. He disappeared while Andie was still trying to right them and she had to run after him. She found him outside on the footpath, his hands stuffed in his pockets as he watched people queuing for pies in the store next door. He didn't meet her eyes.

"Where to, then?" He asked.

But Andie's Friday night mood had deflated and she shrugged. "Home?" She expected a fight or at least an accusation of being lame but George just nodded in agreement. They had been sharing for over a year now in a converted two-bedroom flat with a concrete terrace barely wide enough to hold a few bedraggled herbs in pots. It wasn't fancy but it had immediately felt like home, helped by the fact they had almost a decade of friendship behind them already.

George dropped an arm around her shoulders, pulling her to him. "Sorry, I didn't mean to be a jerk about Leon."

"I'm sorry I'm such a girl," she said, and he grinned at her.

They turned towards home. The light spring wind had kept the sky clear of clouds, and as they walked a quarter moon slowly rose above the streetlights.

***

Andie's uncertainty about her degree felt trivial when she arrived at the University of Sydney the following week. She had never known what the term 'hallowed halls' meant, but when she walked between the buildings that housed the Darlington campus nothing could seem clearer. In a country whose infrastructure was glorified if it was fifty years old, the century-old university seemed impossibly historical.

The campus sat to the south-west of the city with Parramatta Road, a great artery pushing traffic from the city through to western Sydney, along its side. The north-east bordered Victoria Park, a pleasant haven separating the university from Broadway and its strip of grey, mostly closed shops. Running off Broadway was City Road, a street full of traffic trying to get into the city, barren of any attractions until it morphed into King Street further south, the pedestrian-oriented thoroughfare which served the crowds of Newtown.

The campus itself was impressive, and to Andie it always felt miraculous that she could belong in such a place. The sandstone quadrangle, dating from the mid-nineteenth century, seemed like a small cousin of Oxford, less noble perhaps but sitting under a blue sky rarely seen over the English institution.

A jacaranda tree had overtaken one corner of the quadrangle and while its branches were bare for much of the year, the burst of purple each November, signalling the end of the academic year and the approaching summer holidays, more than made up for it. The quadrangle and surrounding halls were the emotional, if not geographical, heart of the university, and provided photo opportunities that the modern, frequently graffitied buildings failed to supply.

The most imposing modern building was Fisher Library, a creation of the mid-twentieth century with an impressive collection at the disposal of humanities students. It was to this building that Andie made her way, to the top floor where desks were lined up single-file and lights within aisles flickered on and off as students came and went. This was where Andie would stay, her head bent over her book and dust floating unnoticed onto the back of her exposed neck, until she had to go to work that evening.

She settled in, casting a cautious glance around to ensure she had no associations with any of the other students, before she began to read the text for her course. It was for a combined art history/sociology course called A Sociological Approach to Culture, Media and the Arts which she had managed to pick up during the week in order to satisfy the requirements of the welfare office. They were already three weeks into the semester, however, and she had had a hard time catching up with the reading. Now, finally, she was on track and the text she was reading, "The Artist in the Non-Artistic World", was for the forthcoming week.

"An artist," her text read, "cannot help but create. Creative thoughts may be common to many people but what sets the artist aside is their ability to channel those thoughts, that everyday material, and create something new. Ordinary thoughts and emotions become extraordinary in the hands of an artist. Some artists take this as a sign that their thoughts and emotions are themselves extraordinary. The truth, however, is that the more mundane and habitual their life is the greater resonance their art can have. That said, many people believe that an artist's belief in their own extraordinariness is what gives them the confidence to create."

She paused, and scribbled in the margins: *artists as necessarily self-delusional?* The lecturer, Enzo, a man with curling grey hair hanging to his shoulders and a heavy Italian accent, had hinted at something like this at the lecture the day before. She opened her notebook with its cracked plastic cover, looking for her notes from the lecture.

Her handwriting detailed aspects of Picasso's life, which was clearly just an introduction to the topic of the self-belief of artists. Her handwriting became sparse, however, a strange collection of words which were now impossible to put together into an argument. She had forgotten what the main ideas of the lecture had been. She removed the hair band from her head. Her hair retained its ponytail shape and she ran her fingers through it impatiently.

She had attended the tutorial the previous week to see if she wanted to sign up for the class, and had been slightly amused by her fellow students. They enjoyed making grand generalisations about the power of art and the misunderstandings endured by artists, something which most of them took quite personally. She had been alternately amused and appalled by their ability to speak openly of their own brilliance, or potential brilliance. Although in some ways she envied these people who could hold their work up to the world and demand a place for it, she was also looking forward to referring them to this passage of the reading. She underlined 'mundane' twice, just for fun.

She reread the passage in the text. "A person who believes their thoughts and emotions are as ordinary and common-place as the next person's will never have the necessary drive to use those experiences to create art." She wrote in the margin again, *Shari, Melanie, Manuel?* The four of them had gone for a drink after the tutorial. The evening had consisted of those three bellowing about how terribly they had been treated by family, or friends, or lovers, and how the trauma informed their art. She had wondered, while listening to their conversation and drinking quickly, if they really thought that being treated mildly worse than they perhaps deserved caused enough emotional damage to make their art better than it would otherwise have been. She had been new to their circle, however, and had remained quiet and sympathetic in the interest of making new friends. Declarations of anguish had always felt false to her, however, and she was looking forward to their next social meeting when she would feel more able to express herself.

The library buzzed with murmurings of people beginning or ending their studies. If she had looked out the window she would have seen a colourful tent being set up, with volunteers trying to entice the passing students into signing a petition. Instead, she stared at the words *self-delusional* in the margins, wondering if such a state could be created in the interest of becoming an artist, wondering if she could ever be brave enough to create such a delusion in herself. She pushed the thought away, sure that the text should have mentioned the need for some natural talent as well and knowing that that, as ever, would be her stumbling block.

TWO

Several others had already made their exits, blaming work or children for their departures, when Caroline began her farewells. They had been a table of twelve friends and dinner had been held in comfortable companionship. Caroline offered her good wishes to Daniel, whose birthday the dinner was celebrating, and looked inquiringly at Lawrence, aware that his attention had been focused on Anya since dessert.

They often travelled separately these days as their aging constitutions handled alcohol and socialising differently. She was unsurprised, therefore, that Lawrence was staying. "Good night, Caroline," he said, and she saw his watery eyes struggle to move in her direction, making a swoop via Anya's cleavage. The woman was young, in her early thirties perhaps, with cheeks flushed pink from the bottles of wine the table had shared during dinner, and the exclusive whisky that Lawrence had presented to Daniel with more pomp than necessary for a good friend.

Caroline leant forward to kiss Penny goodbye, then waved a general farewell to the rest of the table. The few remaining guests farewelled her, including Maggie, Daniel's partner, who smiled sympathetically. As Caroline turned, disentangling her legs from those of the chair, she heard Lawrence's silky drunken voice and a giggle from Anya.

She smiled to the waiter who had served them and was now standing near the door. He was tall, and she felt the slight stoop which had overtaken her shoulders in middle-age cause her neck to twist as she looked up at him. His dark hair swooped over his forehead and covered his ears, each of which sparkled with studs. Below his shirt, unbuttoned now that the manager had left, she spied a gold cross. His 'goodbye' lilted with his Italian accent as he handed her her coat and smiled. She wanted to smile flirtatiously back but was too aware of the decades between them.

The night air had a bite to it after the rain which had swept in off the ocean to cover the city during the afternoon. The footpath was still stained a dark grey from the downpour, and the street lights of Glebe Point Road shimmered off the remaining puddles.

Caroline's shoes made dull thumps against the concrete. It was a thirty-minute walk to City Road and she toyed with the idea of catching a taxi. The rain-freshened air, however, was perfect for the film which had settled over her eyes and so she continued walking.

The timing of the dinner was fortunate. Lawrence had finished the paintings for his new collection and was days away from starting work with the gallery to begin the layout of the exhibition. He had been a ghost in the house for months, flickering into the kitchen occasionally to take tea, coffee, or the cranberry juice his doctor had suggested he start drinking, back to his studio. Most days he would give her a smile or a kiss as he passed. Sometimes he would pause for longer, hold his arms around her, ask her about her day.

The exhibition was an almost guaranteed success thanks to his reputation, and the difference in his mood as he worked now compared to twenty years earlier was astounding. He still, of course, had lapses of confidence when the expectations became a visibly physical burden. At such times his presence was sudden beside her, his eyes drooping from lack of sleep, his breathing shallow. She would stop what she was doing and take his hand. There was little she could do except watch the doubts burn themselves out behind his eyes. Such times were over, for now, and the social evening had allowed him to clear the cobwebs after the solitary work. He was in his element, and she was happy to leave him to it.

Two women, university students she guessed from their age, and two older men fell laughing from the door of a Mexican restaurant. The women wore high heels which quivered from holding up their weight, and colourful jackets which looked warm compared to their bare legs. Caroline slowed her step, trying to avoid overtaking them, but they hailed a taxi and disappeared inside it. She quickened her pace again and the alcohol in her system made the exertion comfortable. Each lungful of air added to her strength and her shoes felt solid on her feet compared to the unsteady stilettos she had just seen. She almost felt young, until she remembered the young woman Anya at dinner.

The junction with Parramatta Road loomed in front of her. A solitary truck sat at the red-light, its indicator flashing orange onto the wet road beneath it.

A Perilous Margin

Normally she would walk around Victoria Park in favour of the safer, longer route which followed the line of the road. Tonight, however, she entered the green space, her feet unable to turn around once she had begun the journey. The trees curved above her, creating the illusion of a forest. The path dipped down towards a small lake which had a thick layer of yellow leaves covering its surface, like a pond of gold. A splash as a duck abruptly changed its position made her heart pound, but her legs remained at their determined pace. She continued on towards the university, whose buildings sat dark and heavy at the edge of the grass. Some shouts of laughter reached her and she relaxed, knowing that others were around. She emerged from the canopied walkway onto the wide pedestrian thoroughfare which ran towards the main quadrangle. It was strange being on the campus without Lawrence. The thirty years since she had graduated hovered in her peripheral vision.

If she turned left she would be on the path towards City Road and her bus stop. She took a right and continued towards the Great Hall which sat on the corner of the quadrangle. The lights from the city were reflected back to earth from the heavy clouds, creating a mixture of foiled night and make-believe day.

She turned left behind the quadrangle and shivered with a momentary claustrophobia as she passed through the connected arms of the building. Empty buildings at night always held their own ghosts, she thought. The area she emerged into was newer but rattier than those she had just left. She strolled down the road gazing at the buildings which had been created since her time as a student.

She and Lawrence disagreed about the first time they had met. He claimed she had been waiting outside a lecture hall, on this road where she was now walking, keeping an eye out for a friend who she usually sat with. He had approached her and asked her for a match, which she had provided, and they had begun talking. She had then ignored him in favour of her friend who arrived to interrupt what Lawrence claimed had been a scintillating conversation. She had no memory of this and enjoyed teasing Lawrence about confusing her with another woman.

What she remembered was a party. It was the launch of an underground art magazine which had made it to its third edition before folding quietly. The launch was raucous, a crowd of people squashed into a terrace house in St Peters, unable to venture far into the building thanks to its dilapidated skeleton. Copies of the magazine were being fawned over then dropped and quickly forgotten as they were mashed into the sticky floorboards. Caroline was there because a friend had contributed a vitriolic page-long poem about the Catholic Church's influence on campus. The friend had squeezed her way into a corner with the editor and Caroline was left to herself.

She had been undecided about the quality of the magazine. The excitement of being a part of something new and shocking appealed to her. The crassness of the writing and the tacky format also spoke to her, calling her to join in the adventure. Sometimes she wondered if the integrity and style which surrounded classic works of art were simply a product of history, a white-washing of the crusty underside that actual artists brought to artistic movements. Or perhaps the dirt she was now experiencing was merely a sign that this gathering was not destined to make it into the annals of art history.

She recognised half the people there from other similarly themed parties. Although she was not in their department, she spent a lot of time socialising with people who were studying politics, visual arts, women's studies. She found them more exciting, more eager for life, than the French students with whom she studied. She made her way through the crowd, smiling greetings at some of the people she knew.

She found her way to the kitchenette, an area only distinguishable from the rest of the living room by dirty tiles on the floor and a gummy bench. A short man with thick shoulder-length black hair was leaning against the bench, his head bent towards a woman much taller than him. The woman gave a ferocious giggle and tossed her hair. Caroline saw the man raise his eyebrows at the ostentatious flirting and turn his gaze away, scanning the rest of the room. Caroline had given a sympathetic smile and moved past him, searching for a proper glass.

"Can I help you with something?"

She had glanced over her shoulder and seen the man now standing alone. She smiled at him. "I'm just looking for a glass."

"You'll be looking all night, darling." His r's rolled, highlighting a Scottish accent he seemed to be emphasising.

"That might be for the best."

"Why would you say that?" He stepped forward as though in concern.

"I have a lot of work to do tomorrow."

"Work for this – magazine?"

"No, no I'm not involved with it."

"Thank god for that. I mean for you, of course. They'd be lucky to have you, I'm sure." His voice was soft but she had no trouble understanding him over the din of the party.

"You don't like it, then?"

"It's attempting to be witty, or perhaps intellectual." He stared at her intently. "In either case, its attempts are failing." The man moved closer, his eyes unwavering from hers.

"They're only twenty years old, I think it's courageous that they're at least trying something new." She was surprised to find herself defending something which she had had no strong opinions about two minutes earlier.

"They're twenty-three years old actually, you can trust me on that." He smiled as though he had inside knowledge. "And they should be trying to be great."

The direction of their flirting started to make her uncomfortable: if he judged them like that, she didn't want to know what he thought of her.

"It was nice to meet you. Excuse me."

"You didn't meet me. I'm Lawrence." He held out his

A Perilous Margin

hand as she tried to squeeze past him. "And I'm sure I'll see you around the sociology area, again." She continued out of the kitchenette, feeling the pressure from his fingers still in her palm.

A few hours later, after she had given up and started drinking the communal punch from a mug, she saw him disappearing with the tall, giggly woman he had been talking to in the kitchenette. She had tried to ignore the slight pull of disappointment in her gut.

It was barely a week later that she saw him again. It was winter and while the sky was a clear blue the wind, which had a lick of ice in it, had everyone wrapped up in coats. Caroline had been on her way home. She had attended her first lecture of the day but was unwilling to sit through another one. She had taken to cutting class frequently, and was embarrassed by what she imagined her mother would say about the wasted opportunities. She was not embarrassed enough to stay, however, since her mother would never know, and so she was heading towards the bus stop which would take her to her sharehouse in Glebe. He was standing outside a sociology lecture theatre. His paint-stained tracksuit pants and stretched black t-shirt contrasted interestingly with her memories of a suave, arrogant man.

He was staring intently at one side of the building. It was a murky gray with some chipped paint near the base and a brown smudge to one side. "Interesting, isn't it?" She said from behind his shoulder. He turned quickly and she stepped back. The eyes that she remembered, blue and brightly lit, were narrowed and impatient.

"Oh, hi." He turned his back to her again.

"Are you working on this?"

"Trying to." He kept looking at the wall as he spoke, muttering without moving his lips. She turned to go as his obvious irritation reddened her cheeks. "Caroline," he called and she stopped, surprised that he knew her name. "Come back in a couple of hours." He was not smiling, and his eyes remained unchanged. But there was something interested, or simply interesting, in his manner. She nodded. Instead of returning home, she found some steps which caught the afternoon sun outside the quadrangle. She leant against the warmed sandstone. A couple of hours felt like a long time.

A presence behind her had blocked the sun for a few moments. Rita, a large woman Caroline's age with a bosom twice the size of most and a lot of smooth auburn hair hanging down her back, sat next to her.

"You're not going either?"

It took Caroline several moments to realise what she meant. "The lecture? I forgot. I guess I could have gone."

"Why are you hanging around?"

"No reason," she answered quickly, her voice a little breathless. Rita raised her eyebrows. "Do you know someone called Lawrence? I think he does painting."

"McGovernor? Of course I do. He's slept with half my cousin's fine-arts class. Why?" A sly smile crept onto Rita's face, "Are you waiting for him?"

"He's doing a painting over in sociology. He told me to come back in a couple of hours."

"To see his painting?"

"– Yes." She suddenly realised that he had not specified why she was supposed to come back.

"His public painting that's on the wall of a public building?"

Caroline smiled nervously. "I had nothing else to do today. It was just an empty wall when I was there earlier. It will be interesting to see what he does with it."

"He's an interesting fellow." Rita stood up, blocking the sun again. "Good luck. Be safe." She grinned broadly.

Caroline wondered if she should leave. Would she turn up in an hour to find half a dozen women, beautiful and nervous and desperate, hanging around, admiring the interesting man and his interesting wall?

"Damn it," she muttered to herself, and hurried, shoulders cowed, towards the bus stop.

Caroline stopped walking and gazed at the side of the building which used to show Lawrence's painting. She had no idea how long ago it had been painted over; it seemed at least a couple of decades since they had showcased students' work in that way. Now, a streetlight behind her shone on the faded, speckled, rain-and-sun-battered grey. She stepped gingerly, her shoes slipping on the slimy dirt disguised by the grass. She placed a hand against the wall. It felt warm. She leant her forehead against it, the concrete was rough on her skin but the sensation in her hand had told the truth: the wall was warm. There was a pressing on her chest, past choices pulled at her as she stared at what was the end of her life as it had been. She had had no idea. She had stood here, staring at the finished work days after Lawrence had sat waiting for her. She had stood here and stared at what she was sure was a portrait of herself.

THREE

Andie squinted as she stepped off the bus. Dirt had been kicked up by the wind and it whirled around her, giving the normally crisp sunlight a dark coating. She slipped on her sunglasses but still had to shield her eyes with one hand. A smattering of pale clouds flew across the sky like clouds in a pop-up book.

The campus was busy but there was a heaviness in the air, as though most of the student population had been out drinking the night before. Students wandered between classes and cafés, their footsteps laboured and their eyes squinting behind sunglasses. It was still early enough in the semester for most people to be attending lectures, though it was difficult to know how much was sinking in. Still, Andie enjoyed this time of semester, when it felt as though knowledge was the aim rather than top marks.

She was the third person to arrive at the tutorial. Marnie and Ying were already standing outside the door. The previous class was still running and the two young women were leaning against the brick wall, waiting. They were both nineteen and lived on campus. Their skirts were short and summery; their arms were long and tanned. Their hair was unbrushed and hung down past their shoulders. They exuded a sexual calm, like most of the kids who lived in the university residences, brought on perhaps by the sense that they had only just emerged from bed. The college fashion added to the image. It was casual, showed a lot of skin, and was backed up by a remarkable confidence. They barely glanced at her as she arrived.

She walked past them and sat down, leaning against the opposite wall. In her peripheral vision she could see their long limbs. She stretched her own legs out on the floor in front of her, aware of wanting to prove that she did not follow their style. She was dressed as she would have been ten years ago; a style not yet old enough to have re-entered the fashion world. It was just old enough to highlight the age difference between them.

More students wandered into the hallway. A couple of them joined Marnie and Ying leaning against the wall; others formed their own group, and Marco, the tutor, hovered to the side. The tutorial which was inside the classroom only emerged at ten minutes past three, after Marco had begun to pace up and down and peer through the plastic window in the door.

Andie stood up in the commotion of students, entered the room last and chose a seat near the middle. She found herself sitting with Shari, Melanie, and Manuel, her one-time drinking-buddies who were deep in conversation and hardly glanced at her as she sat down. She was also near Jackson, a man closer to her own age. He nodded and gave her a cursory "You right?" before returning to his book. The sound of twelve people chatting surrounded them while Marco organised his bundle of papers.

Andie had almost finished the readings in the library but had only skimmed over the last few paragraphs before she

A Perilous Margin

had to leave to go to work. She guessed that Jackson had read them, he looked like that kind of guy, but it was difficult to tell with the other students. It often emerged in her other classes that even the most opinionated students had barely looked at the introduction before the tutorial. She guessed this class would be no different.

Marco straightened and called everyone's attention to himself. He tried to tell a quick anecdote about a mishap caused by the wind, but it fell flat. Andie smiled in sympathy and saw several other students do the same. It was lucky in some ways that few students were actually listening to him. He seemed nice but he had an aura of desperation when it came to dealing with his students. He awkwardly moved on to a brief overview of the lecture then handed around discussion questions. He made them work in small groups while he circulated, occasionally laying a hand on the back of someone's chair and contributing a challenging argument if opinions were becoming too homogeneous.

Shari was leaning back, her loose white singlet allowed the black polka dots on her white bra to be clearly visible. It was a fashion statement that Andie had always found tacky. She saw Jackson glance away, keeping his eyes firmly on the questions in front of him, and felt impatience rise up in her, directed firmly at Shari and her distracting fashion sense.

Melanie started answering the first question immediately. She was doing a gender studies degree and had signed up for this course because she also took photographs in her spare time. In the previous tutorial, she had told Andie that she wanted to take photographs of people in Sydney who were marginalised because of their gender identity. Andie had wanted to suggest she go to Ballarat, or Cowra, or somewhere where the marginalisation was both more acute and more sanctioned by public opinion than in the inner suburbs of Sydney, but she had held herself back.

The first question on Marco's discussion list was about Picasso's political neutrality during war and how it affected his art. Melanie was talking about going to Barcelona and visiting the Picasso museum there. Her voice was low, with a breathy quality that made it seem as though she were worried others would disagree with her. She was skirting the question, but she was very earnest about Picasso's genius. She wound down her anecdote with a flippant, "But of course I just want to go back to Barcelona," and a dismissive flap of her right hand. She sat back in her chair, looking embarrassed to have spoken for so long.

Manuel gazed at her for several moments, ensuring that she had finished, then he started talking. He had obviously been using the time during Melanie's story-telling to mould his own answer to the question. "I think Picasso's neutrality is really a sign of his belief in his own talents, you know? Like Enzo was saying in the lecture. If he hadn't had his art as a way of dealing with the wars, maybe – well, maybe he would have been persuaded to join sides. Instead, I think he probably recognised his unique position in experiencing the wars neutrally, and his ability to create some amazing art out of those experiences – I mean, he is such a strong example of an artist in a non-artistic world, right? When everyone else is focused on war, he was like the only one thinking about how to express those experiences creatively."

"I don't think you can say he was the only one to express his experiences of war creatively," Andie interrupted. "And I don't think a world at war is a non-artistic one either." She felt much more comfortable here, in an academic environment, than she ever did socialising. "For artists, traumatic experiences will always lead to art, and Picasso wasn't the only one to create art based on any of those wars. It isn't the fact that he created war-based art which makes him interesting. What is interesting is that he was one of the only artists who remained neutral. Perhaps you could say he was saving his courage for his art?"

"I know he wasn't the only artist working during the war," Manuel sounded defensive and yet determined to be relaxed. "But I do think his position of neutrality gave him, you know, a unique edge, and I think he was aware of that and really cultivated it. He remained an outsider so his talents wouldn't be eaten up by – I mean, do you really think he'd have been as good as he was if he was working for the French resistance?"

Andie tried to look politely interested in his opinions. She felt Jackson move in his seat beside her, as though he wanted to say something, but she and Manuel had found a rhythm and it was difficult to allow anyone else in.

"The French resistance had a surprisingly large number

of artists working for them. Or not so surprising I guess, considering the French," she said.

"Were they Jewish artists, though?" Shari asked suddenly, still leaning back in her chair, her breasts pointing like headlights at the group. There was a slight pause while Manuel changed quickly from what he was about to say to answering her question.

"Yes, I think so." His eyes flicked briefly to Andie as though for confirmation. "I think a lot of immigrants from Eastern Europe who had immigrated early joined the resistance. And yes, they were Jewish."

"Well, those Jews wouldn't have been living in a non-artistic world, would they? Jewish culture has a huge history of art, doesn't it?" She asked.

Manuel looked at Andie, as though haggling over who had to answer Shari's questions. To her surprise it was Jackson who spoke next.

"There's not much of a culture of visual arts in the Jewish community. Music and writing, of course, but not really painting. It is quite frowned upon."

Andie nodded along to his answer, though she honestly had no idea about the history of Jewish art. She suspected, though could not be sure of course, that if Shari had been less attractive they would have been less inclined to tolerate her diversion. Although Shari would probably have been less willing to voice her questions as well, in that case.

"I didn't think the word 'artist' only referred to visual artists, sorry." Shari's eyes rolled.

Melanie seemed to have recovered from her anecdote, and said, "Of course it doesn't, but they had been talking about Picasso. I know in my head when you were all saying 'war artist' I was really thinking 'war painter'."

"Whatever. I just meant to say I think Andie's right and that war shouldn't be described as a non-artistic world."

"Okay," Andie said, determined to get the conversation back on track. "So war isn't a non-artistic world," she gave a slight nod towards Shari as though she had established this, "but perhaps neutrality in war is?" Jackson once again shifted beside her, so she turned to him and asked, "What do you think?"

He looked stumped by the direct question and half shrugged as his first response. Andie opened her mouth to keep speaking, but, reminding herself to be patient, closed it again and waited for him to formulate an answer.

"I have never lived through a war so it's hard to know how common the experience of it is. I suspect, I guess, that Picasso's inactivity was out of fear rather than any noble thoughts about his art. If he had been more involved maybe he could have created art which spoke more directly to the people involved. As it is, he was probably a pretty poor war artist." His cheeks had flushed red from the attention and he sat back in his chair, his fingers fiddling nervously in his lap. Andie felt a surge of sympathy for him. Despite being older than most of the students in the room, he seemed inexplicably intimidated by them. He reminded Andie of the boys she had gone to school with, the ones who were neither smart enough nor cool enough to be respected in class, but the awkward in-betweeners who paid attention and did the work but received none of the accolades.

The clock on the wall crawled its way towards four o'clock. At ten to four Marco called their attention to the front. He asked a different group what they had said about the first question on Picasso. A soft-looking man, in his early twenties but already balding around the crown of his head, answered; a hesitant whine in his voice made him difficult to listen to. Manuel took the reins for their group when Marco turned to them for input, and Andie, although annoyed, didn't interrupt.

At two minutes to four o'clock Shari closed her notebook loudly, even though the page had remained blank throughout the hour. The zip on her bag screeched over the voice of the last speaker, a young woman with jet-black hair and tattoos creeping up her neck. The speaker flicked her eyes momentarily in Shari's direction, as though daring her to make any more noise, and continued speaking. Marco also glanced quickly at Shari, and increased his show of interest in what the black-haired woman was saying, attempting to make up for Shari's rudeness. Several others in the class followed Shari's example, however. The woman speaking finished her sentence with a pointed, raised voice and sat back, throwing her hands up at the increased noise in the room.

Marco smiled apologetically and began shouting over the top of them. At the words 'major assignment' the general hubbub died out. "As I was saying," Marco said when he had everyone's attention again, "I'll be giving you some information about your field research." He waved a piece of paper at them from a stack in his hands. "I know many of you come from the art history department rather than sociology, and this assignment does try to balance that mixture of experiences. That said, field research is mandatory in a sociology course and so if you are unsure what it means, please come to see me." He shouted some closing comments over the sound of twelve people packing bags and standing up. He rubbed his throat distractedly as he finished, as though massaging his vocal chords after the brief exertion.

"Andie, is everything okay?" Marco asked when he saw her hovering inside the classroom after everyone had left. She was staring at the paper he had given them with details of the assignment on it.

"Sorry, Marco, I just wanted to ask about the report."

"Of course!" Marco looked delighted and gestured for her to sit down at one of the clusters of tables. He took the seat opposite her. "You started this course a bit late, didn't you?" He asked.

"Yes," she nodded. "I'm sorry if you told everyone else about this already. Is it really worth most of the grade?"

"Yes, it is! But don't worry, you can have some fun with it. You have to choose one of the weekly topics and interview an artist about it. For guidance, you could use one of the questions I give out to formulate a hypothesis you want to explore." He waved a piece of paper at her for emphasis. "So we've already done artists as consumers, we'll look at public art and institutions, the impact of media and technology. I heard your group today discussing whether war is a non-artistic world. So for example, you could find a war artist and explore whether the changing nature of war has affected that question. For Picasso, he was living in the war, it was all around him and around everyone he loved. That has an effect on his world which will be different for a war artist these days who actually chooses to go to a war, and is surrounded by other people who have chosen that as well." He looked at her expectantly.

"Right. The thing is, I don't know any artists."

Marco nodded. "I understand. I suggest you find an artist who you could speak to a bit, and then research them or do a general background study of them. That way you can choose a weekly topic about which they will have something to say, rather than trying to fit an artist into a hypothesis you already have."

There was a knock at the door. A young woman with thick glasses was standing there, her arms straining to hold a pile of papers and books. "Excuse me," she said, "I'm holding a tutorial here at half past. Do you mind if I set up?"

Marco jumped to his feet. "Of course not! Andie?" They left together, walking in silence as Andie struggled to think of more questions. These Arts subjects always had such slippery topics though, unlike her Communications ones which felt much more structured.

She had been intending to go to the library and do some reading for her tutorial the next morning, but she decided that starting work on this assessment would help put her mind at ease. She often walked home but that day the sun was still strong, the wind made her clothes feel misshapen and dirt scratched against her skin. As she sat on the half-empty bus she thought about what she had said in the tutorial, and what she could have said. Although she had spoken a lot, and had seemed to have the agreement of most of the other students, she was uncomfortable with her views. She was unsure if they were really her opinions or if she was simply playing devil's advocate to Manuel.

It was a habit she had picked up from her previous boyfriend, Leon. He had been so incredibly sure of himself it had made her work hard to force some proof from him about why he thought the way he did. And now it seemed it was a habit she was unable to break. It disturbed her to think that she might spend her life questioning others' opinions without ever forming her own.

The bus curved itself down King Street through the heavy traffic. The street was divided by traffic lights every two blocks, allowing Andie time to study the flow of pedestrians who were negotiating the footpath on either side. It was predominantly young people, most of whom looked like they were students. At the beginning of each year the street was overtaken by eighteen and nineteen year olds who were new to the university. Many of them were living away from home for the first time and their desperation to fit into the famed alternative scene of Newtown made them awkwardly obvious. By this time of year, however, the nerves had disappeared and their youth and beauty became the envy of the longer-established residents. It was only to last a few months, however, until a new crop appeared in February and the balance had to be reorganised once again.

The bus sank into a stop at a set of traffic lights beside the supermarket. A Big Issue seller, a small woman who had in previous months held a sign asking for money for her children, was standing beside the door. Andie knew that she was giving each passer-by a "God Bless" and a nod as she always did. On the other side of the door was a man sitting on a plastic crate, a lethargic dog with tangled fur leaning against his knees. He was not asking for money, probably aware that he was no competition for the Big Issue, but his eyes were alert as he watched the crowds pass him. Andie usually walked down this street, and seeing it from the bus made her feel like a tourist, trapped behind glass, unable to connect.

Once inside the chill of her house she made a cup of tea and sat down at her desk, the assignment paper in front of her. She had to find an artist in Sydney who would be willing to meet with her. She decided immediately that she only wanted to talk to a genuinely professional artist. She did not want to get stuck interviewing someone whose work she did not respect, and whose opinions she would find it easy to dismiss. She wondered if finding a writer would provide nice common ground.

Writing had become habitual in her early twenties when she was searching for something beautiful to dedicate her life to. It had sat uneasily within her relationship to Leon, however, and perhaps it was not a good idea to revisit such an emotional phase of her life. These days, she kept those short stories to herself, like an embarrassing secret that she refused to share. She was still humiliated by the fact that, despite desiring it so wholeheartedly, she was not very good.

If she did not choose writing, however, then what form of artist should she choose? She immediately dismissed graphic designers and anyone else working in digital arts. While she respected the imagination that went into their work, she knew that she could not feign interest in their creative process, and as such would find it difficult to build any kind of rapport with them. That left a visual artist or a musician.

Within those categories were many sub-categories, and her head began to fill with anxiety. She had seen a lot of installation work recently at an art exhibition opening, and had no desire to talk to anyone involved in creating those huge pieces of work that lacked all the subtlety which made art interesting. She needed someone established, someone who would challenge her to defend her opinions. Someone, she thought with frustration, that she could call an 'artist' without feeling like a fraud. This assignment would be much easier for those people in her class who loved and participated in the strange new forms of art which Andie could not connect with; the people who could sit in a dark bar and watch with rapture a person standing on an empty stage, silently tearing up lettuce. In many ways, Andie wished that she could appreciate work like that. It obviously spoke to a lot of people, not least those responsible for creating it. But it alluded to an emotional intelligence which she could just not see. Emotion in art was important and necessary, and as such should, she thought, be communicated as efficiently as possible. Surrounding important sentiments with triviality didn't make them more real, it only cheapened them.

Her phone rang by her elbow. "Hi Dad."

"Andie, hi. How are you?" Her father's voice was always slightly apologetic on the phone, as though he was embarrassed at having disturbed her.

"I've been at uni all day."

"Anything interesting happen?"

"The work is piling up, that's all. How has your day been?"

"Oh, fine. I walked Charlotte's dog this afternoon. That thing is getting fat and she doesn't seem to care. The poor thing'll die of a heart attack any day now and I bet you she'll cry as though she's surprised." Charlotte was Andie's sister. She and their father, Joey, lived close to each other, in a cosy burrow near the Hawkesbury River. It was a beautiful part of the country, as Joey had always told them. He had grown up there but moved into the city as a young man chasing financial security. After he had met their mother, Celine, there had been no chance to move back: she had been a firm

A Perilous Margin

city person. So much of a city person, in fact, that even Sydney didn't cut it and before Andie had finished primary-school Celine had picked up and moved to Los Angeles, chasing her dream of being the Australian Meryl Streep. By the time Charlotte and her husband Pete announced they were moving to the area that Joey had always called home, it was clear that his wife was not going to return, and he had no reason to pretend to enjoy the city. It was a good decision for all of them, Andie knew, though she was sometimes lonely being the only Hawken left in the inner-west.

"How can it be fat with all that open ground to frolic in?"

"God knows. Charlotte and Pete are distracted, obviously: Fi's finishing year five this year you know, it's a lot of pressure." There was a mixture of fatherly and grandfatherly love in his voice, with a hint of derision at the idea of a ten year old being under pressure.

"Yeah, sure. I guess they have a lot going on. How's Charlotte?"

"She seems well. The job is giving them a bit more freedom, financially, obviously. You should call her, you know. She thinks you think she's boring."

"I don't think she's boring, Dad."

"You should tell her that. I don't want to be the go-between." Their phone conversations always ended like this.

"I'll call her soon, Dad. I promise."

"We'll see you for Fi's birthday in a couple of weeks, anyhow."

"Yes, you will."

Every time she called Charlotte she felt as though the interest she showed in the domestic happenings of the Lee family sounded false, and her descriptions of her own life sounded more adventurous than they were.

Andie turned back to her assignment but couldn't concentrate. Her family had always been closely tied to art – her mother's acting, Charlotte's music, even Pete was a composer – and so this decision felt like it should be easier. All she needed was a person whose interest in art had become a fruitful career. Leaving her desk to make another cup of tea, she wondered if Celine fitted into that category now, and, if she did, what it would be like to talk to her about her art and her choices. Andie wondered what she would do if her mother told her the sacrifice had been worth it.

FOUR

Caroline and Lawrence had moved to a small, three bedroom house in Tempe in the early nineties when the longevity of Lawrence's career finally seemed assured. Tempe was a slice of suburbia hidden between industrial wasteland to the north and waterways to the east. The Princes Highway provided the surrounding streets with the sound of six lanes of constant traffic, which competed with the roar of planes coming in to land at Sydney International Airport.

Caroline's morning start felt early to her, but she was grateful that it was late enough to miss the morning commuters on the train. She had a seat and could use the time to look over the booklet for the exhibition she was going to be instructing tour guides about. They would not be going near the exhibition yet but she liked to be prepared in case of overenthusiastic questions. She had been a volunteer tour guide at this gallery for so long that they had eventually asked her to train the new batches. It only came up a few times a year since the gallery had a slow rotation of exhibitions. She enjoyed the work, generally, as the tour guides were usually respectful of both her experience and her position in the art world. Or at least her husband's position in the art world.

The only real problem had been six months ago. Caroline had noticed nothing special about the woman at first other than that they wore the same shoes: red ballet flats that were plastic, although they looked like leather. The woman, Tara, had spent the morning lambasting Caroline over Lawrence's accepting of a national prize. Caroline was used to strangers having opinions about her husband and had dealt with the attacks professionally at the beginning. The woman, however, began to combine the relentless criticism with personal, snide comments about Caroline's own art. Having a stranger in her proximity who knew about her art sent shocks through Caroline's system. She had left early that day, citing ill health. She had sat on the train and stared unseeing out of the window, her mind elsewhere, until the end of the line, and had to turn around and return to Tempe.

That woman had not been hired. Caroline was proud to say, however, that it was not because of anything she had said. She had kept her distress to herself. The woman, it turned out, had been just as rude to several other, even less deserving employees and had quickly been blacklisted as an unsuitable guide.

"Imagine," one of the offended employees had whispered to Caroline the following week, "if she was saying those things to us, what might she have said to the visitors!" Caroline had smiled, but had refused to imagine it. Lawrence had two works hanging in a permanent exhibition and she knew that their reception would always be mixed. After all, her own reception of his work was mixed, in private at least. And the woman's knowledge and criticism of Caroline's art, which had barely seen the light of day, had no bearing on her ability to be a guide. Caroline had taken responsibility for the disastrous direction the day had taken and was determined not to think ill of the woman. Although she was immensely relieved that she would never have to see her again.

The guides were already standing in a circle when she arrived. She spotted them easily: their excitement, nervousness, and youth were distinctive in the sedate atmosphere of the foyer. She lifted a smile to her face and walked over to introduce herself.

"Good morning. We're a small group today, that's nice. My name's Caroline McGovernor and I'll be taking you through your first day of training." There was the familiar buzz as she said her name. "First, I'd like to take you to my favourite spot in the gallery and we can introduce ourselves to each other properly there." She always started the same way, the routine was a balm for the nerves she sometimes had.

Caroline led the group to an alcove on the second floor. There was a set of windows with a wide view of the city. "Is that the Harbour Bridge!" One of the women said in surprise, and Caroline smiled.

"It comes out of nowhere sometimes, doesn't it? Please, sit down." The leather couches had been arranged in a square, useful for these introductory settings but a bit odd for visitors who usually preferred to gaze absently at paintings rather than at other visitors. "As I said, my name's Caroline. I've been involved in the art world, in some form or other, since the early eighties. I worked as a tour guide here for several years and have recently begun leading these training courses. Please feel free to ask questions during the day. I have encountered every type of visitor that you can imagine."

Two women in their mid-twenties smiled enthusiastically at her. Caroline felt like reminding them that she had no power to actually hire them at the end of the day. They were the oldest in the group and seemed to be the only ones who had come together. The others, Caroline guessed, and was proven correct as they introduced themselves, were still studying and hoped to use this volunteer position to help them with jobs after graduation. The two slightly older women had graduated already, and were finding paid positions difficult to come by. There was some mild banter about the job market and the industry they were in. Caroline noticed one woman, the youngest at just nineteen, staring at her intently. As the group moved on to their first room, the woman, Lucy-from-Adelaide, manoeuvred herself to be beside Caroline.

"I met your husband last week."

"Oh?"

"Yes, at the gallery where his new exhibition is."

"That exhibition hasn't opened yet."

"I know. My cousin works there though and she was showing me round. He's a wonderful artist. The power, the passion, the sex in his work! It must be amazing to see that being created." Her voice was breathy but her eyes, still focused firmly on Caroline as they walked, were steady.

"He's a very private person. I see his work when it's done, like everyone else."

"Oh? He said I could watch him paint one day, he said it might help with my own art." There was an affected confusion in her voice.

"Yes, it might. Lawrence enjoys showing off but he also has a lot to teach." Caroline was aware of a number of the other women listening to the conversation, and so she encouraged Lucy to take her husband up on his offer.

The day dragged. Lucy proved to be a time-consumingly chatty member of the group, and Caroline found it difficult to move conversations along without feeling like she was punishing the young woman for knowing her husband.

After lunch, the group began their practise sessions. The exhibition for which they hoped to be hired was not yet ready to be seen and so they were to practise with the permanent exhibitions. Caroline gave them each information about a different painting and told them they had ten minutes to prepare what they would say. Once the ten minutes was up, the group collected at the painting which Janice, one of the women in her mid-twenties, was going to talk about. Janice had a strip of black and white polka-dotted material wrapped around her head like a bandanna, and Caroline was reminded of her penchant for similar material in the early eighties.

"This painting," Janice began, "is a strong example of colonial Australian bush art. The characters are sat facing away from the audience but also away from each other, symbolising Australia's physical and emotional distance from its European heritage and the impact that distance had on early relationships."

Caroline scribbled notes to give Janice at the end of the talk, trying to keep an eye on the woman at the same time in order to judge her physical presence. She was a confident public speaker, and sure of her interpretation of the painting. The time began to drag, however, as the woman's talk drifted into a general speech about colonial Australian art. Caroline signalled to her to wrap up but Janice seemed determined to look only at the other trainees. After another few minutes Caroline raised her voice, cutting Janice off.

"I'm sorry to interrupt but we really need to keep each painting to five minutes, maximum. That's how long you have during actual tours so it's good to practise it right from the beginning. Well done, you had some interesting things to say. Let's move on." Janice's eyes flickered in annoyance but she smiled as though apologetic.

The next painting was Lucy's to present. Caroline had purposefully given her one of Lawrence's, although she usually excluded them on the first rotation. She expected a touch of nerves from Lucy, and was mildly entertained by the thought of watching her present a painting to the wife of the artist. Lucy, however, seemed delighted with her project.

"Lawrence McGovernor, one of Australia's leading painters, completed this painting in 1987 and exhibited it that year as part of The Midnight Opening, his first solo exhibition. The exhibition was widely reviewed and he was lauded as the most promising young Australian artist at the time. This particular painting was sold to Lord Geoffrey March, a British nobleman whose daughter was visiting Australia at the time and attended the exhibition. She apparently begged her father to purchase the painting for her 21st birthday. At the time it cost close to $2000. Three years later, this gallery bought the painting from her for $55 000, as Lawrence had quickly made a name for himself and the gallery was eager to bring his paintings back to Australia."

Caroline caught herself staring at Lucy, her pen frozen in her hand. The other guides seemed similarly shocked by the level of detail Lucy had at her disposal, none of which was included in Caroline's brief. Lucy's lips curled in a smug smile. Caroline coughed loudly.

"I'm sorry to interrupt, Lucy. But The Midnight Opening wasn't his first exhibition. He'd had one four years earlier which had been unsuccessful."

"I said The Midnight Opening was his first *solo* exhibition. You had work in the earlier exhibition, didn't you?" Caroline nodded slightly, embarrassed to have been caught out on such an obvious and personal detail and panicked at the thought that Lucy might prove to have knowledge and opinions of her art like Tara, the rejected trainee with Caroline's shoes.

"As I was saying, by 1990 Lawrence had become highly respected and well-known throughout Australia. His output of work was phenomenal; he has held a solo show every eighteen months and his most recent one will be opening soon."

Caroline smiled, keeping her teeth well-hidden, and said quietly so that Lucy had to step forward to hear her: "You should refer to artists by their surname, as a rule. Even if you've met them, it's important to be respectful."

"Of course."

"And you haven't begun speaking about the actual painting yet. Five minutes goes quickly, remember." Caroline stood back slightly, feeling like she had re-established her dominance, and feeling petty for being pleased about it. Her breathing, if anyone had put an ear to her chest, would have sounded laboured, as though she had just run up four flights of stairs.

"This painting, simply titled *Rage #5*, is of a local model. She was a visual arts student and McGovernor painted her over several weeks in the summer of 1986. As you can see, she is pictured standing in a half-crouch, with blood flowing from both knees and palms. Beneath her is multi-coloured broken glass which she has evidently been crawling on. Such a painting could be considered violent against women, of course, but the woman's facial expression, which you can see is one of pure rage rather than pain, gives the overall impression of an untamed, wild woman, choosing her own savage path through life. The fact that she is naked adds to her animalism."

As Lucy spoke, Caroline found herself drawn into the

painting. She walked past here every day, resolutely looking in the other direction. Echoes of her arguments with Lawrence during that summer flooded her mind. The model was Bridget, whose spiked afro Lawrence had exaggerated in this painting. It contrasted with her translucent skin and almost purple irises. They had met her in the early eighties when she was a student just beginning her studies. Their group had kept her on the periphery for several years, uncomfortable with her overt beauty, but after Lawrence's first, disastrous exhibition, she had appeared much more often. She had been a life-model and had helped him find work in the industry when he was desperately in need of money and purpose.

The night Bridget had called to tell Lawrence about the possibility of life-model work with her art school, Caroline had been lying on their bed, a pale sheen on her skin leftover from the pneumonia which had dramatically weakened her. It was early 1985 and hot. She had been off work for a week and Lawrence had been intermittently caring for her through the permanent haze of alcohol he lived in during those days.

She had heard Lawrence answer the phone and let her mind wander, presuming it was for her and he would re-tell her school that she was still sick. A few minutes later, however, she had become aware that he was still talking, and in an animated voice she had almost forgotten. She pulled herself up on an elbow, attempting to listen to the conversation through her own ragged breathing. After several more minutes she heard him say goodbye, and he appeared in the doorway of their bedroom. He leaned casually, crossed his arms and feet, and looked at her expectantly.

"Bridget's agency needs models. Dashing, rugged male models, specifically." 'Rugged' was a pointed reference to his now rough, bearded face which seemed to have aged a decade in just a couple of years. He smiled, and he almost looked like he used to. Anything resembling paid productivity seemed like a miracle. She had sat up quickly and had to pause for a surge of coughing.

"Will you take it?" She asked, her voice rough.

"I can't deny the poor art students the chance to get a look at this physique now, can I?" He had gestured towards his stomach, now sitting slightly over his belt, and grinned.

She smiled weakly and lay back down. "No, I guess you can't." He had joined her on the bed, lengthening himself beside her and leaning into her side.

Of course, a month later he had been painting again, and painting Bridget. Caroline, however, who was battling her own demons unleashed by her illness, had barely noticed the long hours he spent away from her in the company of that mysterious and beautiful woman. When she had come back to herself she had realised what he had been doing while she was too ill and distracted to notice. She had never thought of herself as the forgiving type before then.

"And so Lawrence continues to be one of the most important modern painters in Australia." Caroline realised that she had missed the last several minutes of Lucy's talk. She caught the reversion to using his first name, however. She smiled thinly. "Very informative, thanks Lucy." Lucy blushed, her first sign of nerves, and tried to merge herself back into the group of women. They moved on to the rest of the paintings, and Caroline nodded along to each talk, giving advice occasionally and trying not to look at her watch too frequently.

FIVE

The ground floor of Fisher library was in constant movement. When it was raining outside an avalanche of umbrellas and raincoats was dumped just inside the door, the rainwater trickling off the plastic and across the tiles. During exam time its opening hours were extended which caused a strange assemblage of students, some of whom were there to study, others who were tempted by the combination of drinking at the student bar and wandering into a public institution. Even on a normal, sunny spring day, however, clattering trolleys, students complaining, phones bleeping and the rustle of food packaging all contributed to an atmosphere bordering on that of a shopping centre.

The studious atmosphere was reserved for the upper levels with their high windows and cascading dust. These floors were in darkness until a student wandered between the stacks and the lights flickered on automatically. Hours could be lost in those aisles as each book pointed the way to another and another, old and obscure titles rubbing alongside crisp new works.

It was a Thursday afternoon when Andie took the elevator, crammed in beside a trolley piled high with textbooks, to the eighth floor where the art history books were kept. She presumed that this would be where the library kept their own records of art prizes. She had decided, after many attempts to decipher the range of pages thrown at her when she searched online for 'local Sydney artist', that using the university's prizes would be a way of guiding her towards someone who had at least received some formal recognition of their talent.

There were several shelves of books concerned with Australian artists. None appeared useful at first glance, as they were mainly dedicated to large scale art movements rather than local artists she had a chance of meeting. She moved on to search the jacketless spines of the books on the lower shelves, hoping these would be the books published by the university. There was a slim volume written by a lecturer about the history of the arts college at the university, but a flick through the contents showed that it was more about the business side than the students.

Finally, tucked in at the end of the row, she found a single copy of a book which listed the recipients of the Art prizes from 1970 until 1990. The entries included photos of artworks which were difficult to distinguish on the grainy, cheap paper. She found one of the first prizes established and read the list of people it had been awarded to. The names were all unknown to her. It had only been offered for the first ten years, before the college was properly established and had been able to guarantee prizes from outside benefactors. Tucking the book under her arm, she retreated to the computer area.

The floor which was dedicated to computers was even noisier than the foyer: it had the additional sounds of fingers pummelling at sticky keyboards, the buzzing of music from headphones turned up too loud and the groan and beep of the printers.

She found an empty chair and typed the first name into Google but there were no likely hits so she tried the second. Several pages emerged, all linking the name Caroline Simon to the Newtown Arts Centre. It seemed she was a patron there and also ran classes occasionally. Andie was not sure that these results were enough to qualify the woman as 'established', so she continued looking. Ten minutes later, however, she returned to the 'Caroline' search, finding the other names even less fruitful.

The Newtown Arts Centre's web page was out-of-date and unorganised. Andie spent a frustrating twenty minutes attempting to decipher the site plan to see if there was any useful information about the woman. There was nothing, no matter how hard she struck at the keyboard. In frustration, she returned to Google, this time looking beyond the top three returns. Nestled halfway down the page was a link to images which had come up for 'Caroline Simon'.

The first thumbnail jumped to its full size in front of her eyes. Black metal wires were twisted thickly together to create a person, large and rounded and solid. Except that it was not solid at all. Gaping holes had been twisted into the wires, holes that could have looked like bullet holes if it were not for the light streaming through them. There were holes in the hands, shoulders, the eyes, mouth and, largest of all, in the chest. They all allowed the light to shine through. The figure was twisted skywards, its hands raised, its knees bent

A Perilous Margin

and its mouth open as though about to jump and yell at the same time. It was energy: pure, focused and vast.

It took Andie several moments before she read the caption beneath the photo. It was the sculpture which had won Caroline the prize in 1979. She had been 24 years old and completing her final year at Sydney College of the Arts. Other than those two details, however, there was no further biographical information. Andie checked in her book again but it had even less information and the photo was impossible to match with that on her screen. Andie would normally have been annoyed at the lack of resources, but this time she simply scrolled back to the picture.

Time passed as her eyes roamed over its contours. Her gaze twisted back and forward, unable to focus on any one part of the shape. There were several moments when her breathing seemed to cease altogether. She became acutely aware of being lazy, of all the time in her life which she had wasted, of all the things that she still wanted to do. She had created nothing of lasting value and she was three years older than Caroline Simon had been when she created this. The realisation filled her with both a determination to not waste any more time and so much energy she thought she could live off it forever.

She printed the page to take with her, aware of her hand shaking with adrenalin as she removed the paper from the photocopier.

It was after five o'clock when she approached the front

doors of the Newtown Arts Centre. The old-fashioned building, painted salmon pink originally but now so coated with dust it was a sickly fish-scale grey, was set back from the road. It was a prime area for real estate and something other than a government-run centre could have made a fortune from the location.

The entrance was easy to miss. The narrow steps, the dark front door, the small, high windows, all gave the impression of secrecy. Once she got inside she saw that the lighting was bright, the walls were painted cream, there were colourful posters advertising aspects of the centre on the walls. They had done everything they could to lessen the severity of the old building and make it warm and welcoming. There were also many people who looked like they had nowhere else to go, simply sitting in clusters along the walls of the foyer.

A woman with a nametag, Cici, was leaning on the front desk talking to a couple of women, one of whom was holding a small child. The child was bouncing comfortably on the woman's hip, playing gently with the grey curls which hung past the woman's shoulders. Cici glanced up and smiled as Andie walked over. "Hi, can I help you with something?"

"I'm looking to get in touch with a Sydney artist, Caroline Simon. It's for an assignment, and I was wondering if you had any information on how I might go about it. I know she's done some work here."

Cici's smile broadened, heavy freckles expanding on her cheeks. "Of course! I've known Car for years. She does a heap of work for us. In fact," she said, turning around to forage behind the desk for a moment, "she's got a workshop coming up soon." She turned back with a stack of paper. "Yeah, here we are. This is a pamphlet for Car's workshop next month. You'll have to contact her through the centre, I'm afraid. I can't just give out her details." Andie looked up from studying the pamphlet, which was aqua with pink font. Her dismay must have shown on her face as Cici quickly added, "Of course, you could come back next week for Lawrence McGovernor's talk." Andie detected a suggestiveness in Cici's expression as she said his name.

"Lawrence McGovernor. He sounds familiar."

"He should do. He's won every major Australian painting prize at least once in the last thirty years. He's Caroline's husband, she's usually known as McGovernor now. He's giving a talk here on the 17th, six 'til seven." She handed Andie a different flyer with a black and white portrait of a man, heavy brows hanging low over his eyes, centred on it. "It's such a treat that he's coming. Caroline's been involved with the centre for years but Lawrence hasn't been interested before. He must be getting senile!" She laughed loudly again, gesturing to the women who were still standing near her. Though they had started their own conversation they both started laughing along with her joke. Their child squealed and clapped her hands twice. The two women and Cici laughed in delight at the child's involvement and it took Andie a few moments to get Cici's attention again.

"Will I have a chance to speak to Caroline afterwards?"

"If you can find her in the mass of Lawrence's groupies, you can talk to her all night!" Andie left the women enthusiastically speculating about what Lawrence McGovernor would talk about.

She held the leaflets in her hand as she made her way towards Marrickville and the Thai restaurant where she was meeting her father and George for dinner. She knew there was a new café open on the same street that she could pass some time in.

A block away from the café, she could see crates scattered on the footpath, ready to be used as chairs. A trio of young men were sitting on some of them, a scruffy dog attached by a lead to one of their legs. Andie headed to a seat at the back, where a bench running along one wall was covered in dull brown throw cushions. As she passed the counter she paused and asked for a long black. The bearded barista pointed to the different types of coffee bean she could choose from and she chose the single origin Colombian at random, pretending to be discerning.

Once seated at her table with a coffee, she flattened the leaflets out to study them. An artistic couple might be a different approach to the assignment, but if she checked with Marco perhaps it would be okay. The leaflets were the same size but the one for Lawrence McGovernor was double-sided. On the front was the photo of his face. Now she looked at it closely he was older than she had first thought, probably not far off sixty. The text had the details of the talk

A Perilous Margin

that he was giving the following week, including the intimidating title 'Australia's Leading Artist'. On the back was a list of his awards, exhibitions and famous works, and three small images she took to be of his paintings although she could not quite distinguish what they were.

She turned to the second paper, which was even worse quality. The aqua and pink colour scheme was probably designed to be eye-catching but it was painful to look at, the colours jarring against each other and distracting her. She forced herself to concentrate. There were no details about Caroline, however, or her work. Instead, it simply had a list of dates for upcoming workshops. Caroline was described as 'a regular at the Newtown Arts Centre' which did not promise a great body of work like that of Lawrence.

After half an hour of sipping her coffee and looking back and forwards between the pamphlets, a thought struck her. Caroline's advertising was undoubtedly of worse quality, but even Lawrence as 'Australia's Leading Artist' had only semi-professional resources – what did that say about the financial resources of the art industry in Australia? She wondered if it was something she could use in her assignment, or if the poverty of being an artist was a topic exhausted in pop culture.

Joey was already at the restaurant when she arrived. He was talking to a waitress who was giggling as she placed menus on the table. When Joey turned to see Andie approaching his eyes were shining, his grin wide. He was always a flirt.

"Hi Dad," Andie said, smiling at the waitress as she left.

"Andie! How are you?" He stood up to kiss her over the table. "No George?"

"I'm sure he's coming. I was at uni so we came separately."

"Of course. How is uni?" They leant back as the waitress reappeared to pour them each a glass of water. "You read my mind!" Joey said as though all his prayers had been answered. The waitress giggled again and disappeared back behind the bar.

"I went to the Newtown Arts Centre on my way home." Andie was surprised to see Joey's smile fall suddenly.

"Why would you go there?" His jovial attitude had disappeared into confusion, and something like anxiety.

"I have to research an artist for an assignment and I thought they might be able to help. What's wrong?"

But Joey shook his head as though it didn't matter. He seemed relieved. "It was one of your mother's favourite places, don't you remember? Maybe you were too young."

"Hi folks!" George's voice reached them before he appeared at the end of the table. "Joey, good to see you." The two men shook hands. Joey smiled but Andie had the impression it was taking some effort.

"George, grab a seat. Andie was just telling me about a university assignment she's doing on an artist."

"Huh," George was too busy gesturing to the waitress for some water to sound interested.

"And Dad was just telling me that Celine used to go to the Newtown Arts Centre,' Andie said. George glanced up as though checking if it was really her mother she was referring to. Andie and Charlotte had both stopped referring to Celine as 'Mum' after she left.

"They used to have drama classes there, local productions of shows," Joey waved his hand as he spoke as though it was of no importance. "What artist are you interested in?" He asked. Andie considered pressing him on the subject of her mother but decided it was probably unfair to George, who was studying the menu in artificial distraction.

"Her name is Caroline Simon, or McGovernor. I'm not sure which. Anyway, she won a prize at Sydney University in the seventies and I thought I'd try to speak to her, if she's still an artist."

"The seventies? Ancient history there, Ands, a lot can change in three decades," Joey said.

"I know, but I saw the sculpture she won the prize for and it was really amazing. I mean, really amazing. Look," and she pulled the paper she had printed in the library out of her bag. To her annoyance, Joey barely glanced at it before handing it to George, who took a second longer then gave it back.

"What?" She asked. "You don't like it?"

Joey shrugged but George had gone back to the menu. "It's not bad," Joey said. "You know me though, I'm not really one for the arts. Let's order, anyway, I'm starving."

Andie glanced again at the paper as she returned it to

her bag, uncomfortable with the lack of reaction that the sculpture had prompted. It still grabbed her, even through the folds and indentations in the paper. They just didn't get it.

SIX

Caroline barely noticed the spaceship qualities of the gallery anymore – Lawrence had already had half a dozen exhibitions there over the past fifteen years. The sunlight reflecting off the glass of the front made it impossible to see the interior and as she stepped through the door she was surprised to find Lawrence and Sylvia, the gallery manager, leaning on the front desk together, studying something. Sylvia looked up but it was only when she said: "Caroline, hello," that Lawrence also took his eyes off what they were studying.

"Darling," he called, quickly tidying the papers in front of him. Caroline saw Sylvia looking at him with surprise.

"Sorry to come by unexpectedly," Caroline said, her breathing shallow at the apparent secrecy. She didn't wait to close the door behind her, instead she strode to the desk hoping to glimpse what they had been studying. Lawrence held the papers protectively in front of his chest but when he saw her face he sighed slightly. She knew he was a talented liar when he wanted to be, and the thought that maybe he actually wanted to share what he was hiding allayed her suspicions somewhat.

"Syl, give us a minute will you?"

The young woman stood straight and, glancing at Caroline, sauntered into one of the exhibition rooms.

"What is it?" Caroline asked.

Lawrence looked at her for a long moment. She wished

he would get it over with. With a sigh he handed her the papers. They were photographs: streetscapes, river views, a few portraits. They were mainly black and white but had some specific colours added. They were interesting and she felt herself deflate with relief. Just as she was about to ask, Lawrence reached over and turned the top photograph over. Stamped on the back was a name: Bridget van der Wiel, with a date earlier that year. Before she could ask, before she could even look up, Lawrence was speaking.

"She sent them to the gallery, darling. Addressed to me with a note saying she is coming back from New York and is interested in collaborating on a project with me."

Caroline couldn't look at him, she just stared at the name, listening to his voice for a sign as to what he was thinking. She let the silence last.

"She hasn't had much luck in New York lately. For the last decade really, once she stopped modelling as well. You can imagine most of the interest in her was based on her looks rather than her work." He went to take the photographs back and Caroline let them slip out of her hands. Finally, she looked up. His expression was his familiar arrogance with a hint of guilt, or was it fear?

She swallowed with difficulty, feeling as though her face had been numbed at the dentist, and said: "Well? What are you going to do?"

"I was just talking to Sylvia about it," he spoke as though she was precious, as though the wrong word might break her. "Syl thinks the work isn't really good enough for a collaboration. She doesn't think the gallery would want to host it and if this place doesn't, well, I'm not sure who would."

Caroline nodded stiffly. "Yes, they're not great." In her mind, she saw Bridget as she had been thirty years ago: long and lean, fashionably bohemian clothes and impossibly clear skin, bright eyes in a serious expression, a large camera hanging around her neck as she prowled the grim streets of New York City. Bridget must be disappointed to be coming back to Australia without having 'made' it, Caroline thought, to be crawling back to an old, married lover in an attempt to make a name for herself in the country she rejected all those years ago. But Caroline forced the thoughts away, she was not required to understand the woman, no matter how long it had been.

"Are you ready for lunch?" She asked and was annoyed at the relief which swept over Lawrence's face.

"Absolutely, I'll just get my things." As he was crossing the floor towards a back office Sylvia reappeared and he paused to speak to her. Caroline saw him gesturing slightly in her direction, Sylvia glancing at her briefly. Caroline turned and left the building, preferring to wait in the sun than watch Lawrence recount the history she was sure he was using to explain why he had wanted to hide the photos when she arrived. She didn't want to see Sylvia's look of comprehension, or sympathy.

SEVEN

Andie sat down on a bench near the Arts Centre, opposite the train station. She was fifteen minutes early for Lawrence McGovernor's talk. The previous week had passed in a haze of tutorial reading crammed in around long shifts at the clothes store. A part of her knew she should have been researching other artists, rather than pinning her hopes on Caroline and being able to speak to her after her husband's talk. But she had not been able to bring herself to look into anyone else. It would have felt like giving up before she had even started

The sun sank towards the horizon, casting a glow over the commuters hurrying home from the station. Every five minutes a wave of people flooded out of the ticket gates. The traffic on the road was thick, heaving itself from one traffic light to another. She breathed deeply. Despite the traffic, the air in Sydney always felt clean. Perhaps it was the proximity to the ocean. She rarely went out on a weeknight and it surprised her now, watching the pedestrian traffic on King Street, that so many people did. The three pubs she could see, and she could have seen a couple more if she had stood up, were all packed, their music fusing in a cloud of noise over the traffic.

"Andie!" The voice was bright, excited, and she looked up to see a tall man with sandy hair approaching her, a grin on his face and sunglasses needlessly protecting his eyes from the diminishing sun. Simon, Leon's friend. He pulled her to her feet and into a hug. She had last seen him shortly before she and Leon broke up. That made it at least two years.

"How have you been? It's been what, a year? Two? I can't believe I haven't run into you before!" His excitement at seeing her made her squirm slightly, and she bent to pick up her bag to give herself a few seconds before answering.

"Yes, a couple of years. I'm fine, how are you?"

"Don't give me that! What are you up to? How's the writing? I keep my eye out for your name, you know –" he touched her knowingly on the elbow "– I keep expecting to see a review in the Herald!"

Her breath caught in her chest and she had to force herself to answer. "I'm actually not writing much anymore. I'm studying Media and Communications at Sydney Uni."

"Oh," his face fell with genuine disappointment.

"It's not a bad thing," she said, aware of the defensiveness in her voice. "Just a change of direction, that's all." But his expression did not lift. With impatience, she said, "You know, I'm running late for something." She gestured vaguely towards the Arts Centre. "But it was nice seeing you again, Simon."

"I wanted to keep in touch, Andie," he said, his forehead creased in consternation. "But you know how Leon is."

"It's fine, don't worry about it. See you." She forced a cheery note into her voice but the farewell still sounded lame as she turned her back on where Simon remained, disappointment lengthening his face.

Inside, she found the compact hall in which the talk was

to be held. It was three-quarters full. The seats near the front were occupied, so she settled about mid-way, right on the edge. Her knees bobbed up and down with the adrenalin from her unexpected meeting. Simon was one of Leon's closest friends from dental school. She had always got on well with him and they had enjoyed teasing Leon about his stringent view of life. While Leon valued dentistry for the stability it provided, Simon seemed to simply like fixing people's teeth and thought the generous salary was a pleasant bonus. And he had always asked about Andie's writing in a slightly awed voice.

She had never seriously considered writing as a career choice and so for a long time Leon's focus on financial stability had been a minor concern in their relationship. What she had come to understand though was that even writing as a passion outside of paid work didn't fit in with Leon's view of life. The only evening of readings he had attended had made that very clear.

It was a year into their relationship, a month after they started living together. Love had swept Andie along for twelve months and had seen no reason for caution so far. Leon was four years older and it seemed like a miracle that a serious, mature man like him could fall for someone like her. She was a part-time receptionist in a busy dental surgery and he had been taken on as a post-graduate dental student who was studying to be a specialist. He had smooth brown skin and a silky black goatee and he had looked at her intently when he first met her, as though she was someone to be taken seriously. He had taken her out to dinner and made her laugh with stories of his classmates. He had the perfect combination of an adult outlook and a childish sense of humour. But he was not interested in literature.

She was going to be reading two sections of a short story at a small bar which often hosted local artistic evenings and she had invited him along, hoping that he would be able to help calm her anxiety. She was first on the list of performers and had spent a nerve-wracking fifteen minutes before the show wondering when he was going to arrive. She couldn't bring herself to think that he might just not show, and as the time got closer she began to worry that something had happened to him. And then suddenly she was onstage, under the lights and about to start, her trembling fingers holding her papers in front of her, and he was quietly moving behind the seated guests of the bar to stand at the back. He smiled an acknowledgement at her, a colder smile than usual but she didn't notice at the time. After she read her work she felt the applause fix something inside her, some doubt which could not be removed by anything but unbiased admiration.

Her knees had been shaking as she took the stairs off the stage and when she got to his side she had wanted to collapse in his arms. He had taken her hand but kept his attention on the next reader, his body tall and stiff beside her. He hadn't said anything. At the break, he told her he had to go home because he was working the next day. He kissed her but didn't mention her readings.

At the end of the night she had hung around, determined to have the good night that she had been expecting, and had started talking to a young couple who ran a literary journal for Sydney University Press. They told her they loved her stories. They spoke with energy and enthusiasm and an insatiable lust for this hobby of theirs and she had left beaming.

But Leon had been asleep when she got home and had never mentioned the night again. She didn't invite him to the next evening of readings but she told him she was going, hoping he would offer to come with her. He didn't, and after a while he started suggesting that her time might be better used finding a job that would pay more than a part-time receptionist. They weren't short of money – they easily covered the rent and bills even when he had to stop working to do an intensive study course and she was the one working full-time. She didn't see why he was so determined to save for a house when she wasn't yet twenty-five or he thirty. Thinking about it now, while waiting for Lawrence McGovernor, Andie was both angry at the pressure he had put on her and proud of herself for ending the relationship rather than forgoing who she was. She tried not to think about the fact that she hadn't written since.

Six o'clock came and went and no one seemed particularly concerned. Andie's hand pulled at a loose thread on the sleeve of her cardigan, creating a small hole. At twenty past six there was a slight commotion at the door. The audience turned in unison, as though to see a bride's entrance at a wedding. Andie saw a short man with thick grey hair enter the hall. Cici, her smile almost escaping off the edge of her face, and another younger woman were with him, skipping close behind as though they were his entourage. He gazed ahead, unfazed by their presence. Cici made her way onto the stage first, squeezing his arm as she passed.

"I am delighted to be here this evening. I hope you're all as excited as I am." Her voice was high with nerves. "Tonight, as the final talk in our local artists' series, we have Lawrence McGovernor, one of Australia's best known, and best loved, painters." There was a small pattering of applause. "Lawrence has lived in this area for a long time, and I have been lucky enough to know him for several years. But tonight is the first time he has agreed to present for us. So without further ado, I give you Lawrence McGovernor!" Cici stood back, clapping loudly. The audience joined in enthusiastically and the man made his way onto the stage, smiling and waving. He reminded Andie of a politician.

"I apologise for being late. I was held up." His voice was almost unbearably deep but somehow carried easily. "I'm here today to speak to you about my experiences in holding exhibitions in Australia. As many of you know, I'm not originally Australian. I was born in Scotland, but made Australia my home many many years ago."

As he spoke, Andie glanced around at her fellow listeners. The audience was at least seventy per cent female, and everyone seemed to know the personal history which

Lawrence was sharing. They nodded understandingly and smiled benignly at many points. Andie started to lose attention. The painter's personal history did not seem to have much to do with his success in the Australian art world. She found some small papers in her bag and fanned herself. The room was becoming uncomfortably stuffy.

To her left Andie noticed three female friends in their early- or mid-forties. They were all paying close attention to what was being said. The woman sitting in the middle of the trio was clasping a rolled up magazine so tightly that Andie could see the coloured ink staining her skin. Her face, however, had a calm, almost hypnotised look as she gazed up at the stage.

Sitting in the row in front of her was a much older man, perhaps in his late seventies. He had a tweed cap pulled down low over his face, and did not appear to be watching the speaker at all. His hands were clasped together on top of a walking cane which stood between his knees. Despite his age, he was sitting forward on the chair, as though ready to spring to his feet as soon as it was necessary. Just as Andie decided the man was not listening but merely gazing at his own hands, he gave a decisive nod in response to something McGovernor had said. Andie forced her attention back onto the man on the stage, annoyed with herself for losing concentration. Despite the heat and his heavy jacket, McGovernor's face was pale and composed.

"– was in Paddington, one of those tiny galleries with barely room to pass around a food platter, let alone hang

A Perilous Margin

enough paintings to accurately showcase my work. Few people who weren't friends turned up, and the experience left me feeling dejected. Self-doubt, the constant companion of the professional artist, was my best friend. We became inseparable. It was crippling, my hands refused to act on the inspiration they felt. Instead, every time I picked up a brush I would second-guess myself. No line was good enough, no colour was accurate enough, no form was inspired enough. I drank during the day to disguise my lack of progress, or to at least give me an excuse for it. I met with friends every night, although I've never been a social person. I let my paints be forgotten. For two years I didn't touch a paint brush. Moments of sobriety were characterised by thoughts of beauty, shapes and colours I wanted to create, but these were quickly abandoned in favour of the next drink. I was on my way to that place from which few return. This, remember, was because of one negative exhibiting experience. A part of me thought that, if I couldn't handle the minor rejection of an unsuccessful, local exhibition, what chance would I have if I ever managed to host a solo exhibition in one of the city's larger galleries? Perhaps, I thought, my personality was simply not strong enough to cope with the barrage of self-hatred which comes with being an artist." At this point, McGovernor stopped to sip from a glass of water. The audience seemed to let out a collective breath, as though they had all been waiting until they, too, could take a break. This man, with his familiar tale of uncertainty, held their attention for reasons Andie could not put her finger on. He continued with his story.

"This is when I ran out of money." The audience tittered as he smiled at them. "I knew I needed a job, and as my only experience was in painting, I applied to be a life-model." This, apparently, was the funny section of the story, for most of the audience were grinning openly. "Five nights a week, and Saturday afternoons, for months, I stripped off and let a group of strangers draw me. After the initial embarrassment I started to like it. Male life-models are difficult to find so I was in demand. It felt good, to be needed like that. It also felt good, I must say, when I looked at the work being done around me and realised how inferior these people's talents were compared to my own. It was a boost to my confidence to see with my own eyes what average talent looked like. I felt petty and arrogant, but I also began painting again. I bought new paints, and at night when I returned from my classes I worked through until dawn. It was a wonderful feeling. Life-painting, which I had never really enjoyed before, became everything. I filled my studio with pictures of naked women," more laughs, "posing tastefully, of course, and began a series of paintings which would later become The Midnight Opening." There were many nodding heads in the room. The three middle-aged women to Andie's left turned to each other and grinned.

Andie's attention was caught, however, by a woman who was sitting in the front row on the opposite side of the room. She was leaning back in her chair, her arms crossed gracefully over her lap, her long hands and fingers dropping

A Perilous Margin

towards the floor. She had not laughed or even smiled at the joke, and now she looked away at the mention of what Andie took to be McGovernor's first important exhibition. Her eyes were drawn to the window instead, and she seemed to ignore the next few sentences in which he described the exhibition. Her attention only returned to the stage when he moved on to speaking about the process of 'selling' his idea to various galleries, and the thrill of being accepted into a mid-sized inner-city space. Andie could not take her eyes off this woman. She looked so different from the rest of the audience, who were all sitting up, straining to catch every word from the speaker. She was calm, she barely even seemed interested. She seemed, if anything, a little bored by the charisma which had the audience balanced so precariously on the edges of their seats.

"I won't bore you with too many more details," there were more amused smiles from the audience, "but I would like to finish my talk by saying this: it is hard being an exhibiting artist in Australia. The art world can become very small, very quickly, while the rest of Australia barely knows that you're alive. The constant pressure of possible rejections, coupled with the natural self-doubt that comes with pouring your soul into something, these things can make it almost impossible to remain a sane, kind, functioning human. The only way to do it, and I know this goes for a lot of professions, is to have support. My friends, who are artistic-minded but not my immediate competitors, have always supported me. While during dark times, there is really nothing anybody can do, it is nice to have people to come back to once you emerge. My lovely wife, Caroline, is, of course, another person on whom I have relied heavily at times." He gestured to the woman in the front row, looking at her lovingly. "I don't pretend to understand the sacrifices she has had to make over the years, or why she chose to make them for a man such as myself, but I am eternally grateful that she did, and that we have been able to live our lives together for all these years. Thank you." The audience stood to applaud him. Andie rose slower than the rest, clapping slightly out of time with them. There was something about his formality while speaking to these very ordinary-looking people that she disliked, and distrusted.

The people around her had started to move towards the door. The rows behind her were almost empty already. Many audience members were waving to McGovernor, who was on the stage talking to a small group of women, as they departed. He occasionally raised a hand in response. Andie began making her way forward, her focus settled on McGovernor's wife who had remained seated during the exodus. Andie had been waiting so long for this moment that she felt a flutter of nerves in her stomach. The woman was sitting in the same calm way, but was holding her hands up towards her face, studying the skin on her palms.

"Excuse me, Caroline, could I speak to you for a minute?"

Caroline looked up quickly, apparently startled at being addressed directly. Her hair was a darker grey than Lawrence's, but just as thick. It flowed naturally from a part

A Perilous Margin

on the right-side of her scalp, falling in a wave close to her left eye and down to her shoulders. Her shoulders themselves were wide, and were accentuated by the loose neckline of her bottle-green shirt. Her black skirt was a light, stretchy fabric that pulled over the rounded bulk of her thighs. She was not overweight, in fact her collar-bone showed clearly at the opening of her shirt, but middle-age had given a heaviness to her hips and legs.

"Of course. How can I help you?" Caroline gestured vaguely to the seat next to her, and Andie sat down.

"My name's Andie. I'm studying at Sydney University, a Communications degree but also some Arts subjects, and for one of my subjects I have to interview a local Sydney artist."

"Oh yes, we've had requests for that before," Caroline said, her voice suddenly official, secretarial. "Lawrence is opening a new exhibition soon but he might be able to squeeze you in. How many interviews do you have to complete?"

"Actually, I heard that you're a sculptor and I was wondering whether I would be able to interview you? It would be four or five interviews, each of them about an hour long. I'd really appreciate it."

"I haven't exhibited anything in a very long time." Caroline shook her head, her eyes flicking momentarily to the stage where Lawrence still stood.

"Do you still sculpt?"

"Only when I'm teaching." She continued to avoid Andie's eyes, though she was smiling slightly, apologetically.

"If you're willing, I'd really appreciate it. I've seen some of your work and I'd love to know your perspective on a number of things."

"I'm really not an artist anymore. Please, feel free to speak to Lawrence, I'm sure he'd be happy to help you."

"Oh, okay. Thanks for your time." Andie stood up, aware that she had been dismissed. She had thought that Caroline would be both flattered and thankful that Andie had asked her instead of her husband; she thought the older woman would have been impressed that Andie had seen her as equally talented as McGovernor, despite their difference in exposure and fame. Andie felt heat rise through her cheeks. At twenty seven years old she was surprised to still feel like a child sometimes.

She was walking towards the door, too embarrassed to now approach Lawrence McGovernor, when she found herself face to face with him. He had left the group of women standing on the stage and was walking back towards his wife. She smiled at him politely, hoping to simply walk past, but he held out a hand towards her.

"Hi, thank you for coming. What's your name?"

Andie stopped, the interruption making her suddenly nervous. "I'm Andie. Thanks for speaking to us, it was very informative." The adjective sounded cold. She made to keep walking, but McGovernor continued holding her hand. She could feel the light wool of his coat, the sleeves of which hung slightly past his wrists, scratch against her fingers and pulled her hand away, a little too forcefully. He paused a

A Perilous Margin

moment, his large lips pursed slightly. Then he smiled.

"It was my pleasure. Are you acquainted with my wife?"

"No, not at all." She had no intention of saying anything else but as he waited, the pause stretching awkwardly between them, she found herself saying, "I just asked if I could interview her for a university assignment."

"And she turned you down?" Andie was unsure if it showed on her face or if this had happened before, but she disliked the feeling that he knew the conversation that had passed between herself and Caroline.

"Yes, she did. Which is fine, of course, I'll find someone else." There was a false breeziness in her voice. She was intimidated by the thought of changing direction to this wildly popular man so quickly.

"Very good, very good. You know, I'd be happy to talk to you myself." He put a hand to his chest as though offering something very heartfelt. His eyes never left hers.

"Thanks, thank you, that's – I really appreciate it. Thank you." He reached again for her hand and squeezed it slightly. The space between his top lip and his large nose was so small that Andie imagined he could feel his own breath constantly against his skin.

"It would be my pleasure. I have some new works that I'm garnering reactions to. I'd love to know what you think. There's a phone number on my website, call it to set up the times." He let her hand go slowly as she nodded her thanks and turned to go. She could feel his eyes on her as she walked away and the attention made her walk feel clumsy.

EIGHT

The temperature had dropped after the warmth of the afternoon and Caroline wished she had a heavier jacket with her. As she crossed the road at the traffic lights she saw the pub where Lawrence, Cici and a gaggle of women from the centre had gone. She thought she could hear their voices bouncing out onto the street. They had politely invited her to join them but she was not interested in small talk that evening. Her thoughts had been preoccupied since she had heard of Bridget's return, a fixation not helped by Lucy's constant presence at her gallery. She was also unwilling to watch Cici attach herself to Lawrence's arm, her shrill voice cooing in his ear.

The bus stop was quiet. She took advantage of an empty bench and sat down. Her legs had a slight ache below her knees and she rubbed them slowly through the material of her skirt. There was a burst of laughter from the pub behind her, and her shoulders sagged at the thought of her dark, empty house. She found her phone and sent Penny a quick message. The reply was instant and she relaxed back into the bench, comforted by the thought of stress-free company. Her thoughts turned to the young woman, Andie, and the idea of being interviewed.

Four years ago she had said no to being interviewed by a man in his early twenties. She and Lawrence had been at the opening of an exhibition at the National Gallery in Canberra. It was typical of her experiences in Canberra: a

A Perilous Margin

freezing winter night, thick frost promised for the morning, few cars on the wide, tree-lined roads. The exhibition was a retrospective of modern Australian painting. All the artists were still alive and most had made it to the capital for the opening. The curator of Australian art at the gallery, a woman with spiked black hair and green glasses, had a ringing laugh which echoed over the heads of the crowd. It was a relief when a choir, purple silk scarves hung around their necks, began to sing.

The man, Johnny, had sidled up to Lawrence, joining in on his conversation with a group of other artists. The group had shuffled around awkwardly, making room for the uninvited young man. Caroline had watched from across the room as he laughed at Lawrence's jokes, giving him overly friendly smiles at every opportunity. The others in the circle looked bemused at the excessive attention. After ten minutes she had noticed Lawrence point in her direction, and the young man had looked over with interest.

He had interrupted her conversation with a sharp "Excuse me," and what he obviously thought was a winning smile. He had pulled her away, a hand on her arm applying pressure to guide her with him. She had been too surprised to resist. He had black hair hanging over his face, a faded blue suit and black shirt unbuttoned too low, a glimpse of hair on his pale chest. He had peered through his fringe, trying to look intense. His smiles were assured, presuming she would be grateful he asked for her time rather than Lawrence's. She knew from his insistent smile, however, that he was asking her because, despite the buddying, he was intimidated by Lawrence. He did not look like the type of person who could live with feeling small.

She had felt a ray of pride when she refused him and the smile had fallen from his face. She had followed his affected lead, smiling warmly, a hand on his elbow in apology. But inside she was cheering herself on for being less needy than he had expected. She had taken his shock as an opportunity to escape, and had left him standing alone, his cheap wine forgotten in his hand.

When she had told Lawrence about the request he had accepted her refusal without question. She hoped it was because he instinctively knew she had refused because of the man's behaviour and not because she had nothing to say.

She had not disliked the student tonight, however. The student with the over-dyed brown hair, the scruffy jeans, the narrow smile and wide eyes. There had been a hint of condescension in her voice, a certain level of presumption which approached, but did not mirror, that of Johnny. The trouble was not the condescension, however. The trouble was that she was a young woman, and Caroline had stopped inviting young women into her life. It was fine for Lawrence to see them at his gallery or studio, somewhere she did not have to interact with them at all. But inviting a young woman into her own life would raise all those insecurities she had fought for so long. Perhaps she had acted too dismissively though, considering the discomfort in the woman's shoulders as Lawrence had waylaid her.

The bus emptied quickly at the bus stop and Caroline was pleased to have a seat to herself. A man was slouched in the seat opposite her, and had a dark beanie pulled low over his forehead. His eyes looked heavy with sleep, and within one stop his head was rolling down onto his chest. There were two women, young, perhaps thirty, talking with slight slurs in their voices though they managed to keep quiet. There was an interesting difference, Caroline thought, between drunk twenty year olds, who revelled in the feeling of being uninhibited, and thirty year olds, who were slightly embarrassed by the familiar sensation and what it could do to them.

Empty, concreted areas flashed past outside the window. It seemed like a wasteland, the left-overs from the inner-west's heyday as an industrial centre. The bus pulled to a stop beside a construction site. The fence surrounding the deep hole was familiar, it had been in operation for almost a year. The red-brown dirt continued to be removed and the hole expanded, while the fence became tattier and tattier through the ravages of sun and rain. Advertisements for the fence company looked foolish on the sagging wood. The bus pulled away as a swirl of dust was lifted onto the waiting traffic. The bus driver was still swearing at the brown coating that refused to be swept from his windscreen when he stopped to allow an elderly couple off the bus. Caroline watched them begin to walk gingerly down the street, their hands clasped tightly together.

The pamphlet for Lawrence's talk was still crumpled in

her hand. She had used it to fan herself during the talk. The Arts Centre had never managed to overcome the ventilation problems of the old building. She smoothed the pamphlet out on her knee, watching the photograph of Lawrence appear whole again. A crinkle remained over his mouth and she smiled at the difference which smaller lips made to his face. He looked much less self-assured. Below the photograph was a small paragraph explaining that Lawrence would be talking about his career "From his now famous beginning with The Midnight Opening" right up until last year and his award. Caroline had not listened to the part of the talk about The Midnight Opening. She never did, and especially not today.

It was a damp Tuesday in 1987 when he had found out the exhibition would go ahead. She had been home all afternoon, waiting impatiently for him to return with his news. She had tried to ignore the gnawing feeling of being a housewife. Pride at what he was trying to do competed with disappointment in her own behaviour, and a touch of grief at what she might be about to lose for herself. Now, of course, she realised that she had already lost her chance, long before that day had even glimmered on the horizon. Major life-altering decisions often seemed to seep into her life unnoticed. Perhaps it was a lack of self-awareness, or an inability to face change, or simply a symptom of a distracted mind. Conversations had been had about the big events in Lawrence's life. She recalled all of them, generally had while sitting across from each other at a cheap eatery. For some reason, major topics of conversation rarely surfaced within the four walls of their home. It was only once they were out, released into the world, that these real, crucial conversations occurred, and the major turns in Lawrence's life were debated.

She had made potato curry that Tuesday night. It had suited the weather. She had set the table, including some naan bread from the grocer a few streets away. And she had sat at the table, waiting, listening to the rain refuse to tire itself out against the window. It was in their flat in Ashfield, and sitting at the kitchen table she could reach the fridge, the pantry, the cutlery drawer. She could close the door with one hand and open the window with the other.

Lawrence had gone into the meeting at 2pm, it was now edging towards 8 o'clock. She had eaten half the naan bread while thinking about how good he had sounded going into the meeting. He was sure of himself. It was terrifying.

There was a footfall on the step outside and a scrape of the key against the lock. Lawrence had appeared in the doorway of the kitchen, his thick black hair flattened against his forehead. Caroline stood, muscles quivering involuntarily. Lawrence had opened his arms wide as though he could embrace the whole world.

"They loved it." His soft voice easily filled the kitchen. Her muscles became fluid again and she walked into his embrace, feeling the expanse of his chest against her although his arms remained raised to the ceiling.

"Congratulations." Her voice was muffled against his

shirt. The rain on his jacket quickly soaked through her sleeves, and she shivered.

"The Midnight Opening will be on show from September eight, exactly three months from today. They loved it." He had squeezed her, his arms encircling her briefly, then moved away. He removed a half-empty bottle of whiskey from the cupboard above the fridge and leant over to where two small glasses were draining by the sink, white suds still sitting in rings on their bases. He dried them cursorily then poured a large measure into each glass and handed one to Caroline. She smiled at him but he didn't seem to see her, even as they clinked glasses. The whiskey was smooth in her throat. She had moved past him and fetched the ladle from the second drawer by the sink, blowing off a few dustballs before dipping it into the saucepan. She ladled the clumps of curry into two bowls and carried them to the table. Her pretence of normalcy was accepted without question although she felt like a fool.

The half-empty plate of naan bread had looked pathetic next to the full plates of food. She tasted the curry. A piece of potato fell apart in her mouth and the sudden burst of steam burnt her throat. Lawrence continued staring into the bottom of his glass, his mind on his future, his food forgotten. The room was full of exhaustion rather than joy. She told herself it was not the topic of the paintings that made her uncomfortable, she was just scared for him, for what success might mean, or failure. She was being a good, caring and supportive partner by being worried. She tried to ignore the hurt from the day before when she had asked to see the paintings and Lawrence had said no, they were of Bridget, it would not be appropriate. He had said he was trying to protect her from being upset. He had said that even though they had put it all behind them, seeing the paintings would bring it back and he wasn't sure they would survive that. She had seen them eventually of course, at the opening of the exhibition itself. And she had wished she had been able to digest them in private before having to do so in a room full of friends and artists. And Bridget's conspicuous absence.

It was only fifteen minutes on the bus to Penny's house. She had turned on her front light for Caroline, and the door stood slightly ajar. "Hello?" Caroline called out as she pushed the door open.

"Come in, come in!" Penny called from somewhere in the house. Caroline closed the door behind her, feeling the warm air enclose her now goosebumped flesh. She found Penny in the kitchen. Her face was pink and shining from the steam which rose out of the saucepan in front of her. Traces of her indigenous heritage became more prominent around her nose, her brow, as she peered into the saucepan. She was stirring methodically, barely taking her eyes from the contents as Caroline approached.

"Risotto!" She announced proudly. "First time in yonks I've made it. You hungry?"

"Yes, thanks." Caroline realised with surprise that she

was actually very hungry, and it smelled good. Penny had already poured a glass of white wine for Caroline and it stood on the bench, moisture condensing on the outside.

"I love that making risotto gives me an excuse to buy wine. Not that I really need it. I mean, who's going to complain?" Caroline detected a strained edge to Penny's voice and became wary of what was underneath, although she forced a smile. Penny and her partner of twelve years had recently split up. Michelle had moved immediately to Brisbane, and Penny had been trying to make jokes about it ever since.

"How are you going?" Penny glanced up, trying to study Caroline's face without giving any of her own emotion away. This is why Caroline had come over, to talk to someone who knew her well. But now that she was here she realised it was unnecessary. The company was enough.

"Fine really, I'm just tired. Lawrence is out with Cici and the rest of the flock from the centre."

Penny rolled her eyes. "That woman has far too much interest in him for her own good."

"Sometimes I wonder if I should be worried about her."

"You're kidding, right? Laurie's a flirt but he's not going to throw everything away for bloody Cici!"

Caroline knew what Penny meant. He would not risk hurting Caroline for Cici, though that held the suggestion that there was someone for whom he would throw everything away. Caroline wondered if Penny knew that Bridget had been in contact. She looked up from her wine

A Perilous Margin

and found Penny staring at her intently.

"It was only Bridget, you know. It was a crazy time, he was crazy. It's not part of who he is. He's a flirt, that's all." Penny paused, as though checking her message had sunk in. Caroline nodded slightly, unable to tell her friend that that wasn't all that comforting anymore. Penny, obviously satisfied with the response, dipped a small teaspoon into the saucepan. It emerged with thick rice on it. Penny opened her mouth gingerly to taste it. She let her eyes roll skywards. "Heavenly. Let's eat."

They ate in silence for a few moments, each savouring the warm food. They had been good friends since university, and these long silences were comfortable for them. Caroline loved having a friend with whom she could share company without speaking. It was very different from the relationship Penny and Lawrence had. They had been friends since high-school when the fourteen-year-old Lawrence had emigrated with his elderly parents and joined Penny's Brisbane high school. Their conversations were characterised by high-speeds. When they first started spending time together as friends in their own right, Caroline worried that Penny would get bored of her quiet style in comparison to Lawrence, but over time she had come to realise that Penny, too, needed a break sometimes.

"I heard from Michelle," Penny said.

Caroline swallowed her rice too quickly and took a sip of wine to cool down her mouth. "Really? How is she?"

Penny's eyes remained on the slightly congealing rice in

the bowl in front of her. "Loving life, apparently. The new job is everything she always wanted, and everything I was keeping her from in Sydney. The weather is glorious. She's joined a surfing club for women, dykes I presume though she didn't specify."

"Good for her." Caroline tried to make her voice sound both genuine and sarcastic so that Penny could choose the option she wanted to hear. Penny went with sarcastic.

"I know, right? Brisbane in all its banality. I've hardly thought of the place in years. You know, the strange thing is that, since she's moved there, I've started remembering things wrong. I imagine her walking to school, my primary school, down the streets I used to walk down. Ridiculous, isn't it? It's like I'm implanting her into every era of my life. As though she hasn't done enough damage to the parts she was actually present for."

"Oh, Penny."

"I know, I know. I should remember the good times. But she left it all. I still don't understand how long she'd been feeling like that. How long she'd been longing to escape from me." Her rice lay forgotten in the bowl, her voice was thick.

"If she'd been thinking about it for a long time it's just proof of how hard a decision it was to make, of how good the life you two had was."

Penny's eyebrows flicked in disbelief, but she did not meet Caroline's eyes. She was looking for neither advice nor comfort, Caroline realised, but simply a sounding board. Caroline thought she might prefer the unfunny joking

A Perilous Margin

Penny to this morose, self-pitying one.

"It's like she has already grieved and is now ready for a fabulous new life. She was grieving the end of our relationship while we were living together." Finally, Penny looked up. "She was so different for the last year. So sad, so affectionate but distant. She knew, then, I'm sure she did. For all that time she knew it was ending and she didn't bother to let me know so that I could join her in grief. And now, I have to do it alone. I comforted her, damn it! For all those months I worried about her, did everything I could to make life pleasant because she was so unhappy. It's ridiculous, now I think about it."

Caroline had heard this version of events from Lawrence. "You loved her," she said.

"Yeah, well. Only fools, and all that." She poured them each a second large glass of wine and, with a sigh as though her mind had been cleared, she said, "So you're worried about Cici, are you?" Penny's knowledge of Caroline and Lawrence's relationship was disturbing. At times she could do this, apparently ask one question while really asking another. The wine was making Caroline warm, relaxed.

"He just really likes women, doesn't he?"

Penny let out a loud laugh and said, "That he does, but not as much as they like him! You know, you're the only one he ever wanted to marry though."

"It seems he's offering personal lessons to young graduates." She hadn't intended to mention Lucy but the words were loosened by the wine. Penny's eyes were narrowed, the laughter gone. Sometimes it was difficult to tell whether she acted out of loyalty to Lawrence or judgement of his bad behaviour.

"According to who?" Penny asked, her voice sharp. This must be loyalty. Caroline reminded herself to step lightly.

"A girl in my new tour group. She ran into him at the gallery and he offered to let her watch him paint."

"And she told you this?"

"Yes, last week. And again today."

"Sounds like she wants a reaction."

"Maybe."

"Trust me. I know women. If anything was going to happen, she wouldn't have flagged it with you so early."

"That doesn't mean he doesn't want something to happen." She knew she sounded stubborn. She just needed to hear it from someone else tonight. She just needed someone else to defend him.

"He loves the attention, Car! You know that." Penny threw her hands up, apparently exasperated at Caroline's continued doubts.

Caroline shrugged, realising she would not get what she wanted from Lawrence's oldest friend. "Do you think you'll see Michelle again?"

"Hell yes. I'll be with a stunning, young thing and I'll invite her out to be the third-wheel."

Caroline was relieved when she arrived home and saw the lights already on. Lawrence was sprawled low on the couch, a beer bottle in one hand and his head resting on the other. The bags under his eyes were exaggerated by the flickering light of the television. He looked up, his face softened by relief and affection at the sight of Caroline in the room. She felt herself smile at him, finally free of tension after the long evening. She sat and lent into him, his arm curled around her shoulders. He kissed her temple and rested his head against hers. She patted his knee. "How was your night?"

"Those women are painful. I'm so glad you're not like them." He kissed her again. "Where did you go?"

"I had dinner with Penny. She heard from Michelle today."

"Oh right. I missed a call from her at lunch time. How is she?"

Caroline shrugged, Lawrence's arm moving with her movement. "Upset but not disastrously so."

"She's a fighter, she'll be alright." Lawrence offered her his beer bottle and she took a swig. It was already warm.

NINE

Andie returned home from the Arts Centre, her feet aching from the twenty-minute walk in her paper-thin flats, to the welcome sight of George cooking a large pot of green curry. He called out a cheerful 'hello' but was too distracted for more of a conversation, and she took the opportunity to lie down on the couch, her feet resting on the armrest. Her eyes were unfocused and she turned a piece of hair around her finger so tightly that the skin went cold and rubbery.

Her quest to find a professional, local Australian artist had just been solved, although she couldn't help being disappointed that she would not be interviewing Caroline. Lawrence was alluring, that much was obvious from the audience's reaction while he was speaking, but she was unsure if it was a response to his charismatic personality or his actual art. She could not bring to mind any of his works, though she was sure she had seen them before. She found it difficult to believe he was really that much more talented than Caroline, despite his greater success. Her heart-rate accelerated simply at the thought of that sculpture with its twisted limbs and powerful energy. And yet, it had had such little impact on Joey and George.

She picked up her laptop from where it rested on the coffee table, opened the screen and brought up some images. The thumbnails of paintings appeared, at first, to be entirely reds and blues. Andie chose one to look at closer.

It was from the exhibition Lawrence had mentioned, The

Midnight Opening. It was unlike any painting of a naked woman that Andie had seen. It was not like Picasso's explicit, abstract, six-breasted women. It was different to Degas' calm, rounded, soft women. It, and even though Andie knew it was a woman she could not stop thinking of it as an 'it', was rage. An incredible red, blue, realistic painting of a woman enraged. There was a fire to her, there was a sexuality that had nothing to do with her lack of clothes. She was skinny, her ribs on show, sliding beneath her skin. Her mouth was closed, her hair was in streaks behind her, her hands were raised and her fists clenched, as though about to bring the sky down on top of the viewer. Andie sat up, the laptop shifted precariously on her knees and she gripped it tighter. She had never seen a woman depicted like this.

"Food time." George startled her by waving a bowl of curry in front of her face.

"Thanks." She snapped the laptop closed, unable to bring herself to show the painting to George, and swung her legs down to the floor so he could sit beside her. He turned the television on to the eight-thirty news. He was studying political science, and already knowing every major and minor political event that had happened that day was not enough for him. He made several derisive comments about the quality of journalism through mouthfuls of food, but Andie was distracted. She was chewing her dinner slowly and trying not to think about why it was suddenly so difficult to swallow.

She lay in bed later that night, watching the moon rise

through the open curtains. The sky never became completely black in Newtown, there was always a haze of light created by the rows of street lights and night-time traffic. Her eyes settled on the two pictures she had stuck up on the wall above her desk. One was the photo of Caroline's sculpture. The other was the painting of Lawrence's which she had printed after the dinner she had only half eaten. Together, they created an emotional storm within her, and she felt her breathing become shallow. She placed her hands against her ribs in a reminder to breathe. The juxtaposition of the pictures was bizarre, and she forced her mind to concentrate on the discrepancies between them. Caroline's was powerful, energetic and fierce. It also seemed incredibly personal, as though it had been created with no thought of who might see it. Lawrence's too was powerful, but sexual as well, and seemed designed to be viewed, to antagonise. Caroline's could have retained its power even if it had been locked in a dark room away from curious eyes; but the effect of Lawrence's was premeditated and needed an audience to provide the reaction it had been designed for. She was still disappointed that she wouldn't be speaking to Caroline – that first jolt she had felt when viewing the picture the sculpture had left a lasting impression – but she was also excited by the idea of speaking to the man who had created this painting. It was undeniably brilliant.

***

The Friday after she had seen Lawrence speak, Andie was on the bus going to work. She usually walked but it was raining heavily so she had squeezed herself into one of the seats at the back of the bus instead. She sat hunched against the window and gazed at one of his paintings saved on her phone. She had found herself frequently searching for images of Lawrence's paintings. At first she had also tried to find some more of Caroline's but had had to give up that search, defeated. She had saved images of several of Lawrence's paintings and had already spent many bus trips gazing at them. There was a type of life within the works which called to her. She felt as though she had always known it existed but for the first time she was being given a chance to experience it. She had never before been affected by visual art to such a degree.

Earlier that morning, she had called the number on Lawrence's website and spoken to Caroline. She had stuttered a bit trying to explain who she was, but Caroline needed no reminding. Within a few moments, Andie had an appointment to meet with Lawrence the following Monday at the gallery where his new exhibition was opening.

Andie paid no attention to the heaves and whistles of the bus as it stopped to load more people on, and allow a few to extricate themselves from the press. The air was muggy from too many people breathing and the windows closed against the rain, and she turned her face towards the glass.

"Andie!" The voice startled her, and she straightened, searching a moment for the voice. Manuel from her tutorial had made his way through the crush of people. He had spoken over the elderly Chinese woman who was sitting in the aisle seat beside her, a square, rolling shopping trolley between her legs.

"Hi Manuel. How are you going?"

"Oh, you know," he rolled his eyes at the people he was pushed against. "You going in to uni?"

"No, work unfortunately. Have you found anyone to interview yet?"

"I thought I had. Have you heard of Lawrence McGovernor? He's a pretty good painter and he lives locally so I thought I'd give it a shot. He turned me down though, after his wife practically promised me he'd do it." Manuel paused as he squashed himself further against the edge of the seat, the fly on his jeans barely a hands-breadth from the elderly woman's face, allowing several teenagers who had been lounging across the backseat to push themselves out the back door.

Andie swallowed uncomfortably. "Did he say why?"

"I didn't even get to speak to him. I rang the number on his website and his wife answered, told me it would be fine and she'd call back in a couple of days to set up the time. When she called back though it was to tell me he couldn't do it. Or wouldn't. Anyway," Manuel rolled his eyes again, then swung into the seat next to Andie as the elderly woman rose and left the bus. "Have you found anyone?"

Andie shrugged, too embarrassed to admit the truth in the intimate confines of the bus. "Do you like McGovernor's work?" She asked instead of answering.

"It's okay. I don't think it's as good as everyone else seems to think it is." He leaned into her as an overweight man squeezed himself down the aisle and out the door. Manuel looked at the retreating figure with disgust before turning back to her. "He's constantly winning prizes and giving talks about his own genius. I think he has an exhibition opening soon, which would tie in nicely with the art and institutions topic from the other week. It'd just be nice to have a recognisable name on my assignment! Reckon I'd get some bonus marks for that." Andie smiled thinly and gripped her phone tighter.

She got off the bus before him, calling a farewell, and hurried in to work. She said 'hello' hastily to her colleagues and went straight into the back room to change: they were required to wear clothes from the store and she rarely found them comfortable enough to wear all day, preferring to change once she arrived.

After she had switched shirts, she sat and scribbled down the idea of using the art and institutions topic in her interview – it made so much sense she didn't know why she hadn't thought of it before. It was similar to the topic of Lawrence's talk at the Arts Centre but this time she would be able to ask specific questions about the world of institutional art in Australia. She wondered whether her hypothesis should centre on the controversial nature of his work. Perhaps new artists only managed to make it into institutions if their art was provocative like his. Was that why he had been celebrated and Caroline forgotten? Galleries were businesses as well and scandal definitely drew attention, but was it to the detriment of the art world in general? Was Australian art becoming homogenous in its confrontational style?

"Hey, Andie!" Charlie, her mohawked colleague, called. He was due to finish when she started and she was obviously taking too much time getting changed.

"Coming!" She called back, shoving the piece of paper back in her bag. Her thoughts had begun to drift to the short stories she used to write. They had been characterised by gentle, almost poetic descriptions of normal life. No wonder they weren't very catchy.

***

The gallery was designed to harmonise with its surroundings; its sleek grey shell sat between the gumtrees which lined the road as though it had always been there. It was Monday, the day of the interview, and she was fifteen minutes early. She walked the streets around the gallery, not roaming too far lest she find herself running late. Her court shoes began to pinch her toes. She had bought the shoes the night before and liked feeling professional when they clacked against the footpath. They sat awkwardly beneath the black pants she had bought from Kmart, however. The pants were slightly too short, pants always were since she had long legs for her height, but they fitted snugly around her thighs and hips. Her blouse was from her work, a shimmering silver she hoped was not too suggestive.

She strode to fit in with the other pedestrians, as though she too had somewhere urgent to be. The sun pierced through a haze of cloud, making her squint. The air felt thicker in the city centre than it did at the university and her breathing felt laboured.

She arrived back at the gallery at the appointed time. The front wall of the building was glass, including the doors, and she could see a few figures moving within the building. Lawrence and a tall woman, younger than Lawrence but older than Andie, were standing outside the front doors. The woman was smoking, her long fingers held the cigarette with more sophistication than Andie had seen outside of an old Hollywood movie. Andie suddenly felt childish and she wished her shoes were quieter as she approached the steps. Before she had a chance to speak, Lawrence said: "How was your walk?" And he and the woman grinned at her.

Andie tried to smile but felt herself shrink in embarrassment. "I was a bit early."

"So we noticed. You could have come in, you know." The woman spoke with a sleek French accent which made Andie feel even smaller.

"I know. I just wanted some fresh air."

They smiled indulgently at her as a truck belching fumes drove past. The woman stubbed out her cigarette and dropped the butt into a garbage bin hidden in some bushes next to the doors.

"Well, let's get started," the woman said. Andie began to worry that she was going to be joining them for the interview. Andie had prepared questions but she knew she would seem like an amateur, and the idea of this glamorous woman witnessing her attempts to be professional was shameful even to think about. She breathed a sigh of relief when the woman extricated herself from them as they passed the reception area. "Have fun," the woman called as she positioned herself behind the large chrome desk. Lawrence gave her a wave, a signal that already seemed familiar to Andie from the number of times she had seen him do it at the Arts Centre.

"I'm sorry we have to meet here. It's just Sylvia," he gestured back towards the tall woman, "needed to go over some ideas with me. The show opens in a couple of weeks and the paintings are being delivered next week. Time is tight with these things, and the more we can plan before the paintings actually arrive, the better." He smiled warmly, moving closer and tilting his head towards her as he spoke, as though bringing her into his confidence. He seemed to tower over her although their eyes were level.

"It's no problem. Thanks for meeting with me."

"It's no problem." The phrase sounded strange as he copied her intonation, and she smiled shyly, feeling extremely young.

"Let's sit." He directed her towards a set of three armchairs, fitted with coloured tartan, which sat around a coffee-table in the first exhibition room. There was an exhibition being shown but no one appeared to be browsing the rooms. As they sat down Andie tried to remember the first question she had prepared. It was unneeded, however, as Lawrence said, "Have you been to one of my exhibitions before?"

"I don't think so."

He laughed suddenly, loudly. "I hope that means no. I'd hate to think my work is that forgettable."

"I'm sorry, of course that was a terrible thing to say! No, I haven't. I'm sure I haven't." Her voice was not her own. She coughed, trying to bring its tone down to something natural. Her bag was on her lap and she opened it to find her notebook. Lawrence was leaning forward, his elbows on his knees. He was dressed quite formally, Andie thought. His dark navy pants were slightly creased, as though he had been moving a lot during the morning, and his pale grey shirt was unbuttoned at the top, showing dark curls against his chest.

He waited for her to retrieve her notebook from her bag and set her phone on the table between them, before saying, "Will you come to my new exhibition?"

"Yes, I hope so. I have no excuse now, do I? Now that I can say I actually know you!" Her voice was too loud and she stared resolutely at her notebook. She was embarrassed about looking embarrassed.

"No, no excuses. Though I'm not sure you can say you know me. Not yet, anyway. But, that is what this little chat is for! So, ask away." He sat back in the chair, his eyes focused on her and she realised that he must have done this countless times. The realisation did not help her nerves.

"My tutor suggested we start with some questions about the person we're interviewing, but I already feel like I know a lot about your background from your talk at the Arts Centre."

"Oh really? That's good, I guess." He chuckled. "Though I try not to give away too much in those talks so I wouldn't presume you know everything just yet."

Andie looked at the first question she had written down, it looked abrupt and boring. She glanced back up and saw him watching her. "I am interested in hearing a bit more about your experience with exhibiting in Australia," she stuttered. "Did you find it easy or were there any roadblocks you think are particular to Australia maybe?" She held her pen poised to take notes, pretending it was what she had intended to say. Although she had set her phone to record, she had decided to take notes as well as a way of calming her nerves with movement.

"Well I've been exhibiting for over twenty years, now. My first exhibition – which was really my second one but if you remember anything about what I said at the Arts Centre the other night you will forgive me for not including my actual first exhibition –" Andie smiled as though at a private joke, "– was in a gallery just round the corner from here. It was a gallery-restaurant for a while, though I think now it is much more of a restaurant than a gallery. There is more money in food, after all." Lawrence kept speaking as Andie made notes. She had to concentrate to follow what he was saying as he drifted into tangents that bore little resemblance to anything he had previously mentioned. Relaxation came and she settled more comfortably into her seat. After an

A Perilous Margin

hour she was exhausted, although she had barely had to ask a question.

When it felt as though the interview had come to a natural end she dropped her pen and rubbed her fingers over her eyes, pressing on the bone of her eye sockets. The pressure released a dull ache beneath her fingertips and she sighed. Realising what she must look like, she stopped suddenly and glanced at Lawrence. He was studying her, looking amused.

"I'm sorry! I'm not used to this. It's a bit exhausting!"

"That is perfectly fine. Women get worn out easily around me."

She became aware of her gaping shirt as she slouched in the chair, and straightened her shoulders. The material flattened against her skin. She smoothed her fringe against her forehead, feeling the heat from her face and wondering how red she must be.

"You have beautiful hands," he said suddenly, the tone of his voice changed from silky self-control to become hard, insistent. He reached out and clasped her right hand. Andie jumped at the contact, but his eyes were purely professional as he turned her hand in his, studying first her fingers, then her palm. "They look like the hands of a nineteenth-century genteel woman." He gazed, eyes narrowed, at her knuckles, her fingernails. After several moments he looked up at her face again, smiled, and the contact immediately felt personal. "You have that look about all of you, actually. The face, the figure," his eyes dropped momentarily before returning to her eyes. "You would make an excellent life model for classic painters."

Sylvia's voice echoed over to them, calling Lawrence to look at something that had just arrived. Andie jumped up, pulling her hands away and fumbling to close her notebook. He stepped close to her, bringing his cheek against hers in a quick kiss. "It was lovely to see you again, Andie. You'll have to ask me some questions next time."

Andie adjusted the lamp so that its light flooded onto her work. A crackle signalled the death of an insect behind the bulb and she knocked the lamp a few times until the black fly fell soundlessly onto the desk. She flicked it onto the floor. She found the notes she had taken during the interview and opened them. Before she could start reading, however, she was distracted by the painful memory of her arrival, the humiliation of being young and out-of-place was still acute and she wished crawling under the desk would help. Not that she had improved after that, she thought to herself. She hadn't managed to say anything! An inadequate, useless interview, she thought bitterly to herself.

She started reading through the notes, hoping there was something useful. Lawrence had spoken as though reading his autobiography, anecdotes melded easily with explanations of his work, and emotions were explained as though all analysis of feeling had been completed long ago. She wondered whether he really believed what he had said,

A Perilous Margin

or if he had just said it so often that it had become a truth he could not see past anymore.

The information was more similar to the talk he had given at the Arts Centre than she had realised while listening to him. Once again, he had detailed in broad strokes his early years, his first disastrous exhibition, his lost years, his gradual success.

At one point her notes read:

some lucky, others not (Caroline?)

He hadn't actually mentioned Caroline there, it was her addition, wondering if he was referring to her and intending to ask, although she never had. Andie had no idea if they had been competitors at some stage. She did not know how they had met or when they had got married or anything about their relationship. That wasn't that strange, she supposed, considering the interview was about Lawrence's exhibiting in Australia, but she was curious to know who they were as a couple.

Now that she was away from him and the gallery it was difficult to remember why she had felt so nervous, so restrained, so unlike herself and unable to ask questions. It amused her slightly to think about how different she had been in that interview, with a man she was clearly intimidated by, compared with her performance in tutorials when she was frustrated by her classmates. Sometimes it felt like she had no personality but merely slipped from one costume to the next depending on the situation.

A slam from the front door forced her out of herself.

George's footsteps echoed off the tiles in the kitchen as he stamped his way to his bedroom. His door slammed, rattling her own door in its catch.

She ignored the attention-seeking behaviour, trying to pull her focus back to her work. She would go and make him a cup of tea later, she told herself. Overt drama made her impatient and she knew that, if she entered into a conversation at that moment, she would risk trivialising whatever the problem was. She normally had to give herself time to warm up to the idea that someone close to her was hurting about something she could not really understand. Even with George, her best friend, whose problems she knew in detail already.

After another quarter of an hour of studying her notes, searching in vain for new, interesting information, her lamp began to buzz, a sign of overheating, and her hand had a burning sensation from the warmth emitted by the bulb. With an impatient noise she flicked the lamp off and went to discover the reason for George's dramatic entrance.

TEN

Penny flicked off the main lights above the dining table and the ring of candles she had lit leapt into prominence. They were thick and pink with a heavy pot-pourri scent. Too heavily scented for dinner, Caroline thought, but Penny had brought them over especially so she did not say anything, even as the perfume began overpowering the smells from the oven.

Penny and Lawrence were having a ferocious conversation about Sylvia, and Caroline was listening, her back to the oven to allow the warmth to seep through her thin cardigan. It was a surprisingly chilly night.

"How can you not trust me after all these years? I know what I'm talking about."

"Sometimes, of course you do, darling. But you're lonely and frustrated and that is why I do not trust you. I have known Sylvia for years. She is single but most definitely not gay."

"You're just saying that because she's classier than me." They roared with laughter. Caroline turned to the oven and removed half a dozen small potatoes wrapped in foil. Lawrence danced around her, took a second wine bottle from the shelf by the window. He kissed her shoulder as he passed, then danced out of the kitchen to exuberantly pour more wine into Penny's glass. Caroline unwrapped the foil and dropped the potatoes into a bowl.

"In any case, I could probably turn her. I have a pretty

good track record of that!"

Lawrence's pretend shock lasted barely a moment before he once again roared in glee. Caroline returned to the oven for the roast chicken. It smelled of lemon and thyme. It was her mother's recipe and she had made it for the first time in almost a decade. She wanted silence, reverence, for the masterpiece and the memories. It was unlikely to happen, however, once Lawrence and Penny had a few drinks in them.

"Speaking of Sylvia, though," and Lawrence turned in his seat to look at Caroline as she placed the chicken on a tray in the middle of the table. "You should have seen Andie's face when she saw her! She looked like she was meeting a princess."

"Who's Andie?" Penny stabbed a potato with her fork and blew noisily at the escaping steam.

"A student who's interviewing me for one of those assignments. She came by the gallery today."

"How did it go?" Caroline asked, distracted by the large knife she was using to shave off parts of the chicken. She was listening carefully, however, for a change in Lawrence's voice. He waved a hand dismissively then reached for a potato.

"She's a strange girl. She barely spoke at all." His disinterest sounded forced to Caroline and she frowned slightly.

"Just wants a famous name to put on her assignment?" Penny grinned. Lawrence's fame was a running joke.

"There you are, help yourselves." Caroline replaced the knife next to the chicken and sat down. Lawrence and Penny already had mouths full of potato and plates piled high with green salad. Caroline still hadn't mentioned Bridget's reappearance to Penny and she wondered, as she watched the old friends banter over dinner, whether Lawrence had. A few times it was on the tip of her tongue to bring it up but she restrained herself. She wasn't sure she wanted to be present for Penny's reaction – she had had a crush on the young woman herself back in those times. Caroline also wasn't sure she wanted to see Lawrence try to explain why he had not yet told Bridget there would be no collaboration. She trusted that he would tell her, and that that would be the extent of their contact, but she imagined that he was enjoying this: luxuriating in his success story while being tied, even invisibly, to Bridget. Caroline didn't want to see any sign of that enjoyment.

After dinner, they moved to the lounge room. Penny sat in her favourite armchair, Caroline stretched on the couch, allowing her eyes to close against the light above her. She was exhausted from being at the gallery all day with a particularly needy tour group, but also from being on the outer during dinner. As with all groups of three, there was a mismatch of attention which jarred sometimes. She could hear Lawrence, whose movements sounded very drunk, putting a CD on with a lot of clattering. She heard Penny unwrap a chocolate from the box she had brought over. A present, she had said, from an enthusiastic colleague. Soft sounds of Chet Baker and Lawrence's voice crooning along with the recording filled the room.

Caroline enjoyed Lawrence's inebriated personality these days: it was gentle, caring, and had a fluidity which made him seem to embody the beauty he could always see but only usually express with a paintbrush. She had not always felt like this. Those months of his perpetual hangovers and hair-of-the-dog cures had been something else entirely. In those days he had been untidy, loud and opinionated, and his self-loathing had manifested itself as an aggressive arrogance. He had always been tender to her, but his reputation had been something different.

She had tried to ignore it. She had picked up extra work to cover costs after Lawrence had been fired from a full-time sales job. That job had got in under his skin and destroyed him, quickly and spectacularly. Selling expensive leather shoes to gold-wreathed men and women had seemed manageable at first. Or perhaps it had only seemed manageable because it was so necessary: they had wanted to rent a two bedroom flat, and he had wanted a continued break from painting – it had been almost a year since the first exhibition and he had barely produced any work in that time. It all seemed to fit. Except that selling expensive, tacky 'beauty' was a concept he could not reconcile with himself. He began arguing with his manager and then, after a few weeks, with the customers. He was fired unceremoniously one Wednesday afternoon and returned home with dark eyes and no interest in finding a new job.

Caroline had found extra work at a high-school. Spending days alone at home was probably the worst thing for Lawrence, she realised after a while, but a part of her enjoyed the tough love aspect of it. He was an adult with a future to think about and she so desperately wanted him to accept that, through either working or painting she didn't care. Sometimes he would be home when she returned from work and she would ask about his painting. He would make vague generalisations about ideas for new work but he was not actually painting and she did not push it. She hoped that by watching her go to work every day, the reality of his situation would sink in.

Slowly, however, it became more common for him to be absent when she returned. There would be a scribbled note telling her he was 'out' with various friends. Months passed where she barely saw him during the week, although on the weekends they continued to have long, quiet times together. When they met with friends, stories would emerge of recent drunken escapades that she had no knowledge of. She had been glad that since he wasn't working he was at least socialising, and she left the other, darker thoughts for another day.

One Tuesday lunchtime she had returned home unexpectedly. A student had come down with the chicken pox and anyone who had not had the disease was sent home. She had walked up the front path at two o'clock on a Tuesday afternoon, to find the front door wide open. A trail of crusted dog prints ran up and down the hallway, mysteriously at first, and then understandably when she found Lawrence passed out, an arm around a sleeping stray dog he had evidently fed whiskey to, and a pool of joint vomit by the couch. It was a release to finally know the extent of his problem.

The crying had been sudden and swift, finishing as quickly as it had started. She was glad that he had been asleep for that part of it. Then disgust and impatience, in equal measure. She had made a cup of tea and sat on the couch, watching the sleeping creatures. She could smell the vomit; it made her nauseous. She fought the urge to clean it up, or at least spray disinfectant on it.

Her mug was cold by the time he woke up. He had rolled his head, looked at the dog, still sleeping. Then he noticed her shoes, sticking out from behind the coffee table. He sat up with a jerk, his eyes darting for a moment before they found her. His mouth opened, as though to say something, but instead he choked slightly, his throat sounded dry and crusted. She stood, leaving her mug on the coffee table, and went into their bedroom. She felt weak, all of a sudden, and feverish. She hoped that she had the chicken pox and was not having a physical reaction to what she had just encountered.

She had got into the shower, the lukewarm water giving her chills, and then dressed in her pyjamas. She had climbed into bed, and wrapped the blankets around her so that she was cocooned. The shivers continued, and she wished she had taken medicine. She could not bring herself to leave the warmth of the bed. She listened for sounds of Lawrence, but the house was quiet.

She found out later that he had cleaned up the mess from the dog, returned the dog to the outside world, and then left to meet with friends. He had been unaware of her approaching illness, had merely seen the disdain on her face as she walked out of the room, and heard the shower start. He returned in the small hours of the morning, slept on the couch, and awoke at midday to find her still in their bed, feverish and coughing. He had driven her to the hospital and sat with her while her hacking cough caused the other patients to send startled looks their way. It was pneumonia, the doctor said. With antibiotics and someone to care for her, she could recover at home. It was the beginning of a nasty fortnight and she was weakened and distracted for weeks longer. By the time she was back to herself, he had a new job as a life model with Bridget.

In the far corners of her consciousness, Caroline heard her name. Penny's voice was loud and Caroline exaggerated a wince, hoping it would make her be quiet. Then Lawrence's scent, cheap roll-on deodorant and expensive cologne, surrounded her as the soft blanket was pulled from the back of the couch and laid over her body. His face, gentle despite its stubble, pressed against her cheek, and she kissed him back. She had been vaguely aware of feeling cold and the warmth from the blanket allowed her to finally, fully, succumb to sleep.

ELEVEN

It was a ninety-minute train journey to Charlotte's house. Despite the inconvenience, especially on a Sunday with its limited timetable, Andie enjoyed it. It was beautiful wending through towns tucked between groves of bushland. Red and yellow earth forced itself out of the cracks made by the pressure of the train tracks, and the first glimpses of the Hawkesbury River, wide and lush and glinting, always took her breath away. There was a point at which the train track was so close to the water that Andie had to press her forehead against the glass and look directly down to see that they were, in fact, still on land.

Andie was always impressed by the sense of calm in her sister's house. The large expanse of water, gliding calmly by, which was visible from most of the windows, was somewhat to thank. And Charlotte always spoke gently. Sometimes Andie felt as though all that beautiful music that Charlotte had played during her younger years had somehow fused itself into her body, like a second skeleton of soft grey silk which flowed through everything she did.

"Tea?" Charlotte asked. Andie nodded and sunk back into one of the lavender couches that sat in the middle of the living area. In front of her were uninterrupted windows, and she took a couple of deep breaths as her eyes attempted to focus on part of the water sliding past.

"Do you ever get dizzy? Trying to concentrate on all that water?"

"You can't concentrate on it, you just have to let it go." Charlotte sat next to her and they each took a sip of their tea. They both had it black with one sugar like their mother. They looked at each other in silence for a few moments. Andie arched her eyebrows slightly. She had promised to spend Sunday afternoon helping Charlotte organise Fi's approaching birthday. They were simply having a family lunch, however, so she could not imagine what needed to be organised.

"So, what needs to be done?"

"Just the menu," Charlotte said, then, at the look of disbelief on Andie's face, added quickly, "Not actual menus, obviously, but just what food we're going to make."

"Kid food?"

Charlotte's face contorted in distaste. "I don't think I can face a bucketful of mini frankfurts. And anyway, Fi's decided she's a vegetarian."

"Really? Good for her." A burst of pride, not a common feeling for her, swelled in Andie.

"Yeah, not for me though. That's why I need some help. Any ideas?"

"For a vegetarian eleven year old? That's a tough one." The look of panic on Charlotte's face increased and Andie quickly added, "But we'll find something, don't worry. Vegie sausages taste pretty similar I think, wrap them in a bit of pastry maybe and she will never know."

"Pete suggested we just have separate food for Fi, and everyone else can eat meat." Charlotte's face looked pained with the embarrassment of even considering such a suggestion.

"That doesn't sound very inclusive considering it's her birthday."

"I know, I know, but my god this is a lot of hassle."

"Why don't you just do all vegetarian? It'll show Fi you support her decision, and you won't have to think of two sets of food."

"All vegetarian?" Charlotte looked doubtful.

"Don't tell anyone and no one will even notice, I'm sure." Andie smiled, trying to look encouraging while secretly relieved that catering was not a part of her daily life.

They began looking online for recipes. It was surprisingly easy, and Andie was soon grateful to every vegan and vegetarian parent who had planned a children's party and written a blog about it. As she was biting into a sandwich made from fresh bread, a novelty for her as she was used to toasting her bread straight out of the freezer, Andie found a recipe for sweet corn fritters. She exclaimed loudly, and Charlotte joined her on the couch to see what had caused the excitement.

"Remember that birthday, was it for your fourteenth? And Celine made these for you?" Andie turned the computer to show Charlotte the recipe.

"It was my thirteenth. I think we had bacon in ours."

"I was so jealous. You were in high-school with all your cool friends, and you had real grown-up food at your party!"

"It's strange to think of corn fritters as grown-up food."

"You had feta salad too, and some kind of apple strudel instead of a cake. You were so glamorous!" Andie nudged her elbow into her sister's ribs, but Charlotte's face remained focused, drooping with memories.

"What a strange circle life is. Celine makes these for me, I make them for Fi." There was a long pause as they each drifted into their own thoughts. "I didn't celebrate my fourteenth birthday, remember," Charlotte added.

"I know," Andie said quickly. She had wondered if Charlotte had picked up on the mistake. "I didn't forget, it's just the years, you know –" Andie left the words unfinished. She wanted to say that she had been so young, the years had become confused in her memories. Their mother had left when Charlotte with thirteen and Andie was seven. Andie sometimes wished that she had been older, had had more time with their mother. At other times, she was glad that she was so young, it felt like the situation had had more of an effect on Charlotte because she was old enough to understand what was happening.

"You know," Charlotte's voice was thoughtful, "I realised recently that I really should have given up music earlier. Celine used to tell me I had a gift like she did. Those last couple of years, the orchestra, the Conservatorium and the concerts, it was too much for me but I thought I could somehow show her my dedication and bring her back. Take over the world and show her it was possible to be successful at home."

"Oh, Charlotte." Apart from one drunk conversation they

had had after Andie's twenty-first birthday party, they had never really spoken about Charlotte's decision to quit music. Andie found herself on the edge of her seat, waiting for the revelation that would make her sister's life comprehensible.

"No, it's okay. The world lost nothing by me quitting. And I think that's what Dad always wanted me to know – that it was my choice, I didn't owe anyone. Talent didn't have to hold me hostage." Charlotte's face was soft, without bitterness.

"I really thought you loved it," Andie said.

"I did. Sometimes. But it was so hard, Andie. My first year at the Conservatorium was so stressful I hardly breathed for twelve months. Anyway," Charlotte made an obvious attempt to look brighter, "Celine never really made it either, so I guess it's up to you to bring the Hawkens out of mediocrity! It doesn't seem that long ago that you were proclaiming yourself the next Alice Munro! What happened?"

"You know what happened, Charlotte." Andie turned back to the computer, and stared resolutely at the corn fritters.

"Leon?"

Andie grimaced in response, and continued staring at the screen. The website promised a host of other recipes besides the corn fritters and she opened one for mini quiches.

"He was an idiot, Andie, surely you know that by now?"

It was strange to hear her sister talk like this, they had never really spoken about Andie's breakup before. At the

A Perilous Margin

time, Charlotte had gone the traditional route of overfeeding Andie on comfort foods while talking brightly about anything except what had happened.

"He was what he was," Andie said, shrugging. "And I got out in time to stop myself becoming like him. But he was right about some things."

"Like?"

"My stories weren't good enough."

"Good enough for what?"

"To make the poverty worth it."

"You weren't living in poverty!" Charlotte sounded exasperated.

"No. Thanks to him and his full-time wage. But he didn't want to support something destined for failure. I guess no one really does."

"You supported him as well! While he was doing those specialist courses, you worked full-time for him then."

"I know. That was the idea, that we would take it in turns. But when I started talking about trying to get a residency somewhere, it became pretty obvious that our ideas of where life should take us were too different. It was technically his turn to support me but he gave up pretty quickly."

"I thought you broke up with him?"

"It doesn't feel like it anymore." She knew she sounded bitter and wished she could hide it. Next to Charlotte's calm melancholy it felt childish. It was true though, she had broken up with him so that she could pursue writing without feeling guilty but she had never gone on that residency. He had got into her head so much that the breakup seemed to be the catalyst for permanent writer's block. The few stories she had started while mourning the relationship's end were so bitter and forced she had deleted them from her computer. That was two years ago and she hadn't written anything since.

Andie's finger scrolled through a couple more recipes until she found one for chocolate brownies. She gestured at it to Charlotte. "They look pretty good." Charlotte had been looking at her as though waiting for more information about Leon. But she transferred her interest back to the computer, attentive to the aims of the day.

"Excellent. I'm making a cake but I guess one sweet thing probably isn't enough."

A storm blew in at five o'clock and Andie had to run through sheets of rain to get to the station. A disposable poncho from Charlotte protected her from the worst of it and she stripped it off under the shelter of the station, silently thanking her sister's organisational skills, and dropped it into a bin before she boarded the train.

She sat opposite a woman hunched beneath a dark rain-jacket, the hood pulled up to cover her face although occasional droplets found their way down the plastic and dropped into her lap. Her pants were camel-coloured canvas, and the rain had created large swirls of grey just above her knees where she had obviously been walking into the storm.

A plastic bag with Kmart smeared across one side was between her shoes which were once probably white. Now they were brown and the laces looked almost cemented into place by mud.

Andie studied the woman, whose age, body shape and ethnicity were completely hidden under her rain-damaged clothes. As the train lurched suddenly out of the station the woman sat up, arms searching for something to balance on. Her hood slipped and Andie saw a wrinkled, dry face. Her mouth, when she opened it to speak, was empty of teeth.

"Where are we?" Her tongue lisped against her exposed gums.

"We just left Cowan." The woman swore and tore out of her seat, almost tripping on the bag at her feet. She grabbed it with surprising agility and jumped the few steps down the carriage stairs. Her movements were those of a young woman.

The scenery flashed past in a blur of rain-soaked green and brown. The afternoon had not tired Andie as much as she had expected, and with a sigh of relief at the thought of heading home, she took her reader out of her bag. The reading for the week's classes was almost half-way through the thick tome of photocopied pages, and she had to hold it precariously on her knees, her feet resting on the vacant seat opposite, as she settled in for the return journey.

TWELVE

The class was small that Monday night. The rain which thrashed against the window created a constant soundtrack and the light from the traffic on King Street flickered through the glass. Caroline's mind felt too empty to teach. She had been buffeted by the wind on her way in and it seemed to have scrambled her brain. Her students were working, three middle-aged women, a twenty-something woman, and an older man, almost elderly. Missing were the three other young students, including Fred, who wore a tweed jacket without irony and flirted intensely with her. She missed having him in the class. The flirting pulled interest from her apathetic limbs.

Caroline realised with surprise that she had not spoken to a student in ten minutes. Embarrassed at her lack of professionalism, she approached Jenny, one of the middle-aged women. Jenny was bent low over her lump of clay which, unfortunately, still looked just like a lump of clay. Her soft curls covered her forehead. She was one of those women whose age is impossible to tell; Caroline thought she could easily be either ten years younger or ten years older than herself. She had a high, breathy voice and her hands fluttered when she asked questions, but her actual questions, beneath the nervousness, were often pointed and seemed designed to show Caroline's faults.

The chair squealed against the floorboards as Caroline pulled it up to sit next to Jenny. She smiled apologetically at Jenny's wince.

"How are you, Jenny?"

"Oh Caroline, I know you told us to get straight into it tonight but I don't know what you mean. I've just been sitting here pretending to know what I'm doing. How embarrassing!"

"The point of having a fifteen minute time-limit was to try to stop the fear of making mistakes, to make you just jump straight in!"

"It's just not me, I have to say. I need more time!"

"Well," Caroline said and looked pointedly at her watch, "you have four minutes and thirty five seconds like everyone else, see what you can do!" Caroline stood up, unable to bear the passive-aggressive cloud which surrounded the woman.

"Oh I can't possibly do that," she heard Jenny mutter under her breath. The smile on Caroline's face ached.

"How is yours going, Eoin?" The elderly man was pounding his clay. His fingers, thick and permanently clawed, were forcing the clay into odd shapes.

"Very well, thank you Caroline. Just giving my fingers a bit of a stretch. You know, they take a long time to warm up, these days."

Caroline looked around and saw with dismay that none of the students had created anything that looked like anything, despite the twelve minutes they had already had to work.

"You have three minutes, everyone, and then we'll be showing each other our work." Her voice cracked with impatience. She knew that she should both give some specific instructions to help them finish and extend the time limit, but her patience was too thin for that. She wanted to blame them and let herself off the hook. She ignored the shocked expressions and Jenny's mutterings and walked back to her chair where there were several books which she sometimes used as references. She picked one up and flicked through it furiously, as though searching for something. Her eyes were glazed, however; her ears pricked to hear the dissent behind her.

"Okay," she turned back to face the students, all of whom were sitting in front of lumps of clay. "No one's finished?" She asked, incredulity in her voice as though she had been expecting something different. They all shook their heads.

"Perhaps you could explain to us what we're supposed to be doing?" Jenny's voice was apologetic, but her eyes were fierce. Several heads nodded. A wave of guilt swept her stomach as she saw Rosie, a middle-aged woman with loose clothing draped unflatteringly over her large form, close to tears of frustration. Caroline took a deep breath.

"Okay, let's start again. Everyone up here," she gestured to the students to join her at the front of the class. After several moments, they started moving, Jenny rubbing her knee furiously and complaining of pain. Once they were grouped around her, Caroline handed out the books and magazines she had piled near her chair.

"Have a look and find something you either love or hate. No fence-sitting please. Love or hate. You have three minutes." A couple of them giggled slightly with nerves as they started flicking through the pages. Once their time was up, Caroline asked Eion to show them the picture he had found. He held up the book, open to a photo of a sculpture made from what appeared to be raw fish. The group smiled at him.

"Love or hate?" Caroline prompted although she already thought she knew the answer.

"Hate."

"Why?"

"It's unhygienic." A ripple of laughter and Rosie actually clapped.

"That's true. Next?" As each student showed their picture and gave their reasons for their emotional response to it, Caroline hoped that the discussion and movement would help them when they sat back down in front of their clay. The terror of those first few minutes was always difficult to overcome.

Her students watched her as she manoeuvred the tables from separate islands into a semi-circle. No one offered to help. On each table she left the over-worked and misshapen lumps of clay. She asked them to each stand, not sit, behind a table. There was some excited murmurings. This was more activity than they had ever had in a class.

"On the count of three you will each begin sculpting an animal. You will have two minutes to do as much as you can, then you will move on to the next table. Try to guess what the person before you was trying to make, and add as much as you can to it in two minutes. Then you will move again, and again around the circle until we have five beautiful animals. One, two three!" With an excited gasp five sets of hands plunged into the semi-solid masses in front of them. Within a minute Caroline could identify the types of animals being created by everyone except Jenny, who was prodding her work one way and then another. Caroline ignored her and smiled at Rosie, who was giggling at the size of the trunk she had accidentally made for her elephant.

"Okay, time! Move onto the next one." Eion guffawed with surprise at as he came up to Rosie's elephant, and she squealed an apology.

"What's this supposed to be?" Jenny said loudly, prodding a finger at what was clearly some kind of bird.

"I'm so sorry," Natalie, the young woman who had made it, blushed furiously. "I was trying something challenging."

"Good on you, Natalie. It's clearly a bird, though the exact species I'm not sure about. Jenny, perhaps you can give it some more defined features so it's clearer for the next person." The other students seemed unaware of the awkwardness, happily distracted by their new projects. Natalie smiled gratefully.

Caroline turned around to avoid showing her glowered response to Jenny's look of disdain.

"Okay, time. Move around again." By now the figures were easily identifiable and a couple of the students looked stumped as to how they should proceed. "Basic shapes are done now, but we need detail. Think about texture, movement. How can you make it more flesh-and-blood and less clay?" A few nods and they set to work with finger nails and paddle-pop sticks, creating feathers, fur, even scales on a twisted lizard.

The time slowly ran out and by the end even Jenny was crouched over the model of the lizard, adding fine strokes to its tail.

Several smiles came Caroline's way as the students left the studio. Eion waved. His thick fingers had become almost nimble by the end, moving with the grace and force of the zebra he had created. Caroline closed the door behind him, feeling the breath leave her body with the last of the footsteps on the stairs outside. The empty studio yawned behind her, tired from its participation in the almost disastrous class. Her footsteps echoed against the wooden floorboards as she returned to the centre of the room and began moving the tables to their overnight position against the wall. The metal feet scraped and she winced.

On the last table were the leftover clay pieces. They were gritty in her hands, the smooth dirt gristled beneath her fingertips as she rubbed them together. The chair beneath her invited her to sit. Her hands began working the substance, softening it. Time passed. Shapes formed and melted before her, her hands strengthened, the knuckles elongating with the exercise.

She was pleased with how the class had finished. The group activity was one that she remembered from her own university days. It was one of Jay's favourite ways to get them moving on a Monday morning. Jay was a middle-aged lecturer who only worked part time. Caroline had been aware of a faint aura of bitterness around her. She took no pleasure from teaching. The only time she seemed happy was when she herself was sculpting, and she joined in their activities more than was strictly professional.

Bridget had been in that class too, Caroline remembered with a jolt. Caroline had felt old compared to most of the students, although technically she only had a couple of years on them, and Bridget's presence had exacerbated those feelings. Bridget with her dark hair and ivory skin and her ability to make silence seem mysterious and compelling, rather than boring or awkward.

Caroline had been uncomfortable with her immediately and remembered mentioning to Lawrence that there was a young woman in her class to whom she felt strangely drawn and repelled at the same time. Lawrence hadn't paid much attention at the time, but the next class Bridget had sought Caroline out, and the ego boost which came from being wanted by the most desired student in the class had made Caroline put in the effort to become friends.

She had introduced Bridget to Lawrence that semester, and he had been the one to always invite her along to group events, to seek her out for conversations, to tease their friends for being intimidated by her. He didn't tease Caroline, though. It was as if, even then, he knew it was a touchy subject.

With a sigh, she pounded the small crouched woman she

had made back into shapelessness. The waxy paper used to protect the clay had floated to the floor and she stooped to pick it up, feeling her back ache in gratitude of movement. She glanced at her watch. It was nearing midnight. She wrapped the paper around the clay, knowing it was probably overworked by now and she would need to ask Cici for some more supplies.

THIRTEEN

Caroline called on Monday evening to arrange the next interview with Lawrence. Andie apologised profusely, thinking that Caroline had thought Andie had forgotten to call, but Caroline cut her off briskly by saying she was just organising Lawrence's week. Her voice was husky, as though she had been drinking the night before and had not quite recovered. He was still too busy, she said, to conduct the interview at home, but if Andie could be at the gallery at midday on Tuesday then he would speak to her there.

The sweat on Andie's fingertips smudged against the phone screen as she ended the call. She wanted to be strong this time and not allow the man with the deep silk voice to determine what was talked about. It would be helped, she knew, by the research she had been doing about the types of exhibitions favoured by galleries in Australia. While there was a frustrating lack of research, the research that there was hinted at what Andie had already hypothesised – if you were not already a big name, you had better hope to provoke fiery debate.

After her conversation with Caroline, Andie tapped on George's door. It opened slightly at her touch. He was lying on his back on his unmade bed with a political science textbook open face-down across his chest. Ambient, generic Latin-American music was coming from his laptop on the floor. His feet were wrapped in woollen socks. She smiled at him. "Studying hard?"

"Always," he said. "You okay?"

"I've got my next interview with Lawrence tomorrow." The textbook fell with a thump to the floor as he sat up, moving his legs and gesturing for her to sit.

"Are you nervous?"

"Yes." Her eyes roamed the room, unable to settle on anything.

"Do you have some questions prepared?"

"Not yet. Will you help me?"

"Sure." His eyes gleamed with ambition. He had, at one time, wanted to be a reporter. "What approach are you thinking? Andie Hawken: die-hard journalist. Andie Hawken: die-hard Lawrence fan. Andie Hawken: swooning groupie?"

"I don't want to be any of those!" She exclaimed, embarrassed by the memory that the last interview was probably a 'swooning groupie' one, no matter how much her rational side saw his numerous faults. All that had been missing was a breathless request for an autograph, though such a request would not have seemed out of place. She squirmed. "I just want to understand what his life has been like."

"That's a pretty big topic."

They sat in silence for a few moments. Andie's fingers played with the frayed fabric of the doona. He reached a hand out to cover hers, preventing her nervous habit.

"Do you think he's a good artist?" He asked.

"Yes, absolutely."

"Do you think he's a good person?"

"No, probably not."

"But that's not what your assignment is about."

"No." She pulled her hand away from his. "Well, it sort of is. We did this reading about how artists have to consider their lives exceptional in order to create art out of their own experiences. And I want to know if it's true, at least in this case. Other than the fact that he's managed to be a professional artist, his life doesn't sound particularly interesting. He tried to be an artist, freaked out for a while about how difficult it was, then got over it and ended up succeeding."

"I'm sure he'd love to have his life summarised like that." They grinned at each other. Butterflies continued to wriggle in her stomach but an hour later they had written a list of questions designed to get information about why he had created the works that he had, and whether he attributed his success to his controversial art.

***

The clouds were heavy and the lights inside the gallery appeared falsely bright in comparison. The harmony of the gallery's architecture did not extend to storms, a problem for a city with Sydney's tempestuous weather. Andie had arrived five minutes late, intending to make a point, and as she walked through the doors she felt the storm at her back.

She stopped to say hello to Sylvia, prepared this time for the woman's air of sophistication and mystery. She could hear Lawrence's voice as she stood in the reception area, though his words, and who they were being shouted at, were indistinguishable. She glanced uncertainly at Sylvia, who seemed to be watching her for a reaction. Lawrence came striding round the corner and Andie recoiled. A heavy scowl had transformed his face from smugly amused into furiously violent, but he composed himself swiftly when he saw her. It was too late, however: her determination had vanished with his fury.

"Sorry, darling," he said, addressing both Andie and Sylvia at once. "Bad morning but I think it's sorted now."

Sylvia put a hand on his arm. "Is there anything you need me to do?"

Lawrence smiled, back to his usual charming self. "No, it's fine. Shall we?" He said to Andie, gesturing to indicate she was to walk before him. They sat in the same chairs as last time.

"So, mon amie, what would you like to talk about today?" He asked, leaning back with his hands on his knees. He seemed very pleased with himself all of a sudden.

Andie looked down at her notes, breathing deeply. When she looked back up she felt she had recovered some of her steeliness. "I was wondering what you think has changed in Australia about the public's appreciation of art and awareness of it. You mentioned last time that the first gallery you exhibited in is now primarily a restaurant. Do you think that's indicative of the art scene?

"Straight in, huh!" He chuckled. "No, no I like it," he added as though Andie were about to apologise. "The gallery-turned-restaurant I think is indicative of the amateur scene, which I guess is part of the Australian art world. The professional, large-scale galleries are difficult to crack but the smaller ones are often willing to show new artists, especially if it is not their primary way of generating income. Women are more often exhibited in those spaces, if you believe it. Perhaps because their work is less confronting or at least more palatable alongside a nice dinner."

He was smiling as though it were a fun fact but Andie was astounded by his unmoved attitude and forgot to check her follow-up question.

"Do you mean women's work is less controversial? Was that the problem with Caroline's art?"

"Oh god no, darling. Car got the big guns at first. Some of her work got noticed, at my first exhibition actually, and it didn't take long for some of the bigger galleries to buy some for their collections – a representation of 80s Australian women, I think. It was not controversial so much as mildly political. It doesn't get brought out much as far as I know. Sylvia," he suddenly called across to the long, lithe woman still standing at the reception desk. She walked over, flicking her hips to balance on her stiletto heels.

"Yes darling?" she said, dropping a long-fingered hand onto Lawrence's shoulder. He took her fingers firmly.

"Do you know if Caroline still has some work in the basement?"

"I presume so," Sylvia glanced at Andie. "There were

three, I think. None of them have been exhibited though."

"They haven't been exhibited at all?" Andie asked.

"No. It's not that uncommon," she added quickly at the startled look on Andie's face. "Public galleries have far more work than they can show. Caroline's, I believe, were bought with the idea that she would one day be a big name. As she never had a solo exhibition here or anywhere else though, they have just stayed in storage."

"You don't sell them on or something?"

"Of course, if we can get a price for them. Normally the artists come back looking for them if they haven't been on display, but Caroline's never shown any interest."

Andie looked at Lawrence, waiting for some kind of outrage at his wife's treatment. He caught her glance and said to Sylvia, "Would it be possible for us to have a look at them?"

Sylvia shrugged. "There are people working down there at the moment so I'm sure they won't mind getting them out for you. Give me a minute," and she walked back to the desk, her shoes clicking on the tiles. They watched as she spoke on the phone and, as she hung up, gestured to them. "Head on down," she called. "Lucas will show you."

They took the lift to the lowest floor and then walked down two flights of stairs to reach the basement. A man was standing by an open door. He ushered them quickly through the door and Andie had the impression they were distracting him from what he would rather be doing.

"You're after Simon's work aren't you, Caroline Simon?"

He asked over his shoulder as he walked quickly between objects wrapped so completely they were unidentifiable.

"Simon! Ha, I haven't heard her called that in a long time. But yes," Lawrence added at the look of impatience Lucas threw him.

"I'm sorry it's so cramped in here," Lucas said as he showed them into a small room barely bigger than a broom cupboard. "We have the sculptures for you, but please don't touch them. And come and find me when you're finished."

There were three sculptures sitting on a low table. Andie had the impression the room was sometimes used as an office – there was a stack of papers which looked like it had been roughly pushed to the side of the table to make room for the pieces, and an office chair was in the corner of the room. Lawrence pulled it forward and pushed Andie into it. "Sit, sit," he said. "Look at them. I just remembered something I have to tell Sylvia, I'll be back in a moment." He glanced at the sculptures and then left quickly, almost closing the door behind him and casting the room in shadows.

Trying not to be spooked by being alone in a basement, which suddenly seemed like the setting for a horror movie, Andie turned to the table.

Two of the sculptures were made of layered metal wires, like the one she had found online. The first was a metre long and recognisably human, a naked woman reclining on her elbows, her legs stretched before her with one knee bent to the sky. The contours were given such weight by the metal

A Perilous Margin

it was all Andie could do not to reach over and touch it as though it were flesh. The metal of the face was slightly shinier, Andie saw when she looked closer, as though sweating. The woman looked as though she had thrown herself on the floor to rest after some exertion.

Andie stood and shuffled round the table to get a different angle. On the metal of her chest, not the top layer but those buried deep underneath, was a large circle of red, a vibrant colour which came in and out of view as Andie moved, like a beating heart. Andie pulled her phone from her pocket and, glancing quickly at the door, took a couple of photographs. Feeling her excitement growing, she moved to look at the second sculpture.

It too was made of layered metal, but this was not a person. It was an egg shape the size of a small dog and had a curve pushed in the middle, as though it were wearing a corset. It didn't stand up straight, but was tilted back slightly. It was almost like a deformed pear, Andie thought to herself, struggling to see a recognisable form. The metal wires were closer together on this one so there was barely room between them, and they had been polished so they shone. Andie began to feel uncomfortable with it, its elusively feminine form was suddenly like a woman missing her head and limbs and being cinched at the waist. Andie moved on to the next, smaller one.

This was the only one made of clay and Andie was surprised to see it was a man. He was standing with his legs wide, his hands by his side and his oversized fists clenched.

His face was pulled back in a frightening grimace. He looked ready to fight. Except for his clothes, which looked like a parody of 70s fashion: flares with swirls of pattern on them, a slinky button-up top, a chain was around his neck. It was like an eighteenth-century prisoner had become a disco dancer. Andie wished that the sculptures came with notes like in a normal exhibition.

She took a few more photographs then sat down, staring at each sculpture in turn again. She wasn't sure how much time had passed when there was a bang on the door. Lucas half stepped into the room.

"Sorry," he apologised, smiling, as she jumped up. He seemed much more relaxed than he had earlier, and Andie thought perhaps whatever crisis had been happening had been solved. "Is it okay for me to put these away now? I have some spare time, that's all."

"Of course." Andie gathered up her things. As she reached the door she turned for one last look and saw Lucas carefully covering the reclining woman. Andie felt suddenly, intensely sad for the figures that were being locked away again.

Andie took the stairs, holding her jacket close as she wound slowly around the wide, white steps. The warmth of her jacket in her arms provided some comfort from the cold shock she found herself in. Three mesmerising pieces of work were sitting, covered in darkness, in the basement, while their creator received no recognition. As she emerged from the lift into the bright reception area she saw Lawrence leaning against the desk, laughing with Sylvia. Andie's sadness morphed into anger at this man who had not even stayed to look at his wife's work. She tried to keep her hands steady as she approached the desk but felt herself disarmed by the smile Lawrence turned on her.

"Shall we continue then, or do you need to run off?" He asked. He was holding a coffee cup in his hand. Was that the reason he left her in the basement with Caroline's work, to get a coffee? Andie nodded and moved towards the chairs they had been sitting in earlier. She heard Lawrence whisper something to Sylvia, who chuckled.

They sat down and Andie took a deep breath. Before she could speak, however, a man appeared with a sandwich wrapped in greaseproof paper which he handed to Lawrence. The man scuttled away before receiving a thank you. "I hope you don't mind me having lunch while we talk," he said, clearly pleased with the surprised look on Andie's face.

He took a sip of coffee while watching as she tried to regain her composure. She was furious she hadn't been able to launch into the questions that were on her mind, and now had to sit and wait while he disentangled his sandwich from the paper, scooping up fallen shreds of lettuce as he did. He glanced up and noticed her watching him. "I usually hate drinking out of these things," he said, pointing to the cardboard coffee cup, "But desperate times et cetera."

"You're an environmentalist?" She asked sceptically.

"I do what I can."

"When it's convenient?"

"Naturally." He gave her a quick smile but his eyes narrowed as though trying to determine if she was making fun of him. He took another sip and a bite of sandwich. Andie breathed deeply for a few moments and felt composed enough to look into Lawrence's face and meet his eyes.

"This is your fourth major show here, isn't it?" Lawrence nodded, his mouth still full of sandwich. "Did you ever ask the gallery to show Caroline's work?" She hated her voice for cracking instead of sounding strong.

Lawrence looked surprised and took another sip of his coffee before he answered. "No, it's not really my place. Caroline never approached them or pushed for it, she never seemed particularly interested in exhibiting, not after our first exhibition."

"But surely it's normal for artists to waver in confidence – you did, quite significantly. Isn't it possible that she just needed some encouragement to realise her potential?"

His eyes narrowed, transforming his smug face to something approaching ferocity. It was fleeting, however, and when he spoke it was with the same jocular tone. "Of course it is common for artists to doubt themselves. Many artists fail at first and most never stop failing, if you're talking about commercial success. And we all know this when we start out – no one becomes an artist with the thought of being famous. Or happy. Artistic success is as much about learning to play the game as anything else. Few people can play the game without learning the rules first." His eyes stayed focused on her as he raised the coffee cup to his mouth and took a long sip. Andie felt her bare legs sitting between them, stretched towards Lawrence's chair. She drew them back towards her, adjusting her skirt down over her knees. He held her gaze, unsmiling, still chewing.

"Why didn't Caroline learn how to play the game?"

"You mean, why isn't she as successful as I am?" It felt like a rhetorical question, but he looked at her as though waiting for a reply. She kept her lips resolutely closed. She was not going to give him the answer. "If you want me to say that my wife isn't talented, it won't work. If you want me to say that she sacrificed her own talent for mine, it won't work either. Women are as much a mystery to me as the art world is, apparently, to you. This is a large gallery, they choose who they exhibit and who they don't." Andie felt a slight pressure on her solar plexus. It felt like if she just pushed a little more, she might be able to make this charismatic man a little uncomfortable.

"How long have you been married?"

"Thirty years, give or take."

"Did Caroline mind when you started painting naked women?"

Lawrence sucked his breath through his teeth but took a sip of coffee to disguise it. "I think she preferred it to when I was drinking all the time." He tried to smile but it didn't look like his face was working properly.

"Did she ever ask you to change direction, or focus?"

"No." He took another large bite and began coughing suddenly, loud hacking coughs as though a piece of lettuce had become lodged in his airway. Andie talked over the disruption.

"Did you ever consider that your choice to return to art, after the first disaster, was due to her support?"

"Of course I did," he spluttered, reaching for the coffee cup but unable to find space between coughs to drink.

"Did you ever consider that her refusing to push for her place in the art world was due to a lack of support from you?" He stood up, his back to her, and bent over, a hand clasped to his chest. It sounded as though he were about to expel a lung. The man who had brought the sandwich appeared with a glass of water which he passed to Lawrence. After a few moments, Lawrence returned to his chair, his sandwich forgotten on the table beside him, the now empty glass clasped in his hand.

"Listen to me," his voice had dropped to a hiss. "This is not what I agreed to be interviewed about, and I don't have time to answer questions which you have obviously concocted to prove some little theory that you have about the evils of artists, or men, or both. I am what I am, Caroline knows that, and she is still with me. That's all I need to know. If you need to know more, I suggest you talk to my wife." He collected the remains of his sandwich from the table. His fingers looked thick and uncoordinated as he fumbled with the paper. He stood, a sliver of lettuce floating to the ground at his feet, and walked hurriedly away. A few leftover coughs made him pause in mid-stride. He looked small.

Andie's heart was racing as she gathered her few sheets of paper and notebook. She departed the gallery without making eye-contact with Sylvia.

She was breathing normally by the time she arrived at her tutorial. She sat on the floor outside the door and leant her head against the wall. It was cold stone and made a nice change from the increasing warmth of the afternoon. The storm had blown itself out, leaving in its wake a city simmering with humidity.

Her brain was a mess, confusion reigned over any chance to disentangle the truth from what Lawrence had said. Speaking of Caroline, particularly her lack of artistic success, pricked a nerve in him. Was it guilt? And if it was, was it specifically related to something that he had done, or not done, or was it simply the guilt of success? Andie thought about the years he had been successful and wondered if anyone had asked him these questions before, or if he had only been asked to defend his art, not his actions.

As the students filed into the classroom, Andie trailing at the end, Marco called to them; "If you need to you can make an appointment with me to discuss the theory you intend to use for your assignment. But today," he waved a sheet of papers which they all knew had discussion questions on them. The questions were distributed and Andie turned with unease to her usual group. She did not want debate for the sake of debate today.

"I thought this was an odd reading," Manuel said without

looking at the questions. "Odd because what Ashby and Carroll are saying seems so obvious, and yet I've never heard anyone else say it. It's about," he looked around the group with a patient expression, as though presuming no one else had read it, "irony versus sentiment in art and how, since the mid-twentieth century, art, well society in general really, has succumbed to the illusion that irony is somehow cleverer than more sincere ways of looking at the world."

"And because of that," Melanie said, leaning forward in her chair, "we are missing out on genuine insight."

Manuel looked momentarily lost at having the floor taken from him when he was just warming up.

"But political irony is fantastic," Shari said, "and clever." She looked at them as though they were idiots for considering anything else.

"Of course," Manuel said quickly, "the writers do mention that irony in pop culture stemmed from a very real need to disengage with the corruption of politics, to make the public feel smart for knowing when they were being taken for a ride."

"The problem is," Jackson added quietly, and everyone turned to him, "that it's never stopped. It's become the standard for analysing politics and I think what the authors are asking is whether there might be a more thoughtful approach we could take, an approach based on conviction rather than cynicism."

"The political side of the article is interesting," Marco had appeared behind them and now held up his hand as though trying to slow everyone down. He looked very tired, Andie thought. "But what does he say about art? If you look at the first discussion question," he gestured towards the papers he had distributed, "you'll see what I'm getting at." Andie, as the only one who had not yet spoken, had read the question. It asked about the difference between sincerity and sentimentality in art and why sentimentality in particular was so easily ridiculed.

"I think this is a huge problem for a lot of women," Andie said. "When women are earnest in their art it's very easily called sentimentality and dismissed because of it. When men are earnest in expressing those same emotions they are just applauded for being sensitive." Andie thought about the statue in the basement of the gallery, its red beating heart lying open and vulnerable. Was it any more vulnerable than some of Lawrence's women though?

"That reminds me," Melanie said, sitting up a bit straighter, "of the debate about chick lit covers. Some of those writers are good, serious writers, but because they're women and their work deals with love they are marketed with those ridiculous covers of wispy doe-eyed women or stiletto shoes."

"Like when Jane Austen's novels were republished with those kinds of covers," Andie said, feeling for the first time that she and Melanie had something in common.

"Exactly!" They smiled at each other.

Manuel rolled his eyes. "Oh come on. Good art is good art, it doesn't matter how it's packaged." Andie looked at Manuel curiously, wondering if he actually believed the world was a meritocracy, or simply thought it should be. Before she could ask, however, Shari began speaking about a political satire show and the discussion moved on to whether comedy was a type of art. Andie wasn't listening, however, she was wondering whether not having a stereotypical focus had contributed to Caroline's lack of success. Perhaps if there had been something reflecting domesticity or children in her work, she would have done better.

FOURTEEN

An email to her brother was sitting open on Caroline's computer screen when she heard the slam of the front door. She closed the laptop, the catch clicking softly, and watched until the door opened. Lawrence came into the kitchen, his face black.

"Bad day?"

"The gallery is going to be the death of me. Bad management, bad staff, no sense of the aesthetic continuum. They treat me like some sort of god then ignore everything I say." The tiredness in his voice seemed false compared to the anger on his face.

He took the small coffee plunger from beside the kettle and rinsed it quickly. Three teaspoons of dried, ground coffee beans went into the bottom.

"Coffee?"

"Sure." She normally only drank coffee in the morning but he looked as though he needed company. He flicked the kettle on without checking the water level. Harsh spurts came from the dry metal and he swore under his breath. Caroline waited for him to finish stomping around the kitchen. When he was standing with his cup, leaning against the bench and looking slightly calmer, she spoke, holding her own cup tightly in her hands.

"What are you going to do?"

"Nothing. Keep going back. It's the only thing to do."

"Mmm," Caroline made a vague noise of agreement.

"I'm not doing any more interviews with Andie, either."

"Oh?" Her ceramic cup began to burn her fingers but she clasped it tighter.

"I don't have time to be horsing around, thinking up ways to try to convince her that I'm not the devil incarnate because you haven't exhibited in years." Caroline's chair tilted behind her as she stood up. The coffee slopped precariously and she replaced the cup on the table. She tried to disguise her emotion by moving towards Lawrence, arms outstretched in a show of comfort. He let her hug him for a few moments before returning the affection.

"It doesn't matter. She has an agenda, that's all, one that I'm not interested in contributing to. I told her she should talk to you if she has a problem about how we've arranged our life!" His voice sounded light, dismissive, but his eyes looked at her carefully.

"Do you think I should talk to her?"

"You never want to talk to these students," he said.

"Andie was only the second person to ask." Caroline heard the annoyance in her voice and tried to disguise it as she said, "You have committed to these interviews and she does need them for her course. Maybe I should help." She smiled. The idea had lifted something inside her.

"If you want to talk to her, go ahead. But believe me, you won't like what she is attempting to dig up, either." A scowl hung over his eyes as he turned away, coffee cup clenched in one hand.

Caroline waited until Lawrence had closed the door of the

studio before she called Andie. She found herself gushing on the phone. Gushing was not her style and to her own ears it sounded false. Andie, however, appeared to trust it. The exhibition, Caroline explained was just too hard on him at the moment. It had nothing to do with Andie. But, since he had agreed to do these interviews Caroline felt guilty about leaving Andie in the lurch, so how about they meet up instead? The tone in Andie's voice worried Caroline, was it surprise or disappointment? It was impossible to tell over the phone. Andie agreed, however, to interview Caroline at the house on Friday afternoon. Caroline could hear Penny's voice in her head, exasperated with Caroline's distrust of Lawrence, who, as Penny had reminded her, had only deserved her distrust once. This was not about trust, however, it was about a woman who not only resisted Lawrence's charm but seemed to actively repel it. A fascinating possibility.

Caroline knocked gently on the studio door then nudged it open. Lawrence was sitting on the couch, slumped low, Elgar playing softly in the background. He opened one eye, squinting as though a light were shining at him. "I just called Andie," the other eye opened. "She's coming round on Friday. I told her I'd finish your interviews for you."

He sat up. "Does she know you don't exhibit?" She paused, giving him time to correct himself, but the silence stretched.

"She knows. I was the one she wanted to interview originally, remember." His eyes closed again but not before she saw a flicker of disdain in them. He slouched back into the couch, a grunt was his only reply. Caroline closed the door loudly behind her. Not a slam, but with a definite annoyed edge. His self-involvement was not surprising, but it was frustrating.

The guest bedroom had originally been set up for visitors. They had few overnight guests, however, as Caroline's only family also lived in Sydney, and Lawrence's parents were long buried in the dusty earth outside Brisbane. Penny had occasionally crawled in there if she was too tired to return to her own home. Generally, however, it stood empty.

The room, painted in a light green to give the illusion of coolness during summer, had become a de facto study for Caroline. It was not useful for sculpting but there was a desk which Caroline sat at occasionally. The bookshelves had been donated by her brother Damian, who had been going through a wood-working phase. They were by far the most personal aspect of the room. The rest of it felt like a hotel, although that was why Caroline liked it. It was anonymous, separate to the rest of the house and the rest of their lives.

Caroline kicked her shoes off and lay on the bed. One of the things she had first loved about Lawrence was how he made her feel about her work. His support was not traditional in terms of complimenting her or cheering her on through difficult periods. But he took it seriously, and presumed without question that she was as dedicated to it as he was. They had long conversations about art in the abstract, and then each retreated to their own work. His

A Perilous Margin

expectations were so high that she had felt constantly challenged.

Many students she came across while studying sculpture had seemed to delight in creating ugliness, as though that were the way to challenge perceptions of beauty. It came to seem lazy, however. They wanted to whip up masterpieces, which was easy to do if the masterpieces had no need for precision or detail. She had begun to slow down, to take herself and her work seriously, to think about the consequences of what she was creating. She knew now, though she was unsure when the realisation had come to her, that Lawrence had never been particularly serious about her art. It was merely a reflection of what he felt for himself.

The mural he had painted after they first met had caused a stir. It was no secret that he had been with many women, and yet not one of the women he had been connected to seemed to fit the portrait. People had wondered aloud about her identity. Caroline had avoided the area. She skipped a series of lectures and eventually dropped the class to avoid being caught staring at herself.

Two weeks passed like this. Eventually Grace, her sister, had invited her to attend the opening of an art installation project which a friend was holding. Caroline had arrived at the gallery, hair whipped into a ball by the wind, her heavy coat making her sweat in the warmth of the room. Grace had rolled her eyes. "Fix yourself up in the bathroom, then I'll introduce you around." Caroline had retreated to the bathroom, cheeks aflame. She let the water run over her fingertips, and brushed it through her hair, attempting to settle down the flyaway frizz. She removed her coat, the maroon turtleneck underneath was much more suitable to this crowd. She rubbed her cheeks vigorously to get some blood moving. Cold weather always gave her a translucently pale look, and not the sort that was in fashion.

She had emerged ten minutes later and spotted Grace through the crowd. She felt young as she pushed her way through to her sister's side. Grace introduced her to the group of people she was standing with, mainly other students. Older students. A woman, whose dark red hair hung straight down her back, had her mouth slightly open as she stared at Caroline. Grace laughed nervously on Caroline's behalf. "Chi, what's going on? See a ghost?"

"It's you!" The woman's voice had a slight twang to it. Caroline smiled uncomfortably.

"Who?" Grace asked.

"The portrait on the wall of the sociology lecture theatre. It's you, isn't it?"

"No!" Grace's laughter was too loud in the awkward circle, the glasses of sangria she had already drunk gave it a brittle edge. Caroline stayed silent. Grace turned to her, as though to share the joke. "Car?"

"It is you, definitely." Chi said, nodding assuredly as though the matter had been settled. "I gotta tell you, you must have done something special for him to paint a monument like that. Most girls don't even get a second date." Chi's eyes ran up and down Caroline's body, taking her in.

Grace turned to face Caroline, creating a wall of staring faces. Her eyes were fierce. It was difficult to know if a type of sisterly protectiveness was rearing its head, or if she was simply embarrassed to not have known. "McGovernor? Really? I hear he's a total pig."

"I've only met him a couple of times. He was a bit arrogant, nothing special. I don't know why he did the portrait."

"Did you sleep with him?"

"No!" Caroline felt the blood rush to her cheeks. Grace seemed determined to make her uncomfortable. There was no protectiveness in this, only revenge for keeping her in the dark.

"I see. You're holding out on him so he's upped the ante by creating this homage to you."

"I'm not holding out on him, we're just – we've only spoken twice!"

Grace rolled her eyes. "It's obvious what he wants. What are you going to do?"

"I don't know. I haven't seen him since he painted it."

"You won't have to wait long. He's supposed to be coming tonight." Chi rejoined the conversation, looking around eagerly as she spoke, the gleam of a huntress in her eyes. "With his new girlfriend, I'm told. We all presumed it was the woman in the painting, but I guess not." Grace was watching Caroline closely, as though waiting to see what her real feelings were. Caroline shrugged. Nonchalance would not work, she knew, while her cheeks remained tomato-coloured, but she had no recourse to anything else. She had no interesting information about Lawrence, and no interest in speculating.

"I guess that means I can tell him not to paint any more giant portraits of me."

Chi raised her eyebrows and turned away, clearly bored with the lack of gossip. Grace, tired of entertaining her embarrassing, and embarrassed, younger sister, shooed her off towards the drinks table.

The drinks table was laden with beers. Caroline usually avoided beer. The bitterness and bubbles made her ill, especially if combined with food. Tonight, however, it was all that was on offer now the sangria was gone, and she took the first one she saw. The cap was still on, and she turned and tapped a shoulder behind her to ask for a bottle-opener. Lawrence, his hair as wild as hers had been when she had arrived, turned to her. His smile broadened. "Caroline, my favourite muse. How are you?" Behind him a tall woman with ashen-blonde curls framing her face was drinking from a flask. The woman frowned at his greeting.

"That was quite a painting you did." Caroline, the embarrassment of her conversation with Grace and Chi still fresh, was suddenly angry.

"Why thank you." He chuckled, apparently perfectly at ease. "You make for a fascinating subject."

"It seems to have got quite a reaction." The edge to her

voice got harder but he appeared not to notice.

"Meaningless talk by bored people, my dear. What did you think of it?"

"I knew it was me, so it must have been good." The sarcasm made it sound like an insult. The beer was still in her hand, her fingers gripping the wet neck.

"Superficial talent only," he waved his hand, a touch of annoyance creeping into his own smile. "Anyone can copy physical features. What did you think of the rest of it?" She went to make a biting, dismissive comment but paused for a moment. An internal struggle between embarrassing Lawrence to pay him back for her own humiliation, and a desire for him to like her, played within her. She was no good at games, however, so with a deep breath she settled for the truth, consequences unknown.

"I looked like a bit of a siren. Like I wanted to lure people into the sociology theatre." Lawrence bellowed a laugh, causing several people to turn curiously in their direction. Caroline saw Grace look over and frown.

"A siren. I love it. You are, of course, no such thing I take it?"

"Not as far as I'm aware."

"Perhaps you are unaware of your allure." His voice had dropped suddenly, creating an intimacy between them that was quickly broken by his date dropping her arm around his shoulders.

"Lawrence, darling, you said you'd introduce me to the artist."

"I also said to use the term 'artist' with a hint of sarcasm, *darling*." His voice was petty, mean, and the blonde pulled back as though he had struck her.

"Fine. I'll find him myself." She turned and pushed her way through the crowd. Caroline watched her go, her green woollen dress was so figure-hugging that it seemed leaving was her best angle and the sight left Caroline feeling inadequate. Lawrence stepped closer, as close as he could without touching her.

"You didn't come back." His voice was quiet, the note of embarrassment in it surprised her. "The day I painted the mural. You didn't come back." It was more than embarrassment, there was a genuine hint of pain in his voice.

"I did. I was too late. You'd already left."

"You did?" His teeth shone at her from his sudden wide smile. "That's all right then." He slipped a hand against her waist as the crowd jostled them closer together. "How have you been?" She was used to men who didn't hold eye contact, and the connection created by looking directly into his eyes made her hands shake. She looked at the bottle in her hand. His breath smelled faintly of whiskey.

"I've been fine."

"How's sociology?"

"I missed too many classes so I dropped it."

"Perhaps this is your opportunity."

"For what?"

"For doing what you've always loved. You don't look like

a sociologist to me."

"I'm also studying French."

"You don't look French either."

"What do I look like, then?" She asked, impatient with his strange, circular conversation.

"Like an artist. What do you do?"

"I've sculpted a bit. Or I did in Perth. It's been a couple of years now." His hand found hers and pulled it up into the light, removing the still unopened bottle of beer. He studied her fingers in detail, running a finger lightly along the edge of a fingernail.

"Yes, these are sculptor's hands. Strong. But," he needled her palm softly, "too smooth." Caroline smiled nervously and pulled her hand away, aware of the dark rim of dirt edging her nails.

"Like I said, it's been a couple of years." He snapped open her beer with a bottle-opener attached to his keys, and gave it back to her.

"You should come by my studio tomorrow. I'm sure I could rustle up some clay for you."

"You have your own studio?"

"Someone somewhere thinks I'm pretty good."

She had left with him that night. Grace, after too many drinks, seemed to no longer care about his ruthless reputation, and had grinned broadly as she spotted them leaving together. Caroline was nervous. She had slept with two men, both as inexperienced as she was. Both very different experiences, she was sure, than Lawrence had had.

But there was something in the air, fired up perhaps by the fierce winds, which made her feel reckless. As they had walked to the bus stop he had walked close to her, without touching. The space between them seemed magnetised.

He had been sharing a house with several other visual arts students. As he opened the door for her she took his hand, and some of the magic dispersed. The smell of dust, crusted greasy food and something strong and chemical, paint perhaps or even glue, intrigued, and faintly disgusted, her as she entered. Caroline's house was clean, and her room was tidy, she was that type of person. But this elasticity in the bounds of what she knew to be acceptable added to her sense that tonight was different, that she could be different now that she was in his world.

He held her fingers and took her through to his bedroom, which was at the back of the house. It looked like it was supposed to be a study. On the floor was a mattress, larger than a single but not quite a double. Bundled up on top of it was a dark navy blanket, and pale cream sheets were wrapped around the edges, although one corner had come undone, exposing the soft grey material of the mattress underneath. It was not the room of a man trying to impress women.

He had closed the door softly behind her. He seemed completely at ease but her heart was racing. She ran her hands over her hair, hoping to control the frizz which had sprung up again with the journey from the gallery. Lawrence seemed not to notice or care that his shoulder-length hair was sticking up almost at right angles. His nonchalance made it unimportant, and made her movements feel vain.

He was in the corner of the room, squatting in front of a record-player, flicking through a small pile of records. They were all singles, and he chose one without showing her. The needle dropped jaggedly onto it, and the sounds of a heavy guitar riff came out of the speakers. It was the sort of music which should be played loudly, thumping out of open windows. Loud enough to entertain, or annoy, neighbours. He kept the volume down low, however, creating a strangely uneven mood. He turned and saw her standing where he had left her by the door. He laughed, softly, without malice, and gestured towards a beanbag which was sitting to one side of the bed.

"Have a seat. I'll be back in a minute." She waited until he had left the room before she sat in the beanbag, knowing that she would look awkward and uncomfortable lowering herself into the mound of material. He returned with a joint, two glasses and a bottle of whiskey. Caroline had never smoked before, and realised that she had no idea what to do. She reached for the whiskey and poured herself a hefty measure.

He reclined against the side of the beanbag, his back almost to her, and lit the joint. He blew smoke towards the ceiling. She could study the back of his head from this angle. His hair was even thicker than she had thought; it looked as though her hand would get lost if she tried to touch it. The smoke from the joint swirled with the fragrance of the cheap whiskey and she felt nauseous.

"I love this music. Do you know it? It's a Sydney band, though they're from Melbourne originally. Fantastic live performers. So much energy. So much passion." He held the joint towards her and she took it with a shaking hand. He leaned his head against the bean bag and closed his eyes. Relieved that he was not watching her, she studied the end of it carefully. It was moist and unappealing. She put it to her lips and recoiled slightly at the cold damp paper and bitter taste. She hardly breathed it in before she gave it back, taking several large sips of whiskey to remove the taste from her lips. He barely opened his eyes to receive it. His glass was still empty.

After taking a few puffs, he held the joint out to her again but she shook her head, then grunted 'no' when she realised he could not see her. She was surprised, and relieved, that he accepted her refusal without question. Her head felt heavy from the smoke in the room. He took a few more puffs then squeezed off the burning end. He sat up and rested it carefully on an overturned shoebox that doubled as a mini coffee-table.

He lay back, staring at the ceiling. Her glass was almost empty, and her head was pounding. She poured herself more whiskey, wanting to be drunk enough to not worry about what was going to happen. After a few moments the record scratched its way to the end, and the room was silent. A pattering of raindrops hit the window, which had no curtains and let the light from the streetlight outside directly into the room.

"I'm not going to sleep with you."

Caroline held her whiskey in her mouth for a few seconds until she was sure she could swallow it without spluttering. "I'm not going to sleep with you, either."

"But you were going to." He tilted his head back so he could see her. "Weren't you?" She stayed silent, her eyes on her whiskey. She felt rejected but also relieved. She took a large gulp, almost draining the glass. He was still watching her. He leant over, his fingers played with the hair which she had tried to straighten over her forehead. Then they dropped, and held her free hand, his fingers warm against hers.

Caroline sat up on the bed. Night had fallen and the bedroom was dark. There were sounds of cooking coming from the kitchen and Lawrence had turned up his music. He was making sushi, he had said that morning, and was listening to the soundtrack from *Seven Samurai*. She felt like something warm, pasta perhaps, or soup. But sushi was his favourite.

"Sushi time!" Lawrence's voice echoed down from the kitchen. She swung her legs to the floor and felt her toes crack as she stood. She joined him at the kitchen table. They each had three neat sushi rolls on their plate. Several dipping sauces, red black and brown, sat in the middle of the table. Cranberry juice and mineral water bottles were at the end of the table, ready to be combined into Lawrence's mid-week dinner drink.

"Thank you for cooking." She reached over to squeeze his hand. He held it, softly at first then tighter as she went to pull it away.

"Thank you. For everything."

FIFTEEN

It was a quiet Thursday night on King Street. The strangely windless air and empty footpaths created an eerie atmosphere as though everyone was inside waiting for disaster to strike.

Andie and Joey had been to the cinema and were now eating frozen yoghurt and drifting down the street, pausing occasionally to look in the windows of shops. Andie had always got on well with her father, unlike Charlotte. When Celine first left, Charlotte had become a sulky teenager and Joey had struggled to find ways of talking to her. Looking back, Andie thought it was understandable that her reaction to Charlotte's moodiness and the sudden absence of their mother was to become livelier, as though she could fill the sudden spaces in their family with her own personality. Joey had surely noticed what she was doing, but his way of dealing with things was to smile and hope they went away. Not that he wanted her good mood to go away, but he relaxed a lot around her when she stopped performing for them all. She had always felt that he appreciated her good humour through that time, however, like he wouldn't have coped with two sulky teenagers and an ambitious, absent wife.

Joey didn't really understand ambition. The first time Andie saw him really happy after Celine left was when Charlotte had announced that she was going to stop studying music at university. Andie was making sandwiches for their lunches, Joey was doing the breakfast dishes, and they were laughing about something that had been said on the breakfast radio show they were listening to. Charlotte had emerged from the shower, her hair dripping water onto her shoulders, and announced with some defiance that she wasn't going back for her second year. She would get a job she enjoyed, something she could work her way up in. She didn't want any more study, she didn't want any more stress.

Joey had listened, his hands resting in the soapy water in the sink. When Charlotte had finished talking he looked down for a moment, as though calming himself, but when he looked back up it was with tears in his eyes. He had walked over and hugged Charlotte tightly, leaving suds on the back of her dressing gown. "Whatever makes you happy," he had said, and looking up at Andie, he added, "that goes for you, too." Andie had joined them and they had held each other for several long moments. Andie had felt her sister almost shaking with the liberation of finally saying what she wanted. When they pulled away from each other, Joey had looked relieved. Relieved, Andie had guessed, that he wasn't losing another family member to creative ambitions.

Andie, while glad for Charlotte, had also started feeling uncomfortable; although she was only fourteen years old at the time she had already begun harbouring the desire to be some kind of writer. Joey never asked her about that, even when she was in her early twenties and only working part-time to give herself time to write. She always had the impression that he had sympathised somewhat with Leon, although his focus on financial security was not what Joey encouraged either. In any case, ambition, creative or otherwise, had felt taboo in their mother's absence.

Now, as the only middle-aged person she knew, however, Andie wanted his opinion about the McGovernors. Joey dropped his used napkin in a bin after rubbing his mouth vigorously with it.

"I know they call it frozen yoghurt, but it really tastes like ice cream to me."

"Especially when you get the chocolate flavoured one," Andie said, dropping her napkin and last corner of her cone into the bin as well. They kept walking, their hands still slightly sticky from the dessert.

"My last interview with Lawrence McGovernor didn't go very well."

"Hmm? How come?"

"I think I was too antagonistic. I wanted him to tell me why his wife wasn't as successful as he is, if he had supported her like she supported him, but he didn't seem to like that question."

They walked a few steps in silence before Joey answered. "Well, he might not like the question, or he might not like the answer. Or he might not know the answer. No one knows what it's like inside a marriage, remember that." Joey stopped to gaze inside a clothes store full of leather jackets. Andie had the impression that his interest in the apparel was feigned.

"Did Celine ever suggest that she would have been

famous if it wasn't for – us?" Her voice was tentative, high, as though she could ask the question without really asking the question. Joey started walking again, even slower than before. He sighed.

"Oh Andie, your mother and I had so many conversations. I told her she should do whatever made her happy. Maybe I was a fool to think that staying with us would have been a part of that." He was staring at his shoes as he walked. "I was supportive of what she did. You might not remember that but I never told her not to do anything. I told her she had to be present in our family as well though, not go prioritising some theatre people I'd never met over our family." He paused as they waited for a car to pass before they crossed a side street. As they stepped onto the footpath on the other side, he said, "Do these artists you're talking to have children?"

Andie cleared her voice before she answered, "No."

"I think that's different. Children have to come first, there's no question of that. But without children? Maybe it's up to the individuals to do what they have to do for themselves. I'm not sure you can lay the blame anywhere but with the person who didn't follow their dreams."

"If you and Celine hadn't had kids, do you think she would have stayed?" Andie felt strange talking about herself as not-existing, but she was sure it was something that her father had considered.

"Andie," he stopped and took her arm gently. "I would have gone with her." Andie held her breath, confused at the

A Perilous Margin

sudden image of her father as a bronzed, Californian husband. "Without you and Charlotte, I would have had no reason to stay here. But my life would have been emptier. I didn't have the ambition your mother had, but it doesn't matter, because I have you." He was staring at her intently, as though wanting to make her understand. Andie nodded. She wasn't sure if she understood but she didn't want to cause Joey any more pain by arguing with his logic about his life. She linked her arm through his and they continued walking.

For the next half hour, Andie tried to make lighter conversation, but neither of them were in the mood, and when she hugged him goodbye at the train station he held her a second longer than normal.

When Andie opened the door she could hear the sound of water boiling in the kettle.

"Tea?" George called, emerging from his bedroom with a dirty mug in his hand.

"Oh god, yes please," Andie said, dropping her bag on the floor and sinking into the couch. "Charlotte gave me some ANZAC biscuits on the weekend, if you want something sweet with it," she added, lying back and closing her eyes.

"What does Charlotte think of these interviews you're doing?" George asked as he filled their cups with the boiling water.

"We didn't talk about it actually. It was all party party party." Andie struggled to sit up as George handed her the cup and put the container of soft, oat biscuits on the table.

"People with kids always forget that there are other things to talk about," he said.

Andie made a vague noise of agreement. George gave her a strange look, as though wondering why she had not said more. She tried to change the subject. "I have my first interview with Caroline tomorrow," she said.

"That must be nerve-wracking after what happened with Lawrence!" George grinned at her. When she had recounted the last interview with Lawrence he had laughed for a long time. He thought it was exactly what she had wanted to do: ask direct questions that would prompt answers which weren't straight out of the shiny, official version of Lawrence's life. In some ways it was, Andie admitted, but she had not expected it to make her feel petty, and small, and a little bit naïve.

"Actually, I'm much less nervous than I thought I would be. I'm kind of excited that she agreed to be interviewed at all, even though it's kind of a strange situation."

"Does she seem easy to talk to?"

"No, not at all. Actually, it might be quite hard to talk to her! But I do feel like she will understand where I'm coming from. She might even thank me for it!"

"Do you need some help preparing questions?" His eyes gleamed at the thought.

"I already have questions," she said, apologetically. "I think I'll try to make it more of a conversation, though. Caroline isn't used to being interviewed so I think the whole thing can be a lot less professional."

When she went to bed that night she was still thinking about the interview. She knew it was presumptuous to think that Caroline might appreciate the questions, the angle, more than Lawrence had. Knowing it was presumptuous however, didn't stop her being sure that she was right and that Caroline might be glad to have someone who thought about Lawrence's role as a husband as well as an artist. Joey would have been willing to go to Los Angeles with Celine while Lawrence couldn't even lend Caroline a hand in Sydney. She tried not to think about what Celine would have said if Joey had volunteered to accompany her to Los Angeles.

***

The front path to the house in Tempe was lined with banksias. They looked as though they had been there for years and had taken liberties with their position. Andie reached a hand out as she walked past and felt the brittle flakes of the old brushes. On the front veranda were several pots of well-kept herbs. They were sitting strategically for the morning sunlight. Andie recognised mint, coriander, and basil, but the rest had unfamiliar leaves.

Caroline answered the door in clothes as neat as those she had been wearing at Lawrence's talk at the Arts Centre. Dark green trousers of an indeterminate material, a black blouse that moved easily over her skin, and a chunky blue and gold necklace sitting beneath the collar of her shirt. Andie was glad she had worn the clothes she needed for work later that afternoon. The pants, unlike most of her wardrobe, were ironed at least. Caroline smiled politely and gestured for Andie to come into the house.

They moved in silence down a hallway and into a back courtyard. Andie was struck by the realisation that she had not seen Caroline in weeks, despite her almost constant presence in Andie's thoughts. The realisation brought a rush of nerves: her ideas about who this woman was were suddenly based on nothing but speculation and daydreaming. Her presumption that Caroline would not only understand Andie's previous attack on Lawrence but might actually appreciate it seemed not only juvenile but possibly dangerous. Her nerves increased with every step as she imagined Caroline like a lioness, leaping to defend Lawrence against an attack.

Outside, Caroline turned quickly, making Andie recoil. "I hope you don't mind sitting here. I enjoy the afternoon air in Sydney. It feels very crisp at this time of year." There was no smile, but her voice was not aggressive.

"This is lovely."

"I'll make us some tea." Caroline motioned for Andie to sit and returned inside. Andie sat down on a green chair which was part of the garden furniture in the centre of the courtyard, and removed her papers from her bag. She was surrounded by neat rows of flowers. There was no grass, only pavers and plants. Andie had never acquainted herself with types of flowers, all she thought was that they looked foreign: the small, brightly coloured petals of purple, yellow, and pink looked distinctly British to her. Perhaps this was what the banksias out the front had been rebelling against. Caroline returned with a pot of tea and two large mugs on a tray.

"I hope you don't mind the un-dainty kitchenware. I can't stand drinking from teacups. Too many refills."

Andie murmured a note of agreement and reached for her mug, her hand trembling slightly. She saw Caroline notice, and it made the trembling worse. They sat facing each other, their eyes firmly on their tea. Caroline blew across the top of her mug vigorously, and Andie could see the ripples her breath made on the liquid.

"Do you mind if I record?"

"Of course not. I don't expect you to remember everything." Caroline looked up from her tea as Andie sat the phone between them. Her eyes were not unkind, but they were not welcoming either. Andie began to wonder why Caroline had offered these interviews. And then wondered why it had not occurred to her to question the woman's motives earlier. There was a long pause as Andie struggled to remove the cap from her pen. She felt her cheeks flush.

"I might just ask a few background questions first, to understand the kinds of experiences you've had with exhibiting. When I first asked to interview you – and you turned me down –" Andie was shocked that she had said that and began to stutter as she continued on, "– you said that you haven't exhibited in a long time. But you were interested in being an artist when you were younger? When did that interest start?"

"I was born in Esperance, Western Australia, and was always interested in art, for as long as I can remember," Caroline didn't make eye contact as she spoke, and her words were slow in coming as though she had to think about what she was saying. It was very different to the polished performance of Lawrence. "I took classes outside of school as well as for my final year exams, and I did very well. I was originally intending to travel to France after high-school but that couldn't happen in the end. My mother got very sick," Caroline paused, looking away as though unsure why she had mentioned this detail. Andie nodded, trying to look sympathetic and encouraging at the same time. "Anyway, it was a bad time to leave so I started university in Perth. My younger brother was still at home as well so between us we studied and looked after our mother." Andie was finding it difficult to listen and think of the next question at the same time. She realised now how useful it had been that Lawrence talked non-stop during their first interview.

"Did you study art?"

"No, actually. My mother thought it was a flaky career choice so I studied French, intending to be a translator."

Andie wrote her notes slowly, giving herself time to think of some more questions. Caroline sat quietly, drinking her tea. "Why did you start to study sculpture?"

"My brother and I moved to Sydney when our mother died. I transferred my French degree to Sydney University with some Arts subjects as well but I didn't finish it. In my third year, just after I met Lawrence, I transferred to a visual arts degree. He was very convincing about the need to follow our dreams, our passions."

"How did the two of you meet?"

"Is this for your assignment?"

"Oh, sorry," Andie said, embarrassed. "I'm still using his interviews for my assignment as well so I thought it would be good to get someone else's perspective on him when he was young. I'll be writing about both of you," Andie looked down at the pen in her hand, wondering if she had covered up for her nosiness. She looked up when she heard Caroline chuckle slightly.

"He was a PhD student and was involved in painting some murals in one of the newly developed areas of the campus. It was the area in which my sociology tutorials were held. We met, we talked. After a while, we started seeing each other."

"What were your first impressions of him?"

"He was short compared to the Australian men. But his voice was very engaging. He spoke authoritatively about many subjects. I found it difficult to disagree with him, even if I thought he might be wrong. He had a very commanding presence, even as a twenty-four year old."

"And his painting?"

"His painting was under-developed. He was very abstract at that time. Heavily influenced by cubism, although it was deeply unfashionable by then. He was a well-known student although he didn't get along with many people. He hung around various gatherings trying to start arguments with people. He had many rows with the teachers in his department. He was a tough person to talk to."

"He must have done something right, to interest you in a relationship with him!"

"Not really. I was easily swayed, simply because he showed interest in me. I wasn't very experienced, nor very confident."

"So he wooed you?" Andie held her breath, wondering if she had gone too far, but Caroline barely seemed aware of her anymore. She was staring into the far corner of the garden, her tea forgotten in her hands.

"I suppose so. He made me feel like art was interesting, and necessary to the world. He was genuine and his views were sober. We were surrounded by people who would argue passionately about something, but their words were rarely reflected in their actions. Or their art. I guess he wooed me by being a real person, a real artist, in a world of pretenders."

"Did you feel like your art was genuine?"

There was a long pause as Caroline sat motionless. Andie wondered if she should repeat the question but then Caroline said, "No. Not really. I was swayed by all those other people around us. I wanted to be more like him, more confident in going against the grain. And I suppose as we spent more time together that happened to some extent. But the way everyone else spoke, and their view of the world, made the mediocrity of their talent easier to disguise. When I spent time with them, without him, it disguised my mediocrity as well. I think that's what attracts aspiring artists to each other. There's a buzzing around, a lot of talk of things that turn out to simply be fads but which feel so real at the time. Our talent wasn't being tested, and so we didn't know that we were going to fail. We could hide behind our own bluster. Lawrence had nowhere to hide, he was claiming to be totally genuine and free from the fads of the time. There was a quiet calmness around his art. His personality was aggressive but his art was produced in silence. And he had enough talent that the silence didn't matter. It took a while, but eventually his art spoke for itself, and it had a much stronger voice than anyone else's had."

"What did you do after you graduated? Did you want to be a professional artist?

"I did, of course. After our first exhibition there was some interest in my work but I felt uncomfortable that it had come to me so easily, I didn't really trust it so I didn't pursue it. I started teaching art courses instead, keeping my work private. But then we were short of money so I started casual teaching at high-schools. When Lawrence wasn't working at all I took up a full-time position doing administration at a high-school. It was the only full-time work available in schools at the time. I stayed until I was in my forties and we were financially a bit more stable. Now I do various things part-time."

Andie's hand had begun to cramp from trying to write so fast. Caroline sat in silence but her attention seemed to have returned to the present. As she placed a deliberate full stop at the end of a sentence, Andie realised she was unsure of what to ask next. In these few moments she seemed to have lost any semblance of rhythm to their interchange. In haste, she blurted out:

"Did you like it?"

Caroline raised her eyebrows. "Working at the school?" She asked, and Andie nodded. "Not particularly. But unfortunately our finances could only support one artist."

"And it had to be you, doing the financing?" Andie forced her voice to be soft, gentle, trying to counter-act the potential aggression of the question. Caroline looked at Andie hard, her eyes narrowed slowly although she seemed to be gazing through Andie to the pale green of the fence behind her.

"It was me doing it. I'm not sure if it had to be." Andie felt a wall being lowered between them and decided to change tack entirely to relieve some of the tension.

"Do you come from a big family?" Caroline looked up quickly, apparently suspicious of why Andie had not continued on from the previous question.

"No. My father left when I was seven. I have an older sister and a younger brother."

"Do they still live in Sydney?"

"My sister died a few years ago, breast cancer. My younger brother is in Sydney."

"What did they think when you were trying to be an artist?" There was a long pause and then, suddenly,

Caroline looked at her watch.

"Unfortunately, I'm sorry, our time is up." Her voice had a lilt, a dismissal hidden in an apology. Andie glanced at her watch as she gathered her things together. It had barely been an hour.

"Thank you so much for your time. Is the same time next week alright?"

"Yes. Please call on Tuesday afternoon to check."

"Sure. Thanks, thank you Caroline." Andie's voice became formal, a reaction to the quick ending of their interview. Caroline stood, turned quickly, and walked into the house. Andie followed, adjusting her belongings under her arm. The narrow hallway felt longer to exit than it had when she entered. At the front door Caroline turned and offered her hand. "Next week, then." Her rough palm scratched against Andie's soft fingertips.

"Yes. And thanks again." The door clicked shut softly behind her while she was only one step down. Andie resisted the urge, however, to turn back and look. She walked back to the train station, purposefully at first, as though she had somewhere to be, and then slowing into a meander.

She felt windblown, pummelled by something that had gone unnoticed. The touch of regret in Caroline's voice as she had called the interview to a close did not disguise the fact that she had dismissed Andie at a crucial point. Andie had wanted to lead on to how Caroline's family saw Lawrence, his success especially, and whether they were ever disappointed that Caroline had not reached the same heights. Had Caroline guessed that that was where the questions were going, or was she simply on a strict time schedule?

The afternoon felt sloppy. Her non-professional approach had back-fired terribly. It had seemed like such a good idea, a way to make it conversational and, hopefully, more revealing. She knew she had merely looked unprepared and amateur. And nosy. And even after learning some more about Caroline's background, she was still unsure how she was going to tie the interviews in with Lawrence's and link them all to her topic. She had thought institutional art was a good way to go but now that she was speaking to Caroline it seemed so clear that she had little experience with that side of art. Except in a supportive wife kind of way, which was not particularly helpful.

SIXTEEN

Caroline fumbled with the lock as she shut the door behind Andie. She suddenly had no idea why she had agreed to be interviewed. Strangers were draining, and Caroline could feel herself spiralling.

The couch was soft, curving around her weakened legs. She was used to spending time with people who knew her history. She barely had the conversation with anyone anymore, the conversation about where her family were, the conversation about the deaths of her mother and her sister. Mentioning them, even in passing, rattled her.

She ran a hand gently over the bulk of her breast. She was methodical and calm in her self-examinations, although occasionally a touch of panic entered her fingers. Her doctor, a gravelly-voiced woman with ludicrously green glasses, had explained to her, on numerous occasions, as though she needed reminding, that she was in the same age-bracket her mother and sister had been when they had been hit with the aggressive disease. She had felt like hissing that she already knew that, that she had been there, in both cases, to watch the previously strong bodies crumple under the weight of genetics. Unlike most women her age, Caroline longed to be older, longed to be past this danger zone where her mortality was pressed upon her, through her own fingertips, every morning in the shower.

From outside the window she could feel spring trying to get in to her. This time of year, with the floating pollen and the gradually warming days, the crisp grass trying desperately to hold on to its greenery before its inevitable return to golden brown, the changing winds with their promise of burning days and tempestuous fires, made her nauseous with remembered grief. To others, this change of season brought thoughts of Christmas, the time of year when lying on the beach for hours, or in front of the cricket for hours, or in a swimming pool for hours, was acceptable. The last time she had spoken to Damian had been near the end of winter the previous year, the approaching spring an unnamed enemy between them. The city had still been wrapped in its slight chill and its inhabitants were in their winter fashion, trying desperately to mimic the European styles designed for frosted, snowy days that lasted months. Caroline had watched Damian approaching her, older now than she ever thought he could be, his back hunched against the unfamiliar cold. She was unused to seeing him like this, coming towards her willingly. For years it seemed she had been chasing him, always falling short of reaching him but just trying to keep him in her sights.

It had been the last day at their mother's hospital that the chase began. The doors had shut behind them with a solid finality, despite opening moments later for other visitors. Damian, hands shoved deep in his pockets, had said, "I'm going out. See you at home, later." The 'later' was both a farewell and an unspecific time frame. She had watched him leave, his broad back was becoming more like their father's as the years crept by. He was barely seventeen.

A Perilous Margin

Caroline had walked through the grounds towards her car. She had stopped thinking of it as her mother's car since her mother had been unable to drive for over a year. A streak of sunlight had glided over her face, the warmth of spring behind its rays. Life had thrown her a hard few months, and she knew she had struggled on more than one occasion, but now, the tragic end was not creating the devastating grief she had expected. Over the last few months it had occurred to her that she had already lost her mother, a woman who had been a second soul to her for many years. That woman had long since disappeared, replaced by a shrunken shard of pain. The world was now a little freer of suffering, she thought to herself with relief.

The car, a silver hatchback in need of a wash after being pummelled by winter's rain and mud, had come into view, nestled between a red Charger and a rusted Fiat. Her mother had been so excited to buy this car. She had loved it so much she had refused to drive it very often, until, exasperated, Damian, an impatient fifteen year old, had told her that she was actually destroying it by not using it. As though suddenly released, Leanne had begun driving everywhere, reckless with her new-found freedom.

Caroline had found the keys in her bag, the soccer ball keyring a memento from her father's long ago hobby. The key had to be shoved, wiggled and cajoled into working the lock. Eventually, the mechanism clicked and she could open the door. She had thrown her bag over to the passenger seat before climbing in herself.

As the door fell into place with a rusted clink, she was enveloped in her mother's smell – lavender hand cream which still sat in the glove-box, and something more earthy, almost bready. The scent, which Caroline had been sure she had conquered by driving with the window down, had returned with the entrapped heat. And with its return came a sensation of spinning through time, memories cascading as a physical wave. Caroline had frozen, not wanting to move lest the momentary time-travelling disappear. She gripped her legs, just above the knee, and held on as pictures of her mother washed over her. After several moments that had spanned her childhood, her nose accustomed itself to the fragrances of the car and the memories faded away. She opened her eyes and realised tears had run down her face and onto her lap. Her hands had been shaking as she placed them on the steering wheel. She knew she could not drive. She had wished Damian was there, that he would come back from wherever he had wandered off to, that he would take the keys from her and take her home and they could sit together with tea and lemon slice and memories of their mother and their grief, together, shared.

He had returned three days later, when her grief had been drowned out by panic. She had grabbed him as he came through the door, then pummelled him, harder than she thought she could, across his stomach and shoulders as he tried to get away from her. Her sobs had embarrassed her, the older sister falling apart from lack of comfort. The day before, in a moment of weakness, she had called Grace, who was already living in Sydney. She had hung up after two rings. Grace had long since distanced herself from the family, an unspoken disagreement with Leanne had become irreconcilable until it was too late to try, and she had refused to even return for the funeral. During those last weeks and days of Leanne's life, Caroline had thought she would never speak to Grace again. The coldness that emanated from her absence had seemed impossibly cruel. In Sydney a year later she had realised where the distance had come from, as she had seen Grace grip her girlfriend's hand in defiance.

Damian had had no explanation for his absence, nor any words of apology. But Caroline's distress must have been evident because he had hung around the house for several days, and, a few weeks later, he suggested they move to Sydney together. Caroline wondered sometimes whether her fear of losing her entire family had made her agree to the move. If she had been more confident of their bond, perhaps she would have allowed him to go on alone, while she stayed to finish her studies in Perth. The thought of how different her life might have been disconcerted her.

She was brought back to herself with the beep of her phone. It was Lawrence saying he was on his way home. And, almost as an afterthought, he added he had spoken to Bridget and refused the collaboration, but she wasn't coming back to Sydney anymore so it didn't matter anyway. The news seemed too momentous to be included as an appendix to a text message and Caroline felt briefly frustrated with

Lawrence's lack of concern for her feelings. The frustration faded, however, when she realised what it meant – Bridget wasn't coming back. She could continue to forget about her, and so could Lawrence. A weight she hadn't noticed seemed to lift.

Caroline rose from the couch. Lawrence would return tired and hungry and with stories of the incompetence he had encountered at the gallery all day. Perhaps they wouldn't have to even mention Bridget now, it would be a simple understanding between them. She knew, however, that he would be interested in the interview with Andie, but also stubbornly determined to not appear concerned. His interest would stem from anxiety over what Andie had repeated of their own interviews. Caroline wondered whether she had it in her to play with his fears, but quickly knew the answer. She had never been good at games. She began removing items from the fridge in preparation for cooking dinner.

SEVENTEEN

A cup of sweet tea sat by Andie's hand in a café that was more of a diner. She liked the grungy atmosphere here, it was so different to the feeling of academic authority on campus.

She had come to do the readings for her course as she felt like she was falling behind in it. Or not falling behind exactly, since she was on track with her interviews and the assignment, but she had let slide the deeper, theoretical level in favour of concentrating on Lawrence and Caroline as individuals. As she turned to the week's readings, however, she was immediately suspicious of the theme: women in art. Why can't women just be included alongside men in the other topics, she thought to herself. Now it was brought to her attention, the previous weeks had been male-heavy – had they been saving up the women for this week? The first reading was A Room of One's Own. She had read some of Virginia Woolf's other works, but never this one, and she began to read with high expectations. The work was asking what conditions were necessary for the creation of art. Woolf really should not have given away the answer in the title, Andie thought to herself with a smile. Outside the window of the café, the sun was burning through the leftover haze from the morning.

An hour later she closed her reader, her breathing shallow. She sat, barely moving, for a long moment before suddenly opening the reader again, her eyes searching for the line. "...the excuse of lack of opportunity, training, encouragement, leisure and money no longer holds good." If it was not an excuse for not succeeding or at least trying then, Andie thought, less than a decade after women got the vote, then it was certainly no excuse now, after a century of voting and education. Andie wrote a few furious notes.

Are we too easy on ourselves?

Our history is full of women not achieving enough.

And we are products of our history.

But cycles can be broken, if people are willing.

Are women unwilling?

"Those look like some big thoughts you're having," a deep voice said. She looked up, conscious of her messed up hair and wrinkled forehead. She tried to smooth her expression as she smiled at the waiter who had come to take her rubbish away. She knew his job was not to clean up after her, that was what the self-service bins were for. He was probably trying to do something to pass the time before his shift ended.

"Just some reading I'm doing for a class."

"What's it about?" He was handsome, a word she rarely used as it seemed so old-fashioned. But he was the sort of clear-skinned, wide-featured man who featured in black-and-white films.

"It's about women and art." It sounded lame and she stammered on. "It's about why women find it so difficult to allow themselves the time and opportunity to be creative."

"Right, cool." His eyes looked glazed. "Have you found

any answers yet?"

"I'm not sure I agree with the answers I've found."

"Yeah, that happens, doesn't it?" Her Styrofoam cup cracked slightly under the pressure from his hand as he turned away.

Feeling like Marco could have chosen a more sympathetic reading for the week's topic, she turned to the next segment. It wasn't an academic article, however, it was a series of newspaper reports and editorials about a group called the Guerrilla Girls. She had never heard of them before but glancing across the photos of them in gorilla masks and the messages they scrawled outside galleries, she thought she had seen spoofs of them in skit shows.

The group was established in 1985 and were still, apparently, going strong. There were examples of some posters they had produced: famous paintings with gorilla masks over the faces of the naked women; statistics of female artist representation in major New York galleries. After flicking through the first few pages of the group's work, Andie came to a newspaper article from the beginning of the year. It was about London and the comparatively small number of women commissioned for public art or whose work was sold at auction. Andie read it quickly, feeling uneasy by the juxtaposition of this glass-ceiling argument after reading Virginia Woolf's work. It took her barely twenty minutes to get through the reading and when she finished she shut her book, confused and frustrated. There were no neat arguments and it made her uncomfortable.

She left the café and made her way towards her Communications lecture. As she crossed the campus, however, her bag swinging heavily against her back, she suddenly veered off the path which was taking her to the lecture theatre and instead sat by a tree in one of the many common grassy areas. Grass was always sparse under gumtrees and this one was no different, but she hardly noticed the dry earth attaching itself to the seat of her jeans.

She didn't spare a thought for the lecture she was missing: she was falling behind, but something was growing inside her, pulling at the strands of her life. She had always been a little proud of herself for not being angry at Celine for leaving. Disappointed and sad, yes, but not angry. She thought she had understood her mother's ambition in a way that Joey and Charlotte hadn't, and while Andie was sad it had taken her away from them all, she understood that it was what Celine had to do. Why then, if Celine's actions made sense and if her own ambition still sat heavily in the back of her mind, had Andie given up writing? Did she have an excuse or even a reason? It was difficult with Leon, always commenting on pipedreams and phases, on growing up and taking responsibility. But she was proud of seeing through him and his putdowns, of getting out before he had sucked her in. And yet, perhaps she hadn't escaped at all. Two years and she still hadn't written anything, hadn't been to a reading evening or renewed her journal subscriptions. Giving up had felt like falling in line with everyone's expectations – Joey and Charlotte never asked about her writing except with some embarrassment, and the fact that they didn't have to ask anymore seemed to lift a weight from the family. The phase had ended, as they had known it would. And should. She hadn't had the strength to fight against their expectations as well as those of a world in which every second person claimed to be writing a novel but rarely actually did.

She dug her fingers into the tough soil in frustration. Her regret was like a physical weight and yet it was her choice to stop. It had felt easy because there were so many reasons to give up, practical sensible reasons that everyone else followed. Was she really better, more talented than all those other people who had let go of dreams for a real, adult life? Of course she wasn't. She had bumbled along from one attempted style to the next, never finding a voice or a concept that would let her stick out from the crowd. Her lack of confidence was based on the reality of her talent, or lack thereof.

And that, she realised, was where her story differed to that of Caroline: Caroline had been good enough, her talent was all over her early work and a gallery had been interested in her over Lawrence. If Caroline had had someone supporting her, seeing her talent for what it was, perhaps she wouldn't have given up. What was it that Lawrence had done or not done that made it so easy for Caroline to lose her confidence?

***

The lettuce broke with a watery crunch and Andie ate a leaf fragment which escaped the chopping board. The taste contrasted strangely with the sip of coffee she had just taken. She was making a salad for Fi's birthday lunch the next day. She took no pleasure from cooking and a salad seemed like an easy option, although it might be impractical to carry on the train. Her one concession to Charlotte's love of elaborate food was toasted walnuts. She could smell them as they warmed in the frying pan behind her. She would add them to the lettuce with some basil, cucumber and a simplified Jamie Oliver dressing. It was her kind of food, plainness dressed in a decorative coat.

The lunch was the next day and it was only after she had started that she realised it was probably not good to have a salad lying around for longer than necessary. The time combined with the travel and the predictable warmth of the train would make it very limp, she guessed. But it was too late now. Although she loved Fi and wanted to celebrate her birthday with her, her mind had been stuck in an unsatisfied slump since doing the readings the day before. Even her colleagues joking about how her moroseness was repelling customers at work the previous evening hadn't lifted her out of it.

George was lying on the couch, the controller for his Playstation held loosely in his hands. On the screen, flashes of gunfire illuminated a young woman with angular features and a large black afro. She was George's favourite character, and her face was familiar to Andie from the amount of time

A Perilous Margin

George spent playing. While Andie was in the room he kept the sound down, and at the moment they were listening to the radio instead of the sound effects of the guns. It was a current affairs show, and the unfortunately squeaky voice of a female politician who was being interviewed filled the room. George groaned loudly. "She needs a voice coach."

Andie agreed, while moving the frying pan back and forth to even the heat on the walnuts.

"Some things just can't be overcome," she said. "I suspect that voice is one of them. Anyway, it's not as bad as Chris whatshisface, who pauses every two words as though he's saying something really profound."

"That's definitely something he's been trained to do."

"Who would think it sounds good?"

"Someone who doesn't want us to know how dumb he is. Aha!" He sat up, clutching the controller and clacking buttons feverishly. Andie glanced at the television but his character's actions were obscured by a large fireball that suddenly appeared. George swore and collapsed back onto the couch.

Her phone growled against the bench top. "Hi Charlotte." Her sister's voice was almost too soft to hear on the phone and she had to place one hand over her free ear to block out the sound of the radio. A few minutes later she hung up, slightly relieved.

"Everything okay?" George called from the couch, his eyes remaining firmly on the screen.

"Charlotte wants you to come to lunch tomorrow."

His eyes flicked to her, as though gauging her reaction to the statement. He knew Andie's family well and had been included in things which Andie had organised before. An invitation from Charlotte was a new development, however.

"Fi's birthday lunch?"

"Yes." Andie knew she could let him off the hook easily. She could tell him not to worry, that she would make an excuse for him. She wanted to know, however, what he thought of the invitation.

"Do you want me to come?" There was an eagerness in his voice which made it easier for her to answer truthfully.

"Yes, actually. I really do." George was fantastic in social situations, especially if he was nervous. He was funny but not overbearing, and was good at making Fi feel like the most interesting person in the room, something which Andie had never mastered. More than that, however, the thought of spending an extra day with him moved some of the funk which was weighing her down. It even helped her look forward to the party a little bit more.

She had kept her eyes down as she spoke, watching the knife slicing close to her fingers. He appeared on the other side of the bench.

"Then of course I'll come," he said. "Should I bring something?"

"Charlotte didn't mention anything."

"What about gin in a flask," he said with a laugh. "Just for us. Hey, is she too old for balloon animals, do you think?" George was adept at making intricate giraffes, poodles, even a duck once, out of colourful balloons.

"Probably. Though she's vegetarian now, so maybe she'd like a whole farmyard full of animals. Can you do sheep and pigs?"

"If I had fifty hands maybe." There was silence as she finished slicing the cucumbers and moved on to the basil. "What did you get her?"

"Nothing yet. I'll go this afternoon." She had had no ideas about presents and had been dreading trying to find something. With her new buoyed spirits, however, came a sudden, fervent desire to make the next day a pleasant, memorable celebration for Fi. It was strange to think Charlotte probably always felt like this: totally aware of what was going in to her daughter's head and how long it might stay there.

She finished chopping the basil and picked up the chopping board, ready to slide everything into the lettuce. At the last moment she paused and, with a sigh, replaced the board on the bench. She would take the ingredients separately and combine them at Charlotte's house. It would make it slightly more palatable. She opened the bottom drawer and extricated some suitable containers.

The stream of Saturday pedestrians along King Street suited George and Andie's pace. They meandered with the crowd, occasionally stopping to browse in a store. They collected small presents with the intention of making a birthday hamper. There was a sparkly t-shirt, a compilation

CD, a number of small, chocolate animals, a voucher for a frozen yoghurt shop (which they received when they stopped for a free sample from the perky pony-tailed teenager holding a tray out the front of the store). They added the first book of a fantasy series for teenagers and a couple of bottles of nail polish. Looking in the bag of things they had assembled, it struck Andie that she was unaware of Fi's true interests. In previous years it had seemed appropriate to give her a range of things and allow her to decide her preference, but she was quickly moving out of that stage and into teenagehood where having the wrong interests could seem catastrophic. The next birthday, Andie thought, would probably need some research.

George went into a shoe store to pick up some sneakers while Andie waited outside. It was a humid day. They had been promised rain all weekend and the skies were heavy with clouds, although the streets remained dry. A Maltese terrier darted behind her legs, yapping furiously, and an elderly man manoeuvred the leash to allow Andie to try to free herself. They laughed together and when Andie eventually stepped out of the circle the leash had made around her ankles the dog darted away as though desperate for freedom as well.

"So you like dogs now?" Leon, his hair even shorter than it used to be, had appeared, the sun casting him as a silhouette. He was smiling at her but his eyes were unreadable behind expensive silver sunglasses. His hand was clasping that of a small, pretty woman in colourful high-heels and tapered grey pants.

Andie felt her face freeze in the laugh she had shared with the dog owner. "This is Isobel," he gestured to the woman beside him who was smiling a thin-lipped, appraising smile. Andie tried to say hello but her voice caught in her throat. Her body was numb. Neither of them moved to hug or shake hands.

"This is Andie," Leon said softly to the small woman.

"I know," Isobel nodded. "The writer." Isobel's eyes were unshielded but Andie could not read the expression in them. She had the feeling this woman knew every conversation she and Leon had ever had.

"Yes, how is the writing?" He looked faintly revolted by the question, like he was asking how her toe fungus was. The topic seemed to unstick something inside her

She laughed, as though at a shared joke. "Oh I'm studying at the moment," her voice was too fluttery. "So I don't have much time for it." She saw a flicker of emotion crease Leon's forehead but was unsure if it was satisfaction or disappointment. She wished she could see his eyes. There was a moment of silence that felt like it might never end, so she asked, trying to sound relaxed and interested, but not too interested, "How's the practice?"

"Great!" He put his arm around Isobel's waist and pulled her to him. They were both smiling widely, genuine for the first time since they had stopped. "I bought into the business last year so I'm a part owner, and a couple of months ago we bought a house!"

"Wow, that's great. Congratulations." Andie's cheeks were rubbery but she thought she was smiling again.

"Okay, we better be off. It was good seeing you again, Andie."

"You too. Nice meeting you." She jerked her head in a nod to Isobel as they began moving away. With Leon's arm around her, Isobel looked much friendlier. Andie watched them pause for a moment to allow a woman with a twin-pram to pass. They took the opportunity to kiss and Andie had the impression that they knew she was still watching them. The street was long and straight and she knew she could keep watching them for a long time before they disappeared.

"Was that Leon?" George appeared behind her, a large square plastic bag in one hand. Andie didn't answer. "Let's go," George said, taking her arm and turning her so she lost sight of them. He put his arm around her shoulders and the warmth of it unfroze her a little. She leant into him, wanting the present to come back to her and dislodge these memories of being young and naïve. After a block, George said: "Do you want to talk about it?"

Andie shook her head, but then answered: "I kind of hate that he's happy, even though I would be miserable if I was still with him."

***

The next day was wintery and winds tore across the city. The train carriage was full of couples making their way north for a day out, and sleepy adolescents heading home

A Perilous Margin

after a night in the city.

Andie and George walked through two carriages before they found seats together, Andie trying hard not to hit other passengers with all the bags full of Tupperware she was carrying. She had a slight headache and was looking forward to sitting quietly in preparation for seeing her family. George tried to start a few conversations but she could only answer in monosyllables. She took his hand briefly to show him it wasn't his fault, which he seemed to accept. He eventually fell asleep, his head dropping slowly onto her shoulder. The weight comforted Andie and her breathing deepened.

She hadn't slept well and was dreading having to be cheery all day. She wished she was home, just her and George and a lot of chocolate and wine. They hadn't said anymore about Leon when they got home the previous evening. The two years she had been with Leon had been a slow point in their friendship, a sudden dip in what had, since high-school, been a constant source of companionship. In the final year of high-school they had found themselves moving in the same group of friends and, after a few drunken party conversations, where their common interests became apparent, they became closer friends. Best friends, even. The rest of their group used to tease them but there was something about the easiness of being with George that made Andie think it wasn't supposed to be romantic. He was good to her, and for her. He was the only person who could tell her bluntly what he thought and not make her furious at him. And she was the person who could stop him being too lazy. They had shared a drunk kiss once and it had occurred to her that she might have been missing out on something, but Leon asked her out a few days later and George never mentioned the kiss, so she thought he must want to forget about it. He favoured small blonde women who thought he was incredibly intelligent, anyway.

Sunlight came through the window and it made her squint. It glared off the layers of cloud which filled the sky, and Andie wished it would make up its mind whether it was summer or winter. Her hands were folded in her lap, small and freckled with ragged nails. She stared at them, trying to distract herself from her thoughts. Caroline's hands, she had noticed, had been much larger. They had looked strong, the skin rough, her nails short. In the next interview, Andie thought to herself, she would have to ask about how often Caroline sculpted these days. She had not noticed any sculptures in the house which might have been hers. She thought back carefully, closing her eyes against the glare of the sun. She imagined walking down the front hallway. There had definitely been some paintings on the wall, but she had walked straight past them and was unsure if they were Lawrence's or not. There had been no furniture on which a small sculpture could sit. Outside in the garden, as well, there was no sign of her work. Flowers, yes, which Andie presumed were the result of Caroline's cultivation. No other useful memories came to her.

Ten minutes before they were due to arrive at their

A Perilous Margin

station, she gently nudged George awake. "We're almost there," she said. His eyes were heavy with sleep, and he yawned loudly, dramatically extending his arms over his head. He settled back in his seat and looked at her carefully. She wondered if her thoughts were visible on her face and looked away just in case.

When they stepped off the train they were almost blown over. Andie squinted her eyes and turned her face away from the wind, trying to avoid the worst effects. George wrapped his coat tightly around himself.

"Guys!" Charlotte's voice reached them faintly, pulled away by the wind. Andie and George struggled over to her. She hugged each of them. "Shitty day for a birthday, isn't it?" Charlotte said, beaming.

EIGHTEEN

Damian was already sitting at a table in the small Indian curry house. A plate with an over-sized, misshapen samosa sat in front of him, a pool of orange oil leaking from its insides. He looked up as Caroline entered, unwrapping her scarf from her face where she had pulled it up high in protection from the wind and rain. His face was uncharacteristically melancholy, without its usual trace of sullenness. Caroline sat down. He pushed the plate towards her and said, "I've already eaten mine." An exhaling truck on Enmore Road almost drowned out his words. She waited a few seconds until the noise had died down.

"How was it?" She bit into her samosa as she asked. He shrugged.

"I think I'll have the tandoori chicken," he said. She nodded. The restaurant was famous for it. They ordered their meals. Caroline opted for potato and spinach curry, hoping the fiery spices would invigorate her.

"How's Lawrence?" Damian asked, his fingers playing with the rack of sauces on the table.

"Oh fine. His new exhibition opens soon so he's busy, but fine."

"Right, sorry I forgot he had another one coming up."

"That's okay. You don't have to remember." A long pause stretched between them. They had never been good at catching up. Eventually, Caroline decided to broach the reason they were there. "Thirty two years. It feels like yesterday, doesn't it?" She said, watching him carefully. He grunted. "Do you think about her?" She asked.

"Sometimes." He looked at his hands curled on the table. "When I saw Kate doing something that Mum used to do – just cooking or listening to music, anything really – and I thought what a great mother she would have been."

"Do you wish you'd had kids?" They leant back as the waiter, his red polo shirt stained under the arms, placed their meals in front of them and disappeared, returning seconds later with a glass water bottle and two glasses still warm from the dishwasher. The question, so loaded, was hanging between them, but she knew he wouldn't answer now.

They ate in silence for a few minutes. Caroline's curry, the chilli visible on the spinach, burnt her throat and she filled up their water glasses.

"Sometimes I wish we'd stayed in Perth."

"Why?" Caroline was surprised. She always thought that they left because of him.

"My friends were there. I was too young to leave my friends. We should have stayed." Caroline detected a faint accusation in his voice, and felt her defences rising.

"You're the one who suggested we leave."

"You were fading." He looked up at her finally. "You needed family and I couldn't be it. I was seventeen, it was too much pressure."

"You didn't see Grace very often, considering we moved here to be with her."

"I didn't want to see her. We moved so you could make up with her, not me." Their voices became low in their anger. It was a trait from their mother.

"She missed you."

"I saw her at the end."

"And the two decades in between?"

"She didn't come home!" The anger crumpled his face, and he looked like a seventeen year old, broken from the death of his mother, the lines on his fifty-something face adding only sorrow, not age.

Feeling her frustration rise, she said, "She couldn't. You know that."

"She could have. She could have made peace. Mum needed her, at the end. She was the eldest. She was the one Mum would have been proud of." Caroline pushed her plate away, her curry hardly touched. She had never had the opportunity to grow out of needing parental approval.

"What do you mean?"

"Grace was always going to be the one to amount to something. And she did."

"And us?"

He looked up at her, his mouth greased slightly black from the tandoori chicken. "What do you think? I teach high-school chemistry, you teach middle-aged women how to make clay bowls. Do you really think Mum would be proud of us?"

"She wasn't like that. We're good people, she'd be proud of us." Caroline's voice was husky, keeping the tears away.

A Perilous Margin

She hated that she didn't know he was wrong.

"We're not good people. We're the same, you and I. We've hidden behind successful partners because we're cowards." He pushed his plate away, the bones still had flaps of meat and skin on them.

"We supported our partners, we didn't hide. It's hard work and Mum would have appreciated that."

"We were scared they'd run out on us!" He said with a sneer. "We saw Mum's life as a failure because Dad left, and we put all our energy into making sure our lives didn't go the same way. If we hadn't been scared of being alone –" his voice broke and he dropped his head into his hands. Caroline reached a hand over to his arm, his sudden sadness dissolving her anger. His muscles had thickened with age. "She's left me Car," he looked up at her with tears she had only seen clouding his eyes once before.

The waiter appeared again, clearing their plates and depositing the bill.

NINETEEN

Charlotte was an aggressive driver and Andie saw George gripping the backseat armrest tightly as she threw them round the corners, talking non-stop. She had been up since 7 o'clock, she said, though, after the ten minute drive, Andie was still unsure what she had been doing all morning.

Joey had picked up his sister Essie on his way over that morning, and she was settled in an armchair with a cup of tea when Andie and George arrived. Joey was standing with Pete and they were both looking proudly at Fi, who was dressed up for the occasion in a light summery dress and dark brown ankle boots. She looked, Andie realised with surprise, like a mini version of the girls who populated the university campus. Fi sidled over to Andie, hugged her and accepted her present. She waved nervously to George while staying close to Andie's side. He wiggled his eyebrows and whispered "Happy birthday" and she giggled, her eyes flicking to her present and back.

A 'hello' was called from the open front door and Pete's brother Shaun appeared. His wife Julie was behind him holding tightly to the hands of their two small boys. Julie had been a gymnast as a young girl and still had the body of one, though since her sons had been born her narrow hips had become slightly thicker. Jason was seven years old and happy to remain close to his mother. Mark, however, who was five, tore away as soon as he was in the room, seemingly determined to cover every patch of carpet before anyone else.

A Perilous Margin

"There's the birthday girl," Julie cooed, swooping over to Fi and hugging her. Fi could not stop smiling as Shaun then hugged her and Jason fell against her in a sort-of hug.

"Pete, would you mind getting everyone a drink?" Charlotte asked as a way of announcing her entrance carrying two platters of food. On one were the corn fritters, on the other what looked like sausage rolls.

"Here, Char, let me help," Julie took one of the heavy plates from Charlotte's hands. She picked up a pile of paper serviettes from the table, which was covered in a colourful tablecloth and already had cutlery, glasses and plates laid out, and proceeded to offer the fritters to George and Andie. Charlotte smiled after her appreciatively and offered the sausage rolls to Jason, who was standing uncertainly in the middle of the room. He glanced quickly at his mother, who was distracted by George, and took one in each hand. Pete called out for drink requests from the table which had beer, ginger beer, cola and orange juice set up as a mini-bar. George and Andie each asked for a beer.

"Great fritters, Charlotte!" George called out, raising his half-eaten fritter in appreciation. Andie made a sound of agreement, her mouth too full to speak. There was a long silence as everyone accepted their drinks and was busy finishing their first taste of the food. Fi was standing near Pete. She seemed unsure of who to talk to. Pete put on some music and the awkwardness faded along with the silence.

After she finished her beer, Andie went to the kitchen to assemble the salad ingredients. Lunch was, as she had expected, an exuberant spread and she was embarrassed by her contribution next to all that Charlotte had prepared. There were several other salads near her, there were meat and vegetarian kebabs marinating as well as vegie burgers ready to be barbequed. There was a strawberry cheesecake glistening in the fridge and chocolate brownies filling the kitchen with a delicious smell from the oven.

Julie came into the kitchen behind her, Mark's arm clasped firmly in one hand. His face was smeared with brown.

"What happened?" Andie asked, trying not to laugh.

"He decided dirt was better to eat than food." Julie sounded like she was trying to force her voice to be light. There was a crack in it, however. It must be difficult to never have a day-off, Andie thought as she made room at the sink for Julie to wet a sponge. When she was finished, Andie put her salad to one side and waited as Julie made a few final swipes along Mark's now clean face. As they left the kitchen together Andie noticed Julie's face transform from a slight scowl to a wide smile. She guessed it was not genuine, but it was difficult to tell.

Joey was sitting next to Essie. Looking at them, it was easy to see that Essie was the older sibling already in her sixties. Joey was still robust thanks to his years of Iron Man training when he was younger. Until the previous year, Essie had also looked healthy and strong from a life of being busy with children, a husband, volunteering, gardening, playing bridge, gossiping. But during the previous winter she had slipped on some frost on the back steps of her house and since her subsequent hip replacement she had looked small and frail, still quick to smile but with a hint of a quiver behind it.

Julie told the room at large about Mark's mistake in eating mud pies and after the general laughter the room filled with talk as though the story was a release valve. Jason attached himself to Fi who was still standing with her father. Shaun was trying to entertain Mark and stop him reverting to eating dirt. They had found a soft soccer ball and were trying to keep it between them. Andie saw Charlotte throw them a few nervous glances as she sat talking to Julie, whose eyes seemed determinedly not looking at her youngest son's antics. Andie followed Joey outside to help him fire up the barbeque, leaving George to sit with Essie.

The weather was horrible for being outdoors, and Andie pulled her hoodie up over her head, trying to at least keep her ears warm while her beer turned her fingers cold and slippery. The river was in a hurry, charging past the house with a roar, but it couldn't drown out the promising hiss from the barbeque as Joey threw the meat and vegetarian kebabs on the metal plate. They stood in silence for a while, watching the smoke swirl into the air and the meat slowly brown. The vegetables steamed thickly as their juices flowed out until suddenly they turned black. Joey swore and scooped them into a waiting tray. He glanced up at Andie, smiling. "Sorry," he said but she shrugged dismissively. She was enjoying being outside and away from the closed feeling of the house, despite the wind which was pushing her hair into her eyes. She didn't particularly want to speak but she knew being silent might make her seem sulky.

"I can't believe Fi's eleven," she said finally.

Joey shook his head. "I know. Grandpa to an eleven year old, I never would have believed it."

"Why not? You and Celine were young enough when you had Charlotte."

"Oh I know," he said as he rolled the meat kebabs for one last turn and added the vegetarian burgers to the side. Andie saw the meat juices seeping into them but decided not to say anything. "I just never pictured us as the grandparent sort. I guess because of your mother, she was far too glamorous to be so old!"

"Glamorous? I never thought of her as glamorous." Andie knew she sounded sullen but couldn't seem to shift her mood.

"Oh Andie, you've seen the photos. As a twenty year old? She looked like Mia Farrow."

"I guess. But with us she was just so distracted. I can't imagine Mia Farrow burning the kitchen down by forgetting she'd stored her files in the oven before turning it on!"

Joey kept his eyes on the almost burning kebabs. "She didn't forget, Andie."

"What?"

"She was beginning the process, ridding herself of her life. Our marriage certificate was in there, mortgage repayments and all your old school reports, medical information too. She left you your birth certificate, which was surprisingly generous."

It was one of Andie's clearest memories from that time in her life and suddenly, she wondered if she was remembering it wrong. She had been lying on her bed, crying after a fight with Charlotte over possession of a Barbie doll, and Celine had come and held her without speaking. It was so out of character that Andie had kept completely still, trying to hold on to the rare affection. But the smell of burning had driven them from the room, and in the hallway they had run into Charlotte, whose eyes were bright with terror at the palls of smoke issuing from below the closed kitchen door. Closed kitchen door – now Andie thought about it, she had never seen that door closed before.

"Why would she do that? Didn't you need that stuff?"

"Oh sure, but not as much as she needed to not have it, I guess." The kebabs and burgers were done and Joey tipped them all onto the large tray. Without looking at Andie again he carried the tray inside.

Back inside, they all filled their plates with hot kebabs and burgers and piles of salad. Everyone took a polite amount of Andie's limp concoction before heaping their plates with Charlotte's much more impressive offerings. Garlic bread appeared and more beers were opened. Julie led Mark and Jason to a plastic picnic rug on the floor and told them to be extra careful with their cups of soft drink, and then took a precautionary seat beside them. Shaun sat with her. A year ago, Andie thought, Fi would probably have sat with her cousins, but today she claimed a spot on the couch. Charlotte and Pete squeezed in beside her, while Essie and Joey got the armchairs. George and Andie found kitchen chairs and balanced their plates on their laps.

The music swirled about them. Andie made herself smile at a joke of Pete's, hoping the action would prompt her to feel a bit more in the mood. She watched Charlotte, wondering if she should find a time to tell her what Joey had said. Conversations moved around her without pause, however. Julie and Charlotte were talking about the marinade recipe. George, Pete and Shaun were talking about a farewell tour that kept being promised but not delivered. Essie was talking over Joey, asking Fi about school.

Once the plates were empty, and some people had been back for seconds, Charlotte called Fi over to her. Andie saw them in the corner whispering. Fi looked uncomfortable and trapped. Andie tried not to pay too much attention, and saw everyone else, except Pete, do the same. Mark and Jason had been tidied up and Essie pulled them over to her. She held them on either side of her on the armchair. Mark had apparently tired himself out, because he nestled in close, looking ready to sleep. Jason was watching Fi though, and seemed to want to go and join his older cousin. He seemed more comfortable after his food.

"Everyone," Charlotte said, walking into the centre of the room, "Fi has a little surprise for you." Fi was standing behind her, her hands twisting against each other and a nervous smile on her face. Charlotte turned to look at her. "Go on, honey, it's fine." Fi disappeared down the hallway for a moment, and reappeared with her violin case. While Fi was gone, Charlotte pulled a music stand out from behind the couch. It already had music on it. Andie and George glanced at each other but quickly looked away, trying not to smile.

Fi stood in front of her music and raised the violin in her hands. "Don't forget to introduce the piece, honey," Charlotte said. Andie looked around the room. Essie still had an arm around a sleepy Mark. Joey was smiling benignly. Julie seemed to be feigning interest and Shaun was trying to keep Jason still by holding him between his knees. Charlotte and Pete both looked as nervous as Fi.

"This is a minuet, by Bach." Fi looked straight at her mother, who nodded encouragingly. The piece was light and fun. Fi's fingers, trembling with nerves, fumbled a few times but she was a good player and settled down after repeating the first section. Andie glanced at Charlotte, who seemed to be humming along. When she finished everyone clapped, and she took a bow.

"And now," Charlotte said, standing up, "we have a duet."

She stood next to her daughter with her old viola, and nudged Fi to introduce the piece again. "This is Spring, by Vivaldi."

"Well, it's an arrangement of Spring that Pete put together for us," Charlotte corrected her. Everyone smiled politely at Pete, who did not seem to want this acknowledgement. They began playing, and it was a very beautiful arrangement, Andie thought. Pete had done a good job of making Fi's part easy, while Charlotte's was much more complicated but not overbearing.

A minute in, however, and Fi fumbled what sounded like an entire bar. Charlotte kept playing but Fi was lost. Andie fidgeted in her seat as Charlotte tried to tell Fi where they were up to without pausing her own part. Fi looked increasingly stressed and close to tears as Charlotte said bar numbers louder and louder. Andie glanced at George, who had a hand over his mouth, apparently trying to disguise his smile. He was the only one, however, not looking pained. Essie was laughing nervously, as though it would ease the tension. Jason had started talking, apparently taking Charlotte's words as a sign that talking was allowed. Joey had a hand against his head and his face was scrunched up, as though he couldn't look away.

"And repeat!" Charlotte said, so loudly that the music was no longer audible. Fi, able to join in again, was too rattled to play properly, and continued to stumble her way to the end. The room exhaled at the final note. "Take a bow," Charlotte said, seemingly unaware of the tension in the room. "It's okay, honey, we'll just practise a bit more for next time," she said as she caught sight of Fi's pale face and trembling lips. She went to put a hand on Fi's shoulder but the birthday girl fled, using the pretext of returning her violin to her room to avoid the sympathetic audience.

A Perilous Margin

Charlotte was alone in front of her family and looked suddenly embarrassed. "Perhaps a bit much for her birthday," she said, apologetically. She moved the music stand out of the way and Julie asked politely who Fi's music teacher was.

George leaned over and whispered to Andie, "At least she won't forget this birthday." Andie frowned at him and went to find Fi.

The train was almost empty when they caught it back into the city. Andie was relieved that she had found Fi and cheered her up by recounting a similar duet Charlotte had made them play together as children. She had had Fi laughing by the end, as she told her the prank she had played in revenge for what had been a disastrous performance in front of Andie's primary school. The prank had involved Charlotte's new make-up, allowed once she was in high-school, and a dance. It had taken Charlotte months to forgive Andie, but she had never asked her sister to perform with her again either. Andie and Fi had emerged from the bedroom in time for cake, which had dispelled any leftover tension, and the afternoon had finished with Fi and Jason playing happily together. Charlotte's embarrassment had appeared to last longer, but Andie had less sympathy for her and had not endeavoured to cheer her up.

Andie beat George to the window seat for the return journey. Part of her wanted to talk about what had happened, to hear George's outsider analysis of the situation. But a part of her was still angry at his inability to take Fi's humiliation seriously. She stared out the window, barely noticing the rain-lashed bushland. The train curved around the track slowly. It seemed to be travelling gingerly on the slippery tracks, Andie thought, feeling wary at the competence of the old train to cope in the wet weather.

She saw George looking at her from the corner of her eye. She turned to him, ready to have the conversation. A smile was still curving the sides of his lips slightly, but she found, to her surprise, that she did not mind anymore. A small change of distance and time had made her see the funny side as well. As their eyes met they both began laughing. Andie felt the tension release from her shoulders, and her eyes began watering. Their laughter became a howl. She felt the stares of other passengers but they had no effect on her.

Eventually, they stopped laughing. Andie wiped her eyes with her hands, feeling her fingers trembling. She felt like she could easily cry now. The sound of their laughter still seemed to be filling the carriage, and George said loudly, "What was that?" Andie knew he was referring to Charlotte and Fi's performance, and she shrugged. "I get that kids need to be challenged sometimes," he continued, "but it's her birthday!"

"I think it was supposed to be fun."

George started laughing again but stopped quickly when he realised he was alone. Andie had no idea what to say. After a while, George asked, "Is she okay?"

"Fi?"

"No, Charlotte."

"Oh," Andie was surprised by his concern and guilt overcame her, "I don't know. I didn't ask."

TWENTY

Caroline and Damian emerged onto the quiet street. The skies had cleared and sunlight melted between buildings and across the footpath. Caroline shrugged off her cardigan in the warm air. They walked in silence towards the train station, occasionally walking single file for a pram, or a group of friends, to pass them. At the station they could see Caroline's bus approaching. It was like Murphy's Law, she thought to herself, just when she wanted to have to wait, to give her a chance to offer the sympathy to Damian that she had been unable to at lunch, the bus arrived on time. Damian gave her a quick hug.

"Good to see you. When I'm settled into my new place you and Lawrence should come around."

Caroline nodded, wanting to say something, anything to make his trip back to his new apartment less lonely. Her bus sagged to stop beside them. "See you," he said as he squeezed her arm slightly and walked into the station.

Her hand searched in her bag for her wallet. A key buried in the darkness stabbed under her little fingernail and she jerked her hand away. The bus driver smiled at her. "Take your time. I'm running early for once. Beautiful afternoon, isn't it?" She smiled and pushed her ticket into the machine. After several minutes the driver pulled the doors closed and the bus sank into the stream of traffic.

Two stops later her phone beeped with a message from Penny, asking to meet her for a coffee. She put her phone back in her bag, the message unanswered. She needed quiet to digest the conversation with Damian. She needed Lawrence, who saw her family with a clarity she had never achieved. A second message from Penny beeped through; Michelle had called. Caroline pressed the bell and returned to the busyness of the footpath.

The coffee shop was a narrow space filled with too many chairs. The waitress who brought the menu had spiky hair and silver earrings. Tattoos were woven around her neck. She smiled genuinely at Caroline and asked if she would like a coffee. The notepad tucked firmly in the waist strap of her grotty black apron looked like it was only there for show.

Caroline had already drunk half her coffee by the time Penny arrived. Her hair had been thrown into disarray by the wind and she was out of breath. Mascara was smudged beneath one eye.

"Weekend traffic," she muttered, by way of apology, and gestured to the waitress for a coffee. "So Michelle called, nine o'clock this morning." Penny had never understood the need for small talk between friends. "I couldn't believe it. I was half-asleep, nodding along to all the things she was telling me about her new life, how she wanted to call to see how I was doing." Her coffee arrived on the table in front of her and Penny took a moment to take a long drink and exhale. Caroline waited, stirring the last of the foam in her cup.

"She's moving to New Zealand. Did I tell you her girlfriend's a Kiwi? Anyway, she's fucking emigrating for the woman! She's actually packing up and moving, permanently, with a woman she hardly knows. She's such a fucking cliché."

"Permanently isn't usually as permanent as most people expect."

"I know that, don't you think I know that? But she's going with the intention of it being permanent." Penny stared at Caroline as though waiting for her to match her own incredulity.

"Penny, she's moved on. It happens." The words coming out of her mouth felt disconnected to her brain. She understood Penny's distress, but for some reason she could not offer any support. Penny slammed her cup down, her saucer bounced against the table with a loud clatter. The waitress looked over, frowning.

"I'm sorry, Penny. I don't know why I said that."

"What's wrong?"

"Nothing," Caroline said. She was tempted to pretend that she was okay. It would make her feel stronger, although she knew that it would secretly dismantle her strength bit by bit. This was always her problem with friendships: should she feel strong, but crumple inside? Or should she crumple on the outside, and feel weak? After several moments Penny said:

"Is it because Bridget is coming back?"

"What?" Caroline was thrown off guard.

"Bridget, isn't she coming back to Sydney?"

"Lawrence said she cancelled that plan, she's staying in

New York."

"Oh, what's the problem then?"

Caroline wondered whether Penny had heard something new, or if Lawrence had lied, or if Bridget had changed her mind again. But she didn't want to think or talk about Bridget. It took another long moment before she could square her shoulders and say:

"Damian thinks we're failures."

"We?"

"Me and him. He thinks Grace was the only one who amounted to anything, and the only one Mum would have been proud of."

"That doesn't sound right."

"Doesn't it? I haven't exactly amounted to much, have I?"

"You're great, don't say that. You're amazing and talented –"

"And I've been so busy being sensible that I've never given myself the chance to succeed."

"Is this about that Andie girl?"

"What do you mean?"

"Lawrence told me that she's very – forceful."

"I've only talked to her once. She asked why I had given up on being an artist in order to earn money instead of Lawrence. I didn't answer."

"Why not?"

"I don't think I know the answer."

"Caroline," Penny leaned over and took her hand, a patient expression softening the normally hard features of her face. "You were good, don't think that you weren't. But things happened the way they did for a reason. Lawrence needed you to be sensible and stable. And you were." Caroline must have looked doubtful, because Penny sat back in impatience. "How is this an issue? You did a good thing, deciding to back away from that world. You couldn't both have survived, and certainly not together."

"I know it has worked out fine, in the end. And maybe it was inevitable that this was going to happen, Damian certainly thinks it is something inherent in my personality."

"Maybe you're just subconsciously clever enough to know what you have to do. You don't have to make a big effort to do the right thing!"

Caroline smiled slightly, liking Penny's explanation although it was untrue. She knew Penny did not want to talk about it anymore, however, so she smiled broadly, as though the doubts had been cast away.

"So what are you going to do about Michelle?"

"Bitch and moan for a few days, then go find myself a date, I guess." They grinned at each other.

She could hear Lawrence's music playing as she made her way past the dishevelled banksias by the front path. It sounded like the Velvet Underground. He had been listening to them a lot since Lou Reed's death. She had not realised that he was such a fan, but apparently, before they knew each other, he had been to a concert. Caroline suspected that the drugs involved blurred any potential memories, but the emotion of the night was obviously still important. She pushed the door open; she could see Lawrence's feet almost poking out the lounge-room door. It had been something she found herself falling in love with when they were first together: he listened to music, really listened to it rather than just having it as background noise. And he listened from the floor. She had started to do the same, and found that the vibrations from the CD player, which used to be on the ground, gave a different sense of the music. Now it was just habit, since there was no chance of feeling vibrations from the speakers which were sitting in the wall unit.

She paused near his feet, his bare pink toes, nails short and clean, pointing slightly to the sides. His father had been in the army and had drilled good foot care into him from an early age and it showed. He had beautiful feet. His eyes were closed. He must not have heard her come in, or else he was too busy concentrating.

He looked old from this angle. She always had the feeling that he was aging more attractively than she was. His wide, Scottish bone structure held up his sagging skin better than her delicate features did. But from here, his face was relaxed and the folds of skin around his neck sagged towards his ears. The light whiskers on his face made the wrinkles more obvious. He looked old and grey. It comforted her to know that she did not mind. She smiled, and said quietly, "Hi."

He smiled, without opening his eyes, and held an arm out, inviting her to join him. She placed her bag on the couch and crouched down, folding herself into his arms.

His barrel chest always created an enormous amount of heat, and she held him close, pressing their skin together to share his warmth. Oh! Sweet Nuthin' came on. It had always been her favourite Velvet Underground song. She smiled into his jumper. Slowly, he rolled towards her, pulling her closer. He ran his fingers up the cool skin of her back.

She awoke to silence, and a breeze sneaking into the room from under the front door. A shiver ran through her, and she tried to wrap herself more fully around Lawrence, but he had lost his warmth as well. With another shiver, she stood slowly, giving her body a chance to stretch out its muscles. Their dressing gowns were in the bedroom and she retrieved them, wrapping hers tightly around herself and dropping Lawrence's over his still sleeping body.

In the kitchen, she peered out the window. The heavy winds of the morning had transformed into rain. The leaves which brushed against the window were sodden, and created swirls in the water droplets on the glass. A flicker of sunlight tried to find its way between the clouds and for a moment the kitchen brightened, before the premature gloom of the afternoon returned.

She flicked the kettle on, and dropped a ginger tea bag into a cup. She rubbed her eyes. She felt awake now, sometimes sleeping in the afternoon did that, but she also felt hollow. Grief on the part of another person often did this to her, as though her insides had been vacuumed out and all that was left was flesh, struggling to remain taught. Her

A Perilous Margin

own grief was a swarm of fiery snakes in her belly, but she had not felt that for a long time. Her afternoon with Lawrence was a painful contrast with that of Damian, who had had no comfort to return to, nothing to ease the passage from this historically painful day into tomorrow, when the everyday sadness of his separation would return.

She picked up her phone and sent him a simple, "thinking of you" message. He had been so young when their father left that they never spoke of the similarities between them. The dark moods and their encroachment into relations with family members had definitely never been mentioned. She hoped he did not remember the moods that had had them tiptoeing around their own house. From watching their mother, she had thought it was normal for a woman's hands to shake at the slightest raised voice.

Lawrence grunted from the doorway, his dressing gown hanging over his shoulders, his fists rubbing his eyes furiously. He peered at her through half-closed eyes. "Are you okay?"

"Damian and Kate have split up." The news took several moments to sink in, and Caroline swirled her teabag through the hot water in her cup as she waited.

"What happened?" He said through a yawn, pulling his arms into the sleeves of the faded dressing gown. He sat heavily at the table.

"She left him. Or asked him to leave. I'm not sure which."
"Why?"

"I don't think there was a catalyst, she'd just had

enough."

"How's Damian?"

"Sad."

"Hmm." Lawrence's hand reached automatically for the pile of newspapers which were sitting on the table. He pulled a section towards him and scanned it quickly. Caroline watched, waiting for the concern to manifest. After a few moments the gravity seemed to hit him, and he looked up.

"Are you okay?" He asked again.

"Of course I'm not," she said quietly, a touch of impatience in her voice. Her hands shook as she carried her cup to the table and sat opposite him. He pushed the paper away and reached a hand over to rest against hers on the cup.

"Can I do anything?"

She shook her head. "Damian is still angry that Grace didn't come home for our mother's funeral." Lawrence's brow furrowed, unable to follow the train of thought that had provoked the statement but unwilling to risk upsetting her.

"Are you?"

"No. You know that," she said pointedly, aware of how many times they had had this conversation. "I thought it made sense. But Damian thinks she should have made peace."

"Did you ever ask her about it? Grace, I mean."

"No." She rubbed her eyes, her fingers warm from holding the cup of tea. "I don't know, maybe I should have."

"She was a scary woman, your sister. I'm not surprised

you were intimidated by her."

"I wasn't intimidated by her." Her impatience flared again but she didn't want to feed it. "Just forget it. I need a shower." She left the full cup on the table, the ginger fragrance strong in the air.

TWENTY-ONE

Andie arrived at her rescheduled tutorial to find only three others had chosen to come. As well as Marco, the tutor, there was Manuel, Jackson and Shari. Shari was looking much less comfortable than she usually did when Melanie was by her side. As Andie walked in, Marco was just getting the class started. Jackson smiled widely at her, and gestured for her to sit next to him, which she did after a moment's hesitation.

"Has everyone done the reading?" Everyone nodded. "I have some questions here for discussion but since it's such a small group it's probably best if we all just speak together." Everyone nodded again and he handed around the questions. "I'm quite excited about the readings this week," Marco said, his delight evident in his wide smile. He gestured to Shari, who read out the first question. It was about the Guerrilla Girls pieces and Manuel began answering straight away.

"This was really interesting. I've never heard of this group – I don't know if they have a presence in Australia? But it just seems so stereotypical of advocacy groups to spend all this time and money complaining about something rather than producing good quality work which could actually hold its own in these institutions they're protesting about."

"I think we need to take the two readings together," Andie said, speaking slowly to try to formulate her thoughts

A Perilous Margin

as she went. "Virginia Woolf was talking about non-domestic lives as dangerous for women to choose because they go against tradition and expectation, but she also talks about how that was changing and should change. It's so long ago that I think by now it has changed largely – she wasn't even allowed in the university library without a chaperone and we're here, allowed to study," she indicated her and Shari. "A lot of women find it possible now to not follow the traditional domestic route in life. But what the Guerrilla Girls information shows is that these women who are studying and working hard are still not getting recognition or money for it. There are plenty of institutions for artists but the question is, who has access to them and their audience? Because having an audience is crucial to success in art."

"I didn't do the first reading," Manuel waved his hand dismissively. "I can't stand Virginia Woolf's style. I mean, it's just so infuriating."

"I read them both," Shari's voice was sharp. "And to be honest, I just don't get what they have in common."

"Virginia Woolf is writing about the conditions necessary to be creative," Andie said. "Five hundred pounds a year and a room of one's own. It's not good enough to be educated, or to have the vote. What I wonder is what she would have thought of the Guerrilla Girls apparently blaming institutions for not choosing female artists or if she would have understood that they are businesses with their own interests to protect." From the corner of her eye, Andie saw

Marco twitch as though he wanted to add something, but he remained silent.

"I think you're right." Jackson's voice was soft, as though trying to bring the group back together again. His voice shook with nerves but he continued speaking. "I got a very real sense that Virginia Woolf was blaming women for not creating their own foundation for creativity. They already had – and I'm talking about the time when she was writing this – they did have access to university education, they had the vote, and yet they still weren't that successful. She seemed to be saying that society wasn't holding them back anymore, they were holding themselves back." His voice remained soft, and he looked only at his hands and the paper in front of him. It was a similar sentiment to what Andie had felt while doing the reading but hearing someone else, especially a man, say it made her want to leap to the defence of the women.

"Oh please," Shari said, rolling her eyes. "Access to education and the vote? Really? For starters, back in 1900 or whenever she wrote this, it was only aristocratic women who had those things, and even now, what the Guerrilla Girls are doing is clear proof of the glass ceiling!"

"There are no legal boundaries anymore," Manuel said, speaking with deliberation as though pointing out something obvious. "So if Jackson's right and Woolf was blaming women – I mean, if she thought they should have pushed themselves more once they had the same opportunities – then surely it's even more true now. I mean, take this class, it's more than half girls! To my mind, you know, if women aren't succeeding at the same rate as men it's probably because they're either not talented enough or not interested enough. And," he held up a hand as though to silence his critics, "and really I think they're just not interested."

Shari jumped forward in anger at Manuel's words but Andie leant back in her chair, trying to calm her breathing. She glanced at Manuel, his face was animated with delight at the controversy he had caused. Jackson was following the conversation but seemed unsure of how to rejoin it. Andie was feeling nauseous and did not want to speak anymore. She wished she could talk to someone whose opinion she respected so that she could adopt their thoughts and not have to make up her own mind. She was scared by the direction her own thoughts were taking her.

After the class ended, Andie noticed that she had a missed call from Charlotte on her phone. Wondering whether this was her chance to tell her sister what Joey had said about the fire, she stood in the shade of a quiet tree by the side of the chemistry building and called her sister.

"Hi Charlotte, sorry I missed your call."

"Oh that's alright, I know you're busy. Are you in class?"

"No I just finished. Is everything okay?"

"Oh yes, of course," Charlotte said, but the breeziness to her voice sounded strained, and Andie became wary.

"How are you all holding up after the festivities?" Andie asked, easily guessing what was on her sister's mind.

"Fine, we're fine. Did you have a good time?"

"Yeah it was great." There was a long pause as Andie wondered whether to mention Fi and the music.

"Did George enjoy himself?" Charlotte asked suddenly, and Andie detected a note of derision beneath the question.

"Yeah, yeah I think so."

"Oh good. He did look like he was having a good time."

"Well, you know him. He's a happy kind of fellow," Andie replied, aware of the obvious annoyance in her voice. She wanted to avoid the subject of the party altogether if it was going to focus on George and his inability to keep a straight face.

"Well, good," Charlotte said, like she thought it was not good at all.

"Come on, Charlotte, it was an odd situation. Fi was upset, everyone was awkward. He laughs when he feels uncomfortable!"

"Well I'm sorry I made you all so uncomfortable."

"No, Charlotte, I didn't mean –"

"No, no, it's fine. Fi throws a tantrum and I'm what, a tiger mum all of a sudden? She wanted to play for everyone, she really did. I wouldn't *force* her to do something like that, you know. Not if she didn't want to."

Andie took a deep breath. "Okay," she said, exhaling wearily.

"Okay?"

"Yeah, okay. I'm sure Fi did want to play." She did not add her second thought, that it would be very difficult for Fi

A Perilous Margin

to not agree to things that Charlotte suggested. She wondered whether Charlotte's fear of Fi failing – failing to play perfectly or perform with confidence and grace – was a reflection of her own fear that people might have thought she had failed rather than chosen to step away. She thought back to the tutorial discussion and was surprised to realise that Charlotte would probably be most comfortable with Manuel's opinion; it was the only one that acknowledged her autonomy in her decision, and her strength in following her heart. Shari's argument made it sound like Charlotte was simply too weak to fight. Andie didn't mention these thoughts, however, she simply finished with some more placating words to Charlotte and hung up. She hadn't mentioned the fire, but maybe she didn't have to tell her after all. It wasn't a big deal really, was it?

On the way to the library she saw Marco again.

"Hello Andie!" He said.

"Hi Marco."

"How is your assignment coming along?"

"Okay, well sort of. I started off by interviewing Lawrence McGovernor." Marco nodded looking impressed. "But then he had to stop after two so then I interviewed his wife instead."

"His wife? I didn't know she was an artist," Marco said, looking slightly confused.

"She is, or she was anyway. I don't know. In any case, originally I thought I'd be looking at art in institutions because Lawrence has exhibited so much. But Caroline hasn't so I can't really use that topic for her." Andie knew she was looking at him pleadingly, willing him to fix it all for her.

He nodded, his face thoughtful. "That doesn't sound too difficult Andie, even though most people only interview one person." He paused as though clarifying something to himself then said: "What you might need to do is find something that connects them – they're married, that's a pretty big connection. They're both married, both artistic, and Lawrence has managed to succeed. What is it about their world which allowed him to succeed? Perhaps marriage is a 'non-artistic' world like we looked at earlier in the term, and he was able to be an artist anyway but she wasn't. You could use Woolf's arguments for that. Of course, you could use the Guerrilla Girls as well – how art comes to be in institutions rather than the effect of institutional art on the public. But you should try to use your interviews with Lawrence as well, he is an interesting man."

"They weren't very good interviews, actually," she said with a touch of embarrassment.

"Oh no, really? Have you done a sociology course before?"

"No, and this interviewing thing is a bit strange."

"Yes, I imagine so. Did you give him a copy of the questions before you talked to him?"

Andie felt her mouth drop open slightly. "No! Was I supposed to?"

"Don't panic, at undergraduate level it's not expected quite so much, but it is considered best practice generally. It improves the quality of the interview, you see, when the person isn't caught off guard."

"Yes, that makes sense."

Marco smiled and wished her good luck as he departed, but Andie was too distracted by how suddenly juvenile her work felt. She wasn't supposed to catch someone off guard, she had treated Lawrence unfairly for her own agenda with no thought of her actual assignment and what would get her the best answers. She felt like an idiot.

***

Friday morning dawned bright, with a crisp but gentle sun. Andie lay in bed long after her alarm had pulled her from a dream. Her feet were wrapped thickly in the sheet and felt steamy with moisture. She had a strong urge to shower but continued lying in bed. The longer she lay here, the longer she could put off the nerves that had started rumbling around her stomach. She had called Caroline, as requested, on Tuesday afternoon, to confirm their appointment. She had also suggested that this time she send the questions in advance. The conversation was brief, Andie's long introduction and slight ramble as to why she was calling had been cut off unsympathetically by Caroline's "That's fine, see you Friday."

As the clock neared eleven, Andie pulled herself out of bed. She felt mildly hungover. Too much sleep was as powerful as too much alcohol sometimes.

The feral banksias did not hold her attention this time as she walked up the front path to the house in Tempe. Her hands gripped her bag and her folder. She rang the doorbell, her face more serious than it had been last time. Lawrence opened the door, a wide smile on his face. The shock of seeing him caused her to flinch involuntarily, but he did not falter. "Andie, so good to see you again. Come on in." She stepped past him and into the hallway, feeling too hot, her breathing too shallow. She paused, unsure whether to keep walking through the house or wait to be led by him.

The hallway was small and after he had shut the door he had to squeeze past her. She shrank back against the wall. "This way, this way. Caroline was held up for a few minutes but she's on her way. Can I offer you some tea? Coffee?" They were in the house alone and it felt deliberate, though whether it was deliberate on his part or Caroline's she wasn't sure. He led her into the kitchen, which had remained closed to her last time. It was spacious and white. On one wall there was a large colourful painting she was sure was one of his. She turned her back to it and asked for some tea, feeling her strength return. His smile widened with the tenacity of her action.

"How have you been these last few weeks?" He continued smiling, as though the last time they had spoken was not replaying itself through each of their minds.

"I've been fine. Just busy with uni. How's the exhibition going?"

"As difficult and tense as it always is." He gave a melodramatic eye roll. "But it will be ready on time, that is something I have learned. It is always ready on time no matter how desperate it looks. You know, I never asked you if you are an artist yourself?" He framed it as though it had just occurred to him, but Andie had the feeling he had been plotting this question.

"No, I'm not. I used to write short stories a bit."

"Why did you choose visual artists for your assignment? Couldn't bear to face the competition?" His eyes were on the kettle as he filled it to the brim with water.

"I just wanted a different perspective, that's all. One of the first things we looked at was art and consumerism and I thought I would go down that road for my assignment and that short stories wouldn't fit in quite so well as visual arts." She felt strangely transformed by his questions, as though she were in a tutorial rather than his kitchen, and the intellectuality of the conversation allayed her nerves.

"You think painting takes an artist over to the dark side of consumerism more easily than writing does?"

"I think it lends itself more easily to it because it's more easily consumed by non-artists. Anyone can appreciate a painting, it takes a special eye and a level of patience to appreciate good writing."

"I disagree entirely," He beamed widely at her, as though it was all great fun. "Do you think this shallow approach to painting is unique to Australia?" He asked as he pulled two fine china teacups from a cupboard and added the boiling water to a matching teapot. She was unsure if he was genuinely interested in what she had to say or just enjoyed watching her discomfort. She took her time answering.

"I think our education system refuses to acknowledge that having to think hard in order to understand a work of art is not necessarily a failure on the part of the artist to convey the message." Her fingers were tapping the edge of counter, trying to work off some of their extra energy. "Sometimes the most rewarding things are difficult to understand," she added.

"That's a fairly common sentiment. Though not necessarily an accurate one, of course."

He pushed her cup of tea towards her, the tea a pale grey with a pungent smell. It was not ordinary black tea like she had had with Caroline.

She and Lawrence had remained standing throughout the conversation, either side of the metre-wide bench. The bench top was wooden, and as she took her cup, avoiding Lawrence's eyes, she noticed many deep and shallow cuts in various directions within the wood. It was their chopping board, she realised.

"Have you ever painted?"

"Of course."

"Did you find it easy to create what you wanted to create?"

"No. Not at all." She remembered her childhood paintings as indistinguishable blobs, original only in their complete lack of development as she grew up. He looked pleased at her answer, however, so she continued, not wanting to give him any easy answers. "But I have no talent for it. I think the talented painter has an easier job than the talented writer in terms of creating something that people can relate to."

"Or maybe there are just more good painters around than there are good writers."

"Perhaps."

"What do you think of that painting?" He gestured behind her, to the painting of his that she had noticed on entering the room. She was surprised by how genuine the question sounded: it was almost a plea for honesty. Part of her wanted to refuse to look at it, to refuse to tell him he was brilliant. She was, however, a guest in his house, so, biting her tongue, she turned and looked at the painting.

The colours she had first noticed were actually only yellow, purple and a brief splash of green: their contrasting natures made them seem brighter, more overwhelming. The figure was a woman, naked and reclining on a low couch, painted from behind her shoulder so her face was hidden. She was gazing into a tall mirror which reflected another naked figure, although by the haziness of the reflection it was impossible to tell if it was a man or a woman. The reclining woman had one hand tangled in her long hair, and the other tucked under the small of her back. There was no doubt that she was longing for the person in the reflection. Andie vaguely remembered seeing an image of the painting, but it was not one of the ones she had ever looked at closely. She wished she had so that she did not have to suffer its impact in front of Lawrence. She swallowed with difficulty.

"What's it called?"

"Does it matter?" She started at his voice close beside her. His arm was almost against hers. She could feel its heat.

"I guess not."

"Sorry I'm late." They both jumped this time as Caroline's voice, louder than either of theirs had been, came from behind them. "I see you two have made up. Shall we get started?" The first statement was directed at Lawrence with a wry smile. The question was cool as her eyes moved to Andie. Andie followed her quickly, accidentally leaving her tea behind in the kitchen.

Outside, Caroline sat down immediately. She was still wearing a light scarf. Andie sat down as well, carefully arranging her things in front of her and trying not to feel pressured. She looked up and smiled, feeling the strain in her face. Caroline raised her eyebrows. "Is everything okay?" The question bordered on sarcasm.

"Yes, of course," Andie said, trying to widen her smile and feeling it falter.

"Lawrence has a habit of putting young women in a flutter. Even ones who were at one time immune to him."

"Yes, so I've heard," Andie said, uncomfortable with the suggestion that she might be affected by Lawrence, she decided to push Caroline on the subject: "Does it bother you?"

Caroline looked at her steadily for several seconds. "Sometimes."

"Sometimes it bothers you?"

"Yes."

"Which times does it not bother you?"

"You think I should always be bothered by it?" It was Caroline's turn to act confused. "I would be exhausted. It's who he is, he can't help being a flirt."

"Even though it's given him a certain reputation?"

"I know the reputation he has, and I know it has been created by infatuated young women who get slighted by his lack of follow-through. He's an intense, intelligent flirt. Nothing more."

"Are you sure?"

"Yes, I am," Caroline said, her voice terse, impatient. "We've been married for nearly thirty years. Can you imagine the questions that go through a person's mind in that time? Can you imagine knowing someone so well that you rarely have to even ask the question?"

"I just thought that maybe that suspicion – or doubt – might have contributed to the fact that you haven't become a professional artist."

"What do you mean?"

"Just that –" Andie swallowed with difficulty, urging herself to continue, "– that perhaps you thought if you were an artist as well, then you would be distracted, you wouldn't notice if things changed between you two. Perhaps you thought he would get jealous and act out," Andie raised her voice at the end, making herself sound less sure than she was.

"You think that I failed to create art in the way I always dreamed just in case he'd leave me for some silly girl?"

Caroline sat back in her chair, a sudden, genuine smile lighting up her face as if at a delightful idea. She let out a quick laugh and the tension between them eased. "Luckily, I had more faith in our relationship than you do. Besides, these aren't the questions that you sent me, remember?" Caroline said, pushing a piece of paper across the table that she had obviously printed off from Andie's email. "So you think marriage is a non-artistic world, do you?" She added. There was a teasing in her voice and Andie could not quite decide if it was malicious or simply amused.

"Yes, marriage – the jealousies it produces as well as the expectation of a certain level of domestic comfort – seems to me to not be conducive to creating art. Is that your experience?"

"Lawrence is married, and one of the most successful painters in Australia."

"I know. But what about you? Did being married contribute to your decision not to be a professional artist?"

"You seem to think I made a conscious decision at some point to not be the person I thought I was going to be. As though I willingly sacrificed something, a part of myself, in order to be in this relationship. Is that what you think?"

"Yes, in some ways," Andie said, surprised. "Of course I thought you must have chosen at some point not to pursue an artistic career, how else are these decisions made if not consciously?" Andie could not make herself meet Caroline's eyes. She stared into the garden instead, feeling Caroline's eyes on her.

"Neither of us chose it to be this way, life simply flowed along this path and we followed it. There was nothing malevolent going on. But you seem to be blaming my marriage to Lawrence for my 'tragic' life. You think he somehow manipulated me so that I would change my mind, change my life and my priorities. Start making cakes instead of sculptures?" She was staring hard at Andie, who shifted uncomfortably in her seat. Her eyes flicked to Caroline's and away again.

"You sound like you've thought about it yourself," she said stubbornly.

"Of course I have." Caroline's nostrils flared, the first sign Andie had seen of weakness behind the certainty. "Of course I have," she repeated. "But the world isn't big enough to accommodate all the people who think they have something to contribute. Roadkill is necessary."

"And you weren't forced to be −" Andie paused, unsure of the word to use, and decided to follow Caroline's lead, "− to be roadkill?"

"No. Lawrence always told me I could do and be whatever I wanted. To be successful, however, you must be confident that the extraordinariness you see in mundane life is universal and not just the delusional brain of a bored wife." It was the same argument Andie had read at the beginning of her course. It had made sense to her then, now it sounded like an excuse.

"But you were so talented. That sculpture you won the prize for at university is mesmerising. Really, it is. And those ones at the gallery –" Andie forced herself to hold Caroline's eye, to ensure the depth of feeling she felt for the woman's art was conveyed.

"Maybe. But I wasn't interested in only creating art, I wanted Lawrence as well. Perhaps I was greedy. In any case, my twin desires turned mutually exclusive."

"But they weren't for him."

"No."

Andie felt her stubbornness refuse to abate and swallowed her next words, not wanting to put Caroline on the defensive again. She gave herself time, hoping it would pass. When she dared to look at Caroline again she found the older woman staring at her, considering her.

"You really don't like him, do you?" It was not accusatory, merely interested. Even so, Andie felt wary.

"I don't know him."

"And you don't want to get to know him."

"Not particularly, no. He seems like every other man I've ever met who uses his intellect – his charm – to influence people."

"To influence women."

"Specifically, yes. I prefer a gentler approach, I guess."

"A gentler approach to what?"

"To interacting. To relationships. When one person has that much influence, the other person just doesn't have a chance to be everything they can be. Perhaps you're right and it's not a conscious decision on either side, but surely you knew it was happening? Surely at some point you stopped and thought, where have I gone?" There was a long silence.

"I find it interesting that you are here to interview me because I am, as you said yourself, a local artist. And yet so many times today you have accused me of not being an artist anymore."

Andie squirmed for a moment in the contradiction and Caroline smiled. She looked tired. "It's okay, I never know how to describe myself, either."

They sat in silence for a few moments before Andie built up the courage to ask: "Can I see some of your artwork?"

Caroline gazed at her, her face serious but not judgmental or particularly irritated. Then she sighed and glanced at her watch.

"Maybe next week. We're out of time."

Andie apologised and collected her things together. A shadow of movement at a window of the house caught her eye, but she kept her focus on her hands. She thanked Caroline again, and they walked back to the house.

They shook hands at the front door. Caroline smiled at her as at a competitor who had called a time-out.

TWENTY-TWO

The door latch clanged as Caroline closed it behind Andie. Lawrence appeared in the doorway of his studio, leaning against the door jamb.

"That sounded heated."

"She has some strong opinions."

"I thought these interviews were about you?"

"Yes, well, she has some strong opinions about me. And you. But then, you already knew that."

He pretended to be surprised but she ignored it and walked past him into the kitchen and clicked the kettle on. He followed her.

"She has opinions about me, does she? Like what?"

"I think she thinks you're a philanderer, but then, so does the whole of Australia." Caroline looked at him and smiled. There was no malice in her voice. She pulled a mug out of the cupboard, a camomile teabag from the pantry, a teaspoon from the drawer.

"Was she worried about what being married to me might have done to you?"

"She thought I had given up art in order to keep a close watch on the wandering eye of my husband." Caroline rarely used the word 'husband' and it sat uneasily between them. He dismissed the idea with a soft burst of air from between his lips. He left the kitchen and wandered back to his studio. The kettle started boiling.

Her cup of tea was warm against the skin of her hands

as she walked to the shed. When they had first moved in to the house she had thought Lawrence might like to work there. He had taken one look at the dirty cement floor and the cobwebs in the corners, however, and shook his head vigorously. Caroline had decided that she could convert it into a space for herself: somewhere to sculpt without feeling like Lawrence was watching. The conversion never quite happened. Instead, she sometimes deposited work she had made at the Arts Centre here. It had been years, however, since she had been inside.

It was a small, squat structure by the side of the house. The neat backyard ended quickly; the grass becoming thick and overgrown, leaning heavily against the dark brick wall. Caroline pushed the door open. A metal strip at the bottom of the door, designed to keep water out, screeched against the floor. Dust hovered in the air, disturbed by her entrance. She flicked a switch and the bare bulb sprung into life, swinging slightly.

She shut the door behind her. There was an earthy smell from the endless dirt which had made its way in through the cracks of the window. In the centre was a dining table which could have easily sat half a dozen people. On it was a collection of clay figures. She had never bothered firing them in a kiln, although she had access to one through the Arts Centre. They simply sat here, the clay drying and cracking and flaking away; skeletons of ideas which had never flourished. Caroline felt her throat close. It was like a crypt for a family she had not realised had died. She felt tears threaten to fall but could not stop her eyes from roaming over the work. Her work, abandoned to the elements.

A low groan escaped as she saw, lying on its side, the figure of a long-legged woman with a small afro. She remembered the night, twenty years ago, when she had made it, full of furious anger. As her fingers had created the figure, she had imagined the full scale, cast sculpture she intended to create from the small study. She remembered thinking with bitterness what Lawrence would say if he came home to find such a statue in his house. Exactly lifelike, made from bronze to last a lifetime. A lifetime of penance and regret. She had forgiven him more quickly than she had thought she would.

After her pneumonia had cleared she had continued going to the doctor for a long time, certain that there was still something wrong with her. She barely had the energy to get out of bed, to have a conversation with Lawrence. Her school had given her indefinite sick leave but she was unsure if they would take her back after so long.

The doctor told her she was fine, but she was insistent. If it wasn't pneumonia, it was something else. It must be something. It was during her third visit when she had broken down, crying as the doctor, a kind but impatient elderly man, had told her again that there was nothing wrong with her. "You don't understand," she had said, her voice hoarse with tears. "My sister died last year, my mum is dead, it's what the women in my family do! We die when we shouldn't! You have to check me again, you just have to."

He had obliged with a heavy sigh and, when once again he had found nothing, he had written her a referral to a counsellor.

The counsellor was April, a middle-aged woman with soft red hair, colourful blouses and pale green fingernails. She had asked Caroline first about her mother, about caring for her during her illness and for Damian afterwards. About moving to Sydney to be closer to Grace. Then she had asked about Grace's death which had come like a storm, unlike the slow decline of their mother. Grace had been her normal, slightly taciturn but encouraging sister one month, and dead the next. Caroline was still unsure if she had ever grieved properly or if the shock was the type to last a lifetime. April had taken a few weeks to ask about Lawrence and what he had done when Caroline was sick. At first, Caroline had lied and said he had been wonderful the whole time, caring for her, putting her first. But April had eventually encouraged the truth from her.

When the doctor had sent her home from the hospital with antibiotics and instructions to rest, the look of fear had left Lawrence's face. It was as though she was not really that sick if she was allowed home. He did take care of her, sort of. He ordered food in, he moved a bar-fridge into the bedroom so she didn't have to get up for water or juice. But he didn't completely give up his previous lifestyle and at the end of the first week when she was exhausted from coughing, ill from medicine, and he was nowhere to be found, she had called her GP who had arranged for her to go into hospital. Lawrence had arrived home to find a brief note on the bedside table and an empty house, and his panic and guilt had finally been enough to stop the drinking.

He had spent four nights at the hospital with her, sleeping in a stiff armchair and charming the nurses into giving Caroline whatever she wanted. Of course, by this time he had already been offered the life modelling job by Bridget, and when Caroline was finally cleared of pneumonia and sent home to finish recovering, he was leaving every evening to model. She had stopped noticing by then, however, having already withdrawn into her cocoon of fear. It took a month of counselling before she realised he was not just disappearing to go to work and she began to fear that she had lost him entirely.

Caroline lifted the figure and set it on its feet. It wobbled. In her anger she had forgotten to level the soles of the feet. An amateur mistake symbolic of her immature frame of mind, she thought severely to herself. The woman who had made this, who had snuck it home in a large handbag and waited with cruel anticipation for the day when she could surprise Lawrence with it, was long gone. That was a woman who did not really understand Lawrence: a man chased after by endless women but who had chosen her, for reasons she had never been able to see but had come to trust. What, after all, were a few months of distraction compared to decades of dedication?

She carefully returned the figure to its reclining position, partly obscured by the works around it.

A Perilous Margin

She closed the door behind her, plunging the room once more into darkness, unsure when it would see light again, knowing she could not allow Andie to see it.

TWENTY-THREE

Andie returned home to the smell of pizza baking in the oven. George was crouched down, holding a tea-towel aside and peering through the oven door as she walked in. He glanced up. "Hope you're hungry for cheese, I've heaped it on this baby. Should be done in ten." Andie nodded silently. George stood up straight.

"How was the interview?"

Andie shrugged, not to dismiss the question but because she did not know what to say.

"You look exhausted," George said, concern shadowing his face.

"I'm just –" Andie paused, searching for the word to describe how she felt. George waited. After a few moments she could look up at him. "I'm just wound so tightly when I'm near them. It's like they think I'm a child but treat me like an adult – like I should know so much more than I do. And they're completely unperturbed by watching me flounder, like it's a spectator sport."

"Dickheads," he said seriously. She smiled at him as she made her way to her bedroom. He followed, leaning against the doorframe as she sank onto her bed, wrinkling the previously taut doona. She kicked off her shoes and lay down, leaving her feet where they rested on the floor.

"I don't understand her choices, at all," she said to the ceiling, aware of George listening. "And she can't seem to explain them either."

"Do you think she made wrong choices?"

"Either that or she has some source of wisdom I don't know about which explains everything she has done, and why she is with that abominable man."

"Is he really that bad?"

Andie moaned impatiently, unsure how to reply. The timer on the oven beeped and George pulled himself away from the doorway. Andie's eyes trailed over the swirls of water stain on the roof. He was probably okay, she thought to herself. But Caroline's behaviour was so pacifying, so protective of the creative air around Lawrence. It seemed like such an established habit that she could no longer see herself doing it. And it made Andie uncomfortable, that was the word. It made her wonder why when Celine had left a happy family to follow her ambitions, Caroline couldn't even challenge a flirting, possibly cheating, husband. Cause and effect didn't seem connected in Caroline's life.

Andie sat up, suddenly furious with the world. She wanted to bellow at the top of her lungs. It was clearly possible to have creative goals and do everything possible to achieve them, so why were women like Caroline unwilling to even try? Why were they so willing to settle into the shadows of more successful partners?

George appeared in her doorway, a plate with several slices of pizza in each hand. "Pizza solves everything, don't worry so much." He handed her one plate, warmed from the food, and sat on the floor opposite, leaning against her wardrobe. They ate in silence for a few minutes, concentrating on the strings of cheese. Andie's stomach, which had twisted in on itself, slowly relaxed with the warm food.

She knew she was being unfair to Caroline, and judgemental. She knew the whole host of social factors which played a part in life decisions, perhaps sub-consciously, and which probably accounted for the fact that Caroline seemed to have no idea how her life had ended up the way that it did. Andie's thoughts turned to Lawrence. It must be him, she thought to herself, he must have been the one making these decisions without thinking how they would affect Caroline.

She was focusing so much on her thoughts and the hot pizza sliding in her fingers that she did not realise George was looking at her. She met his eyes, surprised and slightly embarrassed by her distraction, and smiled. "Thanks for the pizza." He made a dismissive gesture with his head, his hands busy negotiating the now floppy crust of his last slice.

"What has this woman done to you to make you so distracted?"

Andie frowned slightly, wondering if it would be possible to explain it. "This course is just getting to me. These women, these artists, remove themselves from the world, the wider public world anyway. Do they genuinely stop caring about it? About art? Or is it just so much of a boys' club that they can't get a foot in the door?" She looked at him questioningly, as though he might have the answers.

"What women? I thought you were just talking to the wife

A Perilous Margin

lady."

Andie shook her head, impatient with herself, with him. "Yeah, she's who I'm talking to, but I'm sure she's not the only one."

"It's probably no great mystery, no great battle of the sexes. It's probably just a genuine example of two artists, one a genius and one a tad mediocre, and it just happens to fall along stereotypical gender lines." George spoke dismissively, as though it didn't really matter and Andie felt herself sneer slightly at his response.

"It doesn't explain why these things always 'just happen' to fall along gender lines."

"Unless men are genuinely better, you mean." He smiled teasingly, but her patience had worn out.

"Thanks for the pizza. I'll do the dishes in a little while." She placed her empty plate on the bedside table and reached for her bag, from which several large books were spilling.

"Yeah, whatever." George stood and left, taking his own grease-stained plate with him but leaving hers, with its faint smell of cold cheese, where it was.

Andie opened her reader and stared at the pages she had read the previous week. She wanted to read them again even though it was not the specific topic she was focusing on for her assignment. Her initial reaction when she had read this, to blame women, to blame Caroline, must be wrong. She was missing something in Virginia Woolf's argument, her ideas about social pressures must still be relevant even though most of the examples were out of date now.

Her eyes skimmed paragraphs then stopped as her brain returned to its own conversation. Celine had been talented and driven, and had followed through on her potential to the detriment of her family. Charlotte had been talented but uninterested and had given up and said she was happier for it. And Caroline had the talent, was it possible that she wasn't actually interested in succeeding either? It didn't seem possible considering she had spent her life around art, teaching and sculpting and attending exhibitions with Lawrence. Charlotte had stayed connected to music as well, Andie supposed, by marrying a composer and ensuring Fi learnt the violin. It seemed a new development, however: until recently music was something Pete and Fi enjoyed together while Charlotte stayed away. She didn't know when Charlotte had begun joining in with them. Andie's thoughts drifted to herself but she pushed them away – she had interest but not talent, it was a different problem altogether.

She groaned softly to herself and stood up, feeling a few leftover pizza crumbs fall to the floor. She picked up her plate, with its congealed oil and cheese spills. In the kitchen, George had already tidied up most of the dishes, creating small neat stacks so that it looked like there were not too many of them. He was in his room, Andie could hear the drone of his music through the crack of his almost-closed door. She added her plate to the pile on the sink, sitting it on top even though it was larger and tilted. She turned on the hot tap and held her hands under the water, wishing the

A Perilous Margin

grease would remove itself from the cracks in her skin.

***

After work the following week, Andie returned home to find a silver envelope with her name and address written in round letters in the letter box. She stopped where she was to slide her finger through the flap. It was a pale blue card with a dark blue bird in the lower right corner. She opened it, her eyes looking immediately for the name. 'Caroline' written in round lettering at the bottom, 'Lawrence' was scrawled next to it. She held the closed card carefully in her hand and made her way into the house and through to her bedroom. She dropped her bag behind the door and sat at her desk to read it, holding her breath.

> *Dear Andie,*
>
> *We would be honoured if you would join us for dinner at our home on November 10th. We are hosting a small dinner party with some friends in order to celebrate Lawrence's most recent exhibition. Please reply with the included RSVP card.*
>
> *Kind regards,*
>
> *Caroline and Lawrence*

Andie stared at the invitation for several moments. The RSVP card was a plain white postcard, already stamped and with the address on it. All she needed to do was write her answer on it and drop it in a mailbox. She left the card and envelope on her desk and lay down on the bed, her hands clasped behind her head. Her hair tangled itself around her fingers and she pulled on it slightly, allowing her frustration to escape with the pressure. She had presumed that she would return to interview Caroline that week, but now she thought about it they had never actually agreed on the time for the next interview. She wondered whether to call and check, or to put an extra note on the RSVP. A part of her wanted to keep the two things separate, as though she might learn something more about Caroline and Lawrence and their life if she could use information from a social situation as well as the interviews. With her mind on her assignment and the extra depth such an evening might give it, she sat up quickly and returned to the desk. She wrote, shuddering slightly at her ungainly handwriting next to Caroline's,

> *Dear Caroline and Lawrence,*
> *I would be delighted to attend. Thank you for the invitation.*
> *Kind regards,*
> *Andie*

She grabbed her keys and, before she could reconsider, left the house and ducked around the corner to the post-box. As the card slipped from her fingers she had a sudden urge to grab it back, to not expose herself to a couple who she found both baffling and antagonising. Her hands rested against the warmth of the metal box, but the card was gone. She walked absentmindedly back to her house and rounding

A Perilous Margin

the corner she saw George walking up the steps to the front door. He was bent forward strangely as though trying to listen to something on the other side of the door. His hand rested lightly on the wood, neither pushing it open nor resting idly. Andie, with a flash of memory, realised what he was doing and hurried up to him.

"Sorry," she called when she was still a few metres away. He jumped. As he turned she saw a look of panic on his face.

"Jeez, Andie," his hand had flown to his chest as though clutching at his heart.

"Sorry," she said again. "I just ducked to the post-box, did I forget to lock the door?" She waved her keys vaguely in front of her face in case his terror prevented him from understanding her.

"No, you forgot to close it," he said, "I was seeing horrible images of you lying strangled and the place wrecked." He stepped towards her and she thought he was about to hug her but instead he gently pushed her shoulder. His familiar, comforting scent washed over her and she grabbed his hand, squeezing it in a half apology.

"Oh come on, there's nothing here to steal." She smiled at him.

"They don't know that before they break in," he said, looking at her seriously for a long moment before opening the door fully. He stood aside to let her pass before him. "Anyway, since when do you go to the post-box?"

"Since I got a handwritten dinner invitation from the McGovernors!" She turned to grin triumphantly at him and was pleased to see his mouth drop open in surprise.

"You're kidding? They want you to have dinner with them? Both of them?"

"They sure do. And they wanted a handwritten RSVP card sent back."

"That's so odd! Can you bring a guest? I would love to go!"

"It didn't say, sorry."

George looked disappointed at this news, then suddenly perked up. "Maybe they're planning on seducing you. It's probably not just Laurie who runs around with other women, I bet you anything Caroline's in on it, too!" He looked so convinced but she could only raise her eyebrows.

"I'm not the only one invited. It said it's a dinner party for some friends."

He looked disappointed at this. "That's a shame. It'd be great to know what kind of dynamics they'd have in a threesome."

"For god's sake, George, stop trying to be controversial." She gave him a look of minor annoyance and closed the door of her room behind her.

She sat at her desk, the invitation in front of her. It was a strange thing to have received, but perhaps it was simply a difference of generations, rather than anything ominous or, she baulked in memory of George's suggestions, perverse. She stared at the invitation for a few more minutes then put it in the drawer of her desk and pulled a stack of university work towards her.

TWENTY-FOUR

Caroline faltered as she approached her gallery. Lucy, a colourful scarf wrapped around her neck to protect herself from the wind, was sitting on the front steps. She stood as she saw Caroline approach.

"Lucy, hello." Caroline heard the suspicion in her voice.

"Hi Caroline. I'm sorry to surprise you like this, I was just wondering if we could talk?" It had been weeks since they had last seen each other, and Caroline was conscious of the tension which had permeated their brief relationship.

"Here?"

"Maybe at the café down there, if that's okay?" Caroline checked her watch, as though her time was limited. In reality, she was only there to talk to the manager about the next group of tour guide trainees, a conversation she could have any time. She felt, however, that if Lucy had waited with no specific time to guide her, then she would be impossible to brush off or avoid. It would be better to get it over with. Besides, part of her was curious about the look of humility which seemed to have replaced Lucy's previous smugness.

The café was mainly for takeaway but there were a few tables squashed along one wall opposite the counter. The road outside was so thick with traffic that the buildings on the other side of the street were barely visible through the sliding screen of buses and trucks. Taxis swerved in and out with a constant bleeping from their horns, ferrying passengers towards Anzac bridge or back towards the city centre. Caroline enjoyed having a reason to come into Pyrmont most weeks. Its position beside Darling Harbour gave it a distinctly Australian feel. On Friday evenings, the after-work crowd mingled easily with the shiny, club-going crowd, their combined energies radiating from the throbbing pubs. But this afternoon, from their small table by the window, Caroline was not enjoying the frantic city.

She ordered a short black and a small melting moment. Lucy ordered a long black and a large slice of carrot cake. It will take her an hour to finish all that, Caroline thought to herself, grimacing at the sound of a driver hollering at some pedestrians. Lucy's hands, as she raised her cup to her lips, shook slightly. Caroline looked into the murkiness within her own cup, trying to block out the sound and movement around her.

"What can I do for you, Lucy?" She asked when it seemed Lucy would not be the one to start talking.

"I've been trying to contact Lawrence, actually." Although she hadn't wanted to talk to Lucy, Caroline felt slightly rejected at hearing that the young woman wasn't interested in her either. "Remember, I told you he'd offered to show me his studio, to see him paint? I'd really love to but he won't get back to me."

"And?"

"I thought you might help me." There was an unattractive plea in her voice. Caroline flicked some crumbs off her fingers. The filling of her biscuit was uncomfortably sweet, and her throat ached mildly. Caroline could almost feel Lucy biting her tongue, not wanting to ramble and risk saying the wrong thing. Her eyes were focused on Caroline, creased in worry. One hand self-consciously patted down the fabric of her dress which was pulled oddly by a miss-sewn button over her chest.

"Lawrence is busy. He may simply have overcommitted himself. Don't take it personally."

"I'm not taking it personally. Really, I'm not. I just really want to see him work. I want to work in galleries, this is what I want to do with my life," her voice shook with desperation and Caroline looked away. A woman was dragging a small child on a leash past the door. The child had been distracted by a floating plastic bag that was dancing down the street, just out of reach. "I understand you might be suspicious of me," Lucy's voice was low, falsely understanding. It forced Caroline to make eye contact, "But there's nothing to be worried about. Honestly."

"Do you think I trust you more than I trust my husband? Don't be a fool. I know there's nothing to worry about."

Lucy sat back as though slapped. She also, Caroline was pleased to see, looked slightly disappointed.

"Listen, you have a good understanding of his art. Be satisfied with that. Knowing him as a person is very different." It was unwanted advice cushioned in a compliment, and she was not surprised to see Lucy's frustration as Caroline stood to leave. She dropped some money on the table and paused, wondering whether she should say something else. When Lucy looked up, however, the stubbornness in her eyes made it easy for Caroline to turn with nothing but a cursory "Bye." She stepped out of the café and almost collided with a woman on a motorised scooter, the placid look on her face suggesting she had no idea of the speed she was going.

It was not uncommon for Lawrence to forget something he had promised a young, hopeful woman, Caroline thought as she walked back towards the gallery. She had been surprised, when they first started seeing each other, that he remembered his promise to show her the studio he worked in.

The day after she had slept on the floor of his bedroom in Annandale, she had woken with a crick in her neck. The grime from the floor felt as though it had crawled inside her clothes during the night, but she had not wanted to sound precious or high-maintenance. She had rubbed cold water from the tap in the bathroom vigorously over her face, feeling her skin tighten with the shock of the temperature. She had dampened the fringes of her hair, and ran a finger over each eyebrow. She searched the bathroom cabinet and borrowed some deodorant she found in there, unsure whether it was male or female. Her throat ached from the smoke of the night before. When she returned to his bedroom, Lawrence had changed. He looked fresh, well-rested. Her crumpled clothes seemed to sit at strange angles over her body. He reached over and took her hand.

His studio was in an old building on City Road, opposite

A Perilous Margin

the main part of the university. Caroline had not been to this part of the campus before. Lawrence had held tightly to her hand on the bus, and used it to lead her up a long flight of stairs. The bulb hanging over them was bare, and its light only made it halfway up the stairwell. The last dozen steps were in darkness, and she gripped Lawrence's hand as he continued walking quickly, apparently unperturbed by the inability to see where he was going.

The wood of the door was tight against the door jamb, and Lawrence released her hand in order to shove against it, first with both hands and then with a shoulder. He stumbled slightly as the door gave way.

The room was tiny. 'Studio', Caroline had realised, was a loose term. It was more like a large storage cupboard. There was no window, just another bare bulb. There was a wooden chair in one corner, piled high with old paint-covered sheets, a few empty tubes, a pair of scissors perched precariously on top. There was no chance, Caroline thought to herself, that there was spare clay lying around somewhere. There was no room for any subtle storage but Caroline realised she wasn't surprised or disappointed. Lawrence had left her near the door. An easel was turned, its face to the wall and he was manoeuvring it back into the small space of clear floor. He looked up at her once it was in place, his face expectant. He held out a hand and drew her around to see it.

The first sheet of paper was strange cut up angles of a person's face. Her face. She looked disjointed, unreal. She hated it.

"I don't usually paint people, to be honest. These are just some practise drawings. I'm too late to really change my focus for my degree. But you are such an interesting subject." His hand came up to brush her hair from her cheek. She allowed him to stroke her face, although her body was tense, her eyes on the picture.

"Why did you draw me like that?"

His hand paused, mid-stroke. His eyes stayed on her face although she was staring resolutely at the picture.

"Uneven?"

"Broken."

"I drew you as I see you. One part of how I see you. Remember the siren on the wall? That's also how I see you." He moved a step closer. She could feel his breath on her face. Here, she realised was where he wanted to have sex. Not in his bedroom. She took a step away and he dropped his hands.

"That's not me."

"Okay." He moved so he was in front of the easel, blocking her view of the picture. He raised a hand again, this time to her neck, scooping the hair off her shoulder. She stepped back again, leaving his hand hanging between them.

"You don't know me."

He cocked his head to the side, as though looking at a small child who was trying to tell him the biscuits ate themselves. "You don't!" She said, louder this time.

"Caroline. You're beautiful, and you're lost. What else is there to know?" She clicked her tongue impatiently. "I was

A Perilous Margin

lost, too! For a while. Painting gives my life meaning now. What gives your life meaning?" She shook her head, vigorously. Ready to fight. "Seriously," he dropped his voice until it was gentle, cajoling, asking her to consider what he was saying. She shook her head again, feeling her hair sway in a solid ball around her ears.

"I'm going."

"No. You stay. I'll go." He held a hand up to her and, before she knew what had happened, the door had closed softly behind him. She held her breath, expecting him to come back in grinning, joking, laughing at her look of horror. Moments passed and she exhaled. The picture of her fragmented face remained in front of her. She wanted to leave but found she couldn't. Instead, she flicked the paper over the top of the easel and saw another picture, even less recognisable as her, a female form crouching, a splintered background creating a vortex around her. She flicked it over. The next one was her hands, red and maimed, twists of thick broken skin and buckled knuckles deforming them. She took a step back, then another one, and came up against the wall behind her. Her hands curled themselves in front of her, as though begging for a cure for the painting.

She did not know how long she stayed there. Part of her wanted Lawrence to come back, to fulfil the promise of desire; part of her never wanted to see him again. It was her stomach rumbling that brought her to her senses. In three steps she had crossed the room. Moments later she was outside, a mouthful of dust from a passing bus choked her.

It had taken another month, until the end of the semester, before Caroline had accepted her fate and withdrawn from her French classes. Her transfer to the visual arts department was smooth thanks to a reference she had received from her high school art teacher, including photographs of Caroline's work which the teacher had kept to decorate the art room and inspire future students. She had not seen Lawrence during that month, though his presence seemed to pervade the campus.

Back at the gallery, Caroline had to force her attention on to Barry, the tour guide manager, who was telling her about the new exhibition. He was a small, balding man whose translucent skin always appeared slightly damp. Print outs with information about the exhibition were laid out on his desk, and he eagerly pointed out the show's best points to Caroline, who was uncomfortably aware of how much she towered over him.

"She grew up in Tasmania you see, and her mother was a dressmaker which is why she uses so much fabric. But the fabric and the paint are so perfect at capturing the Tasmanian landscape, you see?" His hands pointed out the photos which showed various aspects of the woman's work and Caroline nodded along. "She's in her seventies now, and is too frail to travel, but her children will be here for the opening. They're the ones who have really pushed for the exhibitions. This is the fourth one in five years, all with different work. She must have just worked non-stop for decades!" He beamed up into Caroline's face, delighted to share with her this new, Australian artist. Caroline tried to smile but it felt like a grimace. Her mind found its way back to the collection of work which lay in the darkness of her garage. Such a small collection for so many years work. And, now, almost all ruined. Caroline smiled back at Barry and made her excuses to leave.

Scattered over the kitchen table, rustling slightly in the breeze from an open window, were sample programs for Lawrence's new show. Caroline watched them flutter from the doorway, unsteady with the sudden déjà vu.

"Darling!" Lawrence said from behind her, nudging her into the room. "Sylvia asked us to look over these tonight." He led her over to the table. Once she was closer to them, Caroline realised the poor quality of the samples. The gallery, for all its big talk, was not throwing money at Lawrence. He pulled one off the top of the pile and held it out to her, one hand still clutching at her elbow. "I think this is my favourite, but tell me what you think." Her keys were still clasped in her hand so she let Lawrence continue holding it for her. It was a large photo of his face with a small amount of text. He opened it and flicked through the pages for her. Each page had three or four photos of different works. He had created so much for this exhibition. He had for all his exhibitions. Her mind was stuck, unable to process the potential of the pamphlet to assist exhibition goers. To disguise her lack of opinion, she moved her eyes over the rest of the samples.

"Don't they have a standard format for this kind of show?"

"Darling," Lawrence clasped a hand to his heart in shock, "I am sure they do but how could I possibly accept 'standard'?"

She smiled faintly but could not bring herself to join in his exuberance. She nodded back to the one he was still waving about in his hand.

"You're right, that's probably the best." She turned and retreated from the kitchen, wondering why she suddenly found it difficult to fulfil her part in his success. This was what she did, normally: assist with the peripheral decisions which had to be made. They were a team when it came to these things.

She put her bag in the wardrobe and carefully hung her scarf up. The silk had become tattered over the years but it was one of the few presents she had received from Grace which she felt her sister had chosen carefully. Grace was a kind and generous person, most of the time, but giving presents was not something she had been naturally gifted at doing.

Lawrence came to the doorway as she turned. "Is everything okay?"

She sat on the bed without answering, and pulled off her shoes. The socklets she was wearing had slipped under her foot, and the back of her heel was rubbed slightly raw from the thick leather of her sturdy flats. The bed dipped beside

A Perilous Margin

her as he sat. "Do you ever go into the shed?" She surprised herself with the question. He looked confused.

"No, I thought we just kept old junk in there. Are you thinking about converting it into something more useful?"

She shrugged, trying not to let the pain show when she knew she could not explain it. "I'm just thinking, that's all."

TWENTY-FIVE

The days before the dinner party passed quickly. Caroline had called and left a voicemail advising that they postpone the next interview. Andie had agreed via text, which meant when they saw each other at the dinner it would be almost two weeks since the last interview. Andie was nervous that any slight rapport which had been created by the truce of their last meeting might have disappeared.

George sat on the couch, calling out helpful suggestions, as she got dressed, though she felt self-conscious parading each outfit in front of him. She had given herself a lot of time but was finding it difficult to know what to wear and his enthusiasm about everything she chose, while flattering, was not particularly helpful.

The dinner party was starting at eight o'clock and she hated to be late, so by the time the clock hit seven-thirty she decided to leave wearing what she had on: skinny black jeans and a fitted dark blue top, which showed more cleavage than she wanted but looked better than anything else with the jeans. Several pieces of large silver jewellery hung around her neck and wrists, and as she left her room she felt them jangle against her skin. George whistled and she gave a half-curtsey on her way to the door, acting more comfortable than she felt. "Give 'em hell!" he called as she pulled the door shut behind her. The muscles across her shoulders were tight and her walk to the train station felt stilted. She hated the fact that her attempts to fit in with a different crowd were so unnatural.

It was barely five past eight when she arrived at the front door of the house in Tempe. It was a reasonably familiar place for her now, but the atmosphere was markedly different in the fading twilight. She had the momentary feeling of being mature, free. The doorbell rang loudly in the evening air and her nerves swarmed back. There was a hurried rustle from inside the house, and several moments passed before Lawrence opened the door, his collar unbuttoned and his hair untidy.

"Welcome, early bird! Come in, come in. We are nowhere near ready, I'm sorry, but come in, make yourself at home. Can I get you a drink?" Lawrence was a natural host and he ushered her in to the house with a large smile and a faux kiss on each cheek. Andie smiled in return but her embarrassment at arriving first made it feel strained. She would have loved to turn around and disappear for an hour but her instinct was always to downplay awkwardness in a desperate bid to quash it. She stepped into the house, continued smiling slightly manically at Lawrence, and asked for a glass of red wine.

Lawrence led her into the kitchen and poured her a small measure in a bulbous glass which sat awkwardly in her hand. He poured himself an equal measure and raised his glass to hers. The glasses made a low chink against each other. The wine was warm and she wished she had asked for white. To disguise the heat which refused to leave her face she turned around, her gaze roaming over the kitchen. "This is such a nice place. How long have you lived here?"

"Thank you, Andie. It works for us." He smiled before he bent down to open the oven, reaching in to turn a dish around. "We've been here for over twenty years now," He said, speaking into the oven. "It's very different to Brisbane, but it's certainly home now."

"Do you still have family in Brisbane?"

"Oh no. My parents died a long time ago and I'm an only child. My extended family I presume is still in Scotland but my parents were not very good at keeping in touch."

"But Caroline has family in Sydney?" Andie asked, aware that she was trying to get more details about Caroline's family, details that Caroline had avoided during the interviews. Lawrence, however, seemed to know what she was doing and simply made a small noise of agreement.

Then, nodding towards the painting behind her, he said, "You know, I never heard your opinion on that piece." He had put her on the spot like a punishment for her question. As she looked at it she felt her nerves return. The wine in her hand, however, seemed to give her permission to take her time, to relax into an opinion.

She let her gaze follow the flow of the woman's body, the slight change in hue between the rise of her breasts and the length of her thighs. The figure in the mirror appeared both sensual and menacing. Perhaps it was the reclining pose of the woman which gave her a vulnerability and hence the other figure was endowed with a sense of strength.

"It's about power, is it?" She said and Lawrence smiled

slightly but continued staring at the painting rather than Andie. "I can't decide who has the power, though."

"Does only one have to be powerful?"

"No, I suppose not." Andie fought her instinct to say what she thought Lawrence wanted to hear. "The colours are beautiful, but it makes me uncomfortable. I don't think I could have it hanging anywhere quite so prominent." She laughed, forcibly. He looked at her this time, and nodded with a slight smile.

"The relationship between sex and power is an uncomfortable one, especially when it's reflected back to us. You have a good eye." It was a parting comment rather than a genuine compliment and Andie felt her opinion of the painting dismissed as Lawrence went over to the stove to stir something in a large pot.

"Do you like mushroom soup? This is a recipe I picked up in France when I was travelling there. It never fails me."

"It smells delicious." The segue into small talk was peculiar and the presence of the painting remained behind her, its topic unfinished, as she watched Lawrence at the stove. His shoulders were very broad. There was a lick of grey hair hanging over his collar.

In the silence Andie heard a few thumps and a muffled groan from somewhere else in the house. She saw Lawrence smile to himself. The silence stretched out so long that it became natural, and Lawrence hummed slightly as he moved around the kitchen.

"Andie, welcome," Caroline said, appearing in the

doorway.

"Thanks. Sorry I'm so early." Andie gripped her glass tightly, afraid her sweating fingers would let it slip, but Caroline made a dismissive gesture with her hand.

"Not to worry. We've just gotten used to our tardy friends, I think." A pause of a few seconds as Caroline and Lawrence shared a look which Andie was unable to read. The oven timer beeped and the three of them seemed to let out a collective sigh.

"Cheesy puffs. Would you like one?" Caroline swept the small, golden balls of flaked pastry into a colourful salad bowl and offered it to Andie. The particles of pastry broke away from the ball as Andie bit into it and cascaded down her front. She brushed them off hurriedly while Caroline and Lawrence pretended not to notice.

The conversation moved between Lawrence's exhibition, and where the food which they were going to eat that night was from. Andie relaxed, feeling the wine soak into her muscles. Watching Caroline and Lawrence together, she felt unexpectedly comforted by their obvious affection for each other as they continuously found small ways to make contact, to smile and laugh with each other. After half an hour she surprised herself by realising she was enjoying herself.

It was almost nine when the doorbell rang. Several people, three at first though a fourth soon bounded in after parking the car, were shown into the kitchen by Lawrence. Introductions were made and the noise level escalated as several conversations started at once. Andie realised how quiet the house had been until then. Someone put on some music, loud brassy jazz that was not Andie's style, and the atmosphere became jovial. Andie's glass was refilled and she was ushered in to the lounge room.

The couch was large and cushioned and she sank several inches as she sat down, the low position making it difficult for her to join in the conversations. Everyone else was sitting at various places around the room and banter bounced around her, private jokes that further isolated her. She sipped her wine. To her left was a tall man, Paul she thought his name was, who looked like a once handsome man whose muscles had softened with age. His jowls wobbled as he laughed and he kept plucking at the buttons over his stomach as though they were too tight. His partner was Mai, who had a strong Australian accent despite her Vietnamese appearance. She was standing to one side talking to another woman, Penny, who was tall and had to bend slightly to talk to her. Penny was the best-dressed person there: a formal navy cocktail dress and gold jewellery made her stand out.

Sitting on an armchair opposite Andie was Colm, who had parked the car. He seemed the least comfortable and Andie guessed that he was not very well acquainted with Caroline or Lawrence. He kept looking around at the room, as though it was the first time he had seen it. Andie's cheeks remained flushed from the wine and the close atmosphere and she held her cold fingers against her skin as the conversations swirled around her. Caroline stood with

Penny and Mai for a few minutes, smiling over to Andie at numerous points as though including her in the conversation.

Lawrence disappeared for a few moments and his absence created a conversational hole. He was back quickly, however, carrying a tray of large mismatched mugs. He gave the first one to Andie, and the smell of the mushroom soup overpowered her. She waited until everyone had received their soup before she started. A loud groan of appreciation caught her attention and she looked up to see Penny smacking her lips.

"Best mushroom soup, ever. Whatever this secret recipe is, I've got to get it when you're dead."

Lawrence laughed loudly. "I'll put it in my will tomorrow, darling."

He must have used a wild species of mushroom because the liquid was almost black. Andie took a tentative taste. It was creamy but not from dairy, and tasted more of garlic than anything else. She took a quick sip of wine and realised they complemented each other perfectly.

The dinner table was large, a dark mahogany oval that easily accommodated the seven people. Lawrence, who had retreated somewhat from being the exuberant host he had started out as, had laid out three bowls. One was a salad of rocket and parmesan; the second was fat pieces of roasted chicken; the third a mound of roasted potatoes, pumpkin, onion, sweet potato, parsnip. A fourth, flat pan was placed on the table which looked like it held a spinach quiche.

A Perilous Margin

Glasses were filled and a resounding 'cheers' given. As they began to serve themselves from the bowls, Penny, who had put a pair of red-framed glasses on, leaned forwards, resting her elbows on the table and looked at Andie. "So, you're the student who's been interviewing Lawrence and Caroline."

Andie's hand, which was holding a large spoonful of roast vegetables, gave an involuntary jerk at the direct address. "Yes, that's me."

There was a strange silence around the table. Even Lawrence was looking steadily at Andie. She replaced the spoon in the bowl after tipping the vegetables onto her plate, and sat with her hands in her lap. "It's for an art history and sociology course I'm doing at university." A few polite nods, but Penny's gaze was steady.

"And what does the course cover?"

"It's fairly broad in its scope. We've looked at art in consumerism, institutions and also the gender disparity of successful artists."

"The gender disparity? As in, it's easier for men to be successful?"

"Maybe, I don't know. We try not to be that black and white about it!" Andie threw out the line in an attempt to deflect attention away from herself, and a few people including Lawrence smiled for her.

"Why did you choose the course?" Penny barrelled on.

"It sounded interesting," Andie shrugged.

"Are you an artist?"

"No, I'm not."

"But she writes short stories," Lawrence contributed with a wide smile, Andie was unsure if he was supporting her or feeding a bit more of her to the lion. Penny's eyebrows raised.

"Have you been published?" She asked.

"No, no. It's more a hobby than anything else."

"Do you want to be able to make money out of it?"

"Ideally, maybe, one day." Andie could feel her already flushed cheeks redden further. "But for the moment I'm still studying and focusing on that."

"Is it difficult being a mature-aged student?" Mai jumped in with a kind smile, artfully moving the conversation to more neutral territory.

"Oh Mai, she's hardly mature-aged!" Lawrence said, and everyone laughed.

"Older than the other students then!" Mai corrected herself.

"Sometimes it's hard," Andie was aware that everyone else was eating and she had barely had time to draw breath. Penny skewered a piece of pumpkin and ate it. "It can be frustrating. This course, my whole degree, means a lot to me but it seems for some of the eighteen and nineteen year olds that it's just a way to pass some time."

"Weren't you like that, when you were just out of school?" Penny again, between mouthfuls.

"I went to work straight away, part time so I could concentrate on writing."

"Where did you work?"

"I was a receptionist in a dental practice." Andie felt her answers becoming terser. She quickly shoved a piece of potato in her mouth, hoping to halt Penny's interrogation.

"You wanted to be a dentist, didn't you Colm?" Lawrence came to the rescue this time. Caroline was leaning back in her chair, eating slowly and looking between Penny and Andie. She seemed unconcerned. Colm started slightly, he had obviously been focused on his food rather than the discussion.

"Oh no, no I wanted to be an orthodontist until I was about seventeen."

"What put you off?" Mai, looking politely interested.

"Bad breath. I have a very sensitive nose." Everyone chuckled and Lawrence passed around the wine bottle. Andie had had a chance to eat several more mouthfuls, as had Penny, though her eyes had barely left Andie's face. She pounced again.

"How long did you work there?"

"Eight years."

"Do you still work?"

"Yes, at a clothes store on King Street in Newtown." Andie had the feeling that her wine was dismantling her senses. It felt as though someone else was answering for her.

"But you don't write anymore?"

"Between studying and working it's hard to find time." Andie was embarrassed to find she was sweating.

"Don't you think artists will always find time for what they love?"

"Penny, Penny, let the poor girl take a breath." Lawrence laughed to cover the awkwardness, and passed around a plate of ciabatta he had just removed from the oven. Penny did not reply, but continued to look at Andie. Andie smiled at the other guests nervously. Only Mai seemed to be aware of the tension. Caroline's eyes had dropped to her plate, as though contemplating an unusual seasoning. Colm had returned to his daydreaming state, and Paul was distracted by trying to disentangle the bones from his chicken.

"Caroline, I meant to ask you, why did you use snail mail invitations? I don't even remember the last time I saw one of those!" Mai beamed brightly at Caroline, who looked faintly surprised.

"Lawrence thinks they give a sense of occasion. I don't mind either way really, but as it's for his celebration I thought I could put the extra effort it."

"Of course, your exhibition!" It was as though everyone had only just remembered the reason they were there. "When does it open?" Mai leant forward as though barely able to contain her excitement.

"Next week at Ford's exhibition centre in the city."

"Wow, big space." Paul's voice was dry when he spoke.

"How long is it running for?" Colm asked, looking more interested now.

"Four months, but really we don't have to talk about it. It was just an excuse for a party." Andie was surprised to see Lawrence blushing from the attention.

"Of course we should talk about it. Andie probably has a

lot of questions she'd like to ask you." Penny managed to speak while chewing without sounding disgusting. Andie had to chew for a few seconds and swallow.

"No, not really. This is a social occasion, after all, not part of my assignment."

"Will you go to see the exhibition?"

"I don't know. Hopefully, I guess."

"That's not overwhelming enthusiasm."

Andie wanted to slither under the table and stay there. She didn't know why she had sounded so unsure when she knew that she would go. Her brain was becoming foggy with the wine.

"Andie and I have already had some interesting conversations about painting." Lawrence jumped in, smiling at Andie as though it did not bother him at all if she went to see his paintings.

"So you have opinions about painting, do you?" The obvious hostility of the question caught everyone's attention, and Paul actually rolled his eyes.

"What's the deal with you tonight, Penny?" He asked. There was a moment of silence as Penny refused to take her eyes off Andie.

"Penny, I think, is trying to determine why I have not been myself since Andie here began her interviews a few weeks ago. She thinks, perhaps, that I am being poisoned by young blood and new ideas. When Penny suggested we invite Andie along tonight, I wasn't aware that it was for her own agenda. I'm sorry." Caroline's voice was cool and slightly detached but the apology was warm. Andie held her breath. It was the first sign Caroline had given that the interviews were affecting her. There was a pause in the conversation and it occurred to Andie, as she saw Penny cast an unreadable look at Lawrence, that there was more to these old friends than she had realised.

Penny sat back in her chair for the rest of the evening, creating an odd cone of silence in the middle of the table. Caroline also seemed uninclined to talk. Mai tried hard to keep the conversation going by asking first Colm and then Andie a series of harmless questions about their lives. Paul, Andie realised at one point, had finished a bottle of wine by himself. He was very quiet, however, so his drunkenness was not too apparent. Lawrence became merry, though he seemed to be forcing it by speaking too loudly.

Colm began to lounge in his chair, his long legs jiggling restlessly, and just after eleven he actually yawned audibly. He gazed into the shocked silence that followed and said, "Oh, sorry. Guess I'm tired. I'd better head off now, if that's alright by you guys?" Mai and Paul, although obviously surprised and faintly embarrassed, nodded and drank the last few mouthfuls of their wine. Penny, however, had just refilled her glass.

"Don't worry about me, I'll get a train in a little while."

"Sure," Colm shrugged, "How about you?" He asked Andie.

"Oh that's okay, I got the train in so I can get it back. I live close to the station." She had the strong desire to stay in the same house as Caroline, to investigate this discomfort the older woman had apparently been feeling since their acquaintance began.

"You're on the Bankstown line, right? We can get the same train if you'd like." Penny smiled quite genuinely as she said it, but Andie wasn't fooled. Now that she knew she had been invited at Penny's request, the series of questions seemed planned and purposefully daunting. She wondered why Caroline was friends with someone who would sabotage a gathering like that.

Colm hastened the departure of his friends, and within ten minutes just Andie, Penny, Caroline and Lawrence remained. To avoid sitting across from Penny again, Andie began clearing the dishes. Caroline started to help her, while Lawrence and Penny immediately started a hushed conversation which Andie was pleased she could not hear. In the kitchen, she and Caroline were silent for several moments.

"I'm sorry if Penny upset you tonight. As I said, she has noticed some changes in me that she is not altogether happy about," Caroline said, leaning against the bench. Andie could not bring herself to make eye contact.

"How long have you two been friends?" She asked as she filled the sink with water.

"Since university. She and Lawrence went to high school together though. I think they even dated for a while, before Penny came out, of course." Andie nodded. She ran her fingers over the smooth surface of a dinner plate as water from the tap trickled lukewarm down the back of her hand. She shook the plate and handed it to Caroline, who began drying it with a muted blue tea towel.

"I presumed you and her were closer, I guess just because you're women."

"Lawrence has never had a problem finding women to get along with. You already know that, though."

Andie reached for the heavy-bottomed oven tray which the chicken had been cooked in. It was smeared with chunks of sauce.

"I'm sorry if I went too far during the last interview," Andie said, as she took a large steadying breath. "I never meant to cast aspersions on your relationship, or presume that I could understand it. I've just noticed that women often change during relationships, change direction I mean. I guess I was taking my curiosity out on you." Andie looked at her fingers, covered in slight suds. She could feel the skin wrinkling in the warm water.

"It's okay. Strangers can sometimes see things more clearly. Though sometimes they only see things they want to see."

"Caroline," Andie turned and looked her in the eye for the first time since they had entered the kitchen, "I know we don't know each other very well, and I know that I'm probably bringing a whole lot of personal judgements into my view of your life, but I just feel like there's something missing from the happy-wife image that you project."

"Andie," Caroline said gently, "what gives you the right

to have a view of my life in the first place? Take my word for it, my art was always going to be mediocre. I have attached myself to a man of genius and been lucky enough to get some semblance of the life I always dreamed about but which my talents would have failed to provide for me. That is it. That is the extent of the drama." Caroline smiled slightly, almost apologetically.

"Yes, but –"

"No, no 'but'. Almost certainly I have made wrong decisions in my life. You'll be a rare person indeed if you get to my age and don't say the same thing. But there was no hidden agenda forced on me. My motivations are my own even if my decisions seem so terribly ordinary to you."

"But how can that be?" Andie was embarrassed by the sudden emotion in her voice, contrasted with Caroline's low, sedate words, and turned her face away to hide just how emotional she felt.

"I did things I thought would make me happiest," Caroline shrugged. "I realised a long time ago that life is fragile and priorities are important. The things I've prioritised, love and yes stability, have kept me safe. That doesn't mean I have failed. And I certainly haven't failed *you*, which is the impression I continue to get." The dishes in need of washing had ended and Andie emptied the sink, the loud suck of water disguising the awkward pause. She felt her face distorting with emotion. She understood what Caroline was saying, and could even see the logic in it. But it created a rush of anger in her belly which swept up her throat, constricting her breathing. She was angry at the world for forcing people to choose between livelihoods and living. Was it really the world though that had forced Caroline to choose, or was it Lawrence?

"You're so angry, Andie. It's been a long time since I've seen a young woman so angry about these issues."

"You don't know the right young women." She heard the impatience in her voice but Caroline's quick light laugh eased the tension of the room.

"Yes, that's probably true. I must say, it's nice to see." Andie looked up and saw gentleness in Caroline's face. "I was angry too, for a long time. I wanted to be so different, to make such changes in the world. But that can come at a terrible price. And I decided I wasn't willing to pay it."

"What price?"

"Loneliness."

Andie shook her head, vigorously. "No, I don't believe that."

"Lucky for you you've never had to make the choice." As Caroline turned away, Andie remembered waiting in the living room for Leon to return from work, waiting with shaking hands as she rehearsed what she was going to say. She never told him, specifically, that his lack of support for her writing, his lack of belief that something could be important and necessary for her happiness if it did not contribute financially to their life, was the reason she was breaking up with him. She just said she needed to be alone.

"Come on," Caroline said gently, "I'll drop you home. I

don't think either of us particularly wants to know what they —" she gestured with her head towards the room where Lawrence and Penny were still talking, "— are going on about." They smiled gently at each other, without judgement.

TWENTY-SIX

When Caroline returned home Penny was just leaving the house. "Goodnight," Caroline said and kissed her on the cheek. It was an automatic action that felt strange after the tension of the evening. The smell of wine was strong on Penny's breath.

"Wait," Penny's hand clasped at Caroline. Her wide face shone slightly with the reflected light from the front windows. Her red glasses suddenly annoyed Caroline.

"What?"

"Look, Lawrence and I had coffee this afternoon, all right? And he was upset, angry more than anything. He was saying that you've been different. I've noticed as well, of course, but the fact that it has been distracting him so much." Penny threw her hands up, unconsciously mimicking Lawrence's gesture of frustration. "He has an exhibition opening next week and he called me to have coffee this afternoon. It's not right, Car." She shook her head slightly, as though in disbelief at Caroline's behaviour.

"So you decided to destroy his party by picking on one of his guests?"

"Who cares what Andie thinks," Penny said, jerking her head impatiently. "It's you guys I'm worried about."

"Really? Both of us? I couldn't tell." Caroline waited a moment but the alcohol had slowed down Penny's reflexes so that she simply stood, staring. Caroline turned, leaving her friend on the front path. Caroline knew they would have

A Perilous Margin

it out, eventually. But not tonight.

The rubber soles of her boots made soft beats on the wood of the hallway as she walked to the kitchen. The streetlight which shone over their back fence barely made a dent in the darkness, but the room still seemed to sparkle after her and Andie's clean. She moved towards the bedroom, listening out for a sound from Lawrence. The door to his studio was standing ajar so she nudged it open. He was slumped low on the couch; a faded corduroy sofa-bed leftover from the early days of their marriage. He had sunk several inches into the soft cushioning. His eyes were closed behind his reading glasses, though his hand gently swirled a small measure of whiskey in a glass. The light from the lamp on the desk caught the amber liquid and created soft light patterns on his face.

"Are you okay?" She asked. He did not answer, but held out one hand towards her, inviting her to join him on the couch. She breathed into the calmness as his arm encircled her shoulders.

"Penny thinks it's my fault that you're distracted," she said.

"Penny only just met Andie."

She smiled. He did not sound distracted. She watched his whiskey swirl in the glass for several moments until she realised he had opened his eyes and was looking at her. "Have I been in your way this whole time?" There was a soft plea in his voice, his breath a fusion of whiskey and garlic.

"What do you mean?"

"Andie seems to think that I made you give up everything. Your art. Did I?"

"No." She was reassured by the conviction in her voice. Her gaze was firmly on the liquid which continued to tremble in his glass. In his speeches he often mentioned the sacrifices she had made, but they had never spoken about it, not explicitly.

"Why did you stop?"

"I had to," she shrugged, hoping to deflect further conversation but Lawrence was not finished.

"Because of me?"

"Because I love you."

"I love you, too, and I didn't stop."

"Perhaps we love in different ways." Moments passed. She stole a glance at him. His eyes were closed; he looked peaceful.

In the bedroom, she put a Dave Brubeck album on softly, and cleaned her teeth. She climbed into bed, aware of her crimped skin folding over the elastic of her underwear. She spread out in a large star shape, the smooth cool cotton sheets were soothing against her skin. They loved in different ways, she had said. It felt true. Who loved more? She knew most people would probably say she did. She had somehow forgotten her own dreams in the midst of watching him create his own. The truth is, she thought to herself, I love selfishly; so selfishly that there is no room for anything else. Whereas his heart is bigger, and it can cope with multiple demands. Somehow, his dreams could cope with

A Perilous Margin

the constant demands that love had brought; whereas hers crumbled at the first sign of competition.

She had not always been like that, she knew. But something had changed after her illness. The summer of 1985, the summer which had heralded the start of Lawrence's recovery had also begun her creative demise.

He had been circling in gloom for two years, and she had held on to him, and to her job, so tightly for all that time. But a part of her, she knew, always expected it to be temporary. At some point, she had thought, she would return to the rest of her life, including sculpting. They just had to get through the bad patch. But the bad patch was not just a patch, it was not a grim speck which could be rubbed away when the time came. Although she knew that technically her pneumonia was exacerbated by the weakness in her lungs from a childhood of bronchial infections and years of smoking, she felt as though it was really the result of the prolonged grimness. And while supporting her had given Lawrence the strength to become sober and look to the future, to her, being sick had merely proved to her the fragility of life. When faced with life's blackness, she had clung ever more strongly to the one thing that gave her some security. Even when he had been sleeping with Bridget.

She had returned home after lunch with Penny and an afternoon of sculpting. She was due to start back at work the following week and was trying to make the most of her last weekend. She had known what was going on, she must have known. But she had never put words to it. And it was only when Lawrence let slip Bridget's name while they were having dinner that everything clicked and she had finally been ready to deal with it. Her plate had smashed against the wall before he had finished the sentence – something about a new café they had eaten lunch in. Their eyes had met with a sudden understanding that they both knew what was going on, and both knew they knew. She had expected apologies and begging but Lawrence had calmly placed his knife and fork back down on the table, looked up at her and said: "Caroline, I love you."

She threw her glass against the wall. He had turned his head away, wincing slightly at the shattered glass, but had looked back at her with the same, calm expression.

"Caroline, I love you. I want to be with you. But you haven't been here, not really. I needed someone. You know that I am no good alone. If you're back now, I'll end it with Bridget."

She couldn't believe his matter-of-factness. She could tell that he wanted to continue eating, that he thought that was that and she had no idea how to show him that it was not okay. She couldn't find words. She was out of things to throw. They sat in silence for several long moments and then Lawrence picked up his fork and ate another mouthful of pasta. She had grabbed his plate as though to throw it but he had put a hand on her wrist, gently. "Please," he said, and for the first time there was fear in his eyes. "Please," he said again. "I need you. I only want you, Caroline. Please come

A Perilous Margin

back to me." She had frozen, half standing, holding his plate.

"I needed you," she said, her voice almost a hiss. "I have been trying so hard to get better, and I needed you. Where were you? With her," she spat the words out.

He was looking up at her and something in her elevated position made her feel powerful and made him look small. She expected him to admit wrongdoing and plead for forgiveness. But he didn't follow the script.

"I needed you too," he said, his voice still calm but with a current of anger through it. "You think it's been easy for me? I have been black for years and all you've done is go to work and leave me alone. You never tried to help me, you kept your own life going. And now when I do the same, it's all my fault?"

"I was keeping us afloat!" She shouted, unable to believe he could blame her after all she had done. He had stood up, his chair falling with a crash behind him.

"No, you couldn't face the fact you had married a loser. You could barely look at me. You've been ashamed of me for years. Do you know what it's like living with someone who thinks you're useless?"

She sat, the sobs coming quickly, knowing that while what he said wasn't true, it was entirely possible that that's what it had felt like to him. After a long moment he had moved to sit next to her. He had held her hand. They had sat, talking and yelling for the night before collapsing into bed, exhausted, the next morning.

They had spent the following fortnight treating each

other as if they were fragile, the future uncertain. Caroline didn't know what she wanted. She knew she wanted Lawrence but didn't know if she was going to be the kind of person who could forgive a betrayal. And yet, according to him, she had betrayed him as well. Perhaps not with someone else but emotionally, he had also felt abandoned. And for a long time. She hated herself for making him feel like that, and hated him for making her feel it as well.

Two weeks later and neither of them had managed to leave. The relationship felt stronger, as though the longer they stayed the harder it would be to leave. And with the news that Bridget was moving to New York to pursue fashion photography, it seemed it had been decided for them, and Caroline was relieved. Life was fragile, her still weak lungs were proof of that, but together they could be strong. Together, they could be successful.

And so she had held on to Lawrence while he worked harder and harder, and she had sculpted less and less. She was not giving up, she told herself, she was simply ensuring she was available to him when he needed her. She was not going to abandon him again because she knew that he would not betray her again either. She allowed herself to become a dabbler and after years of that, her talent matched the challenges she set it, and she lost any chance of being anything more. The proof of that was sitting quietly in the darkness of the shed, a constant reminder of her mediocrity.

The door of the bedroom clicked open, a sliver of light

accompanying the sound. Lawrence's shadow moved into the room. She pulled her limbs back onto her side of the bed and rolled over, allowing Lawrence to curl his body around hers. He would never know, she realised, what it felt like to live with a reminder of your own failings, your own deficiencies. His self-doubt was prompted by himself alone, not by comparing himself to the person he loved the most.

TWENTY-SEVEN

Andie crept into her house, as though disturbing the quiet would affect the dark rooms. George snuck in a few moments after her, however, and they smiled to each other, the shine of the kitchen tiles diluting the darkness. "How was your night?" Andie asked, trying to remember what his plans had been.

"The band was pretty shit but the pub has some good new beers." He looked at her closely. "How was dinner?"

"Exhausting," she said as she filled the kettle and got out some mugs for tea. "Their friends hate me. And Lawrence is so —" she paused, searching for a word before giving up. "I don't know. He's done something to her though, to Caroline. He must have. She was so talented and now she's just so —" she paused again, but the wine of the evening had caught up and she simply shook her head.

"Was she really *that* good?"

"You've seen her work!" Andie exclaimed, her voice suddenly loud in the quiet house.

"Yes, I've seen it."

"And?"

"It's good." He shrugged again, sounding tired, but she waited, sure there must be something else coming. "What, Andie? I said it's good. But just because she did one or two fantastic pieces doesn't mean she was cut out for living as an artist. You should know, I mean, you gave up as well!"

"What do you mean? That was different, I wasn't any

A Perilous Margin

good."

"According to Leon."

"And every publisher I ever sent a story to."

"Yes, those uni students volunteering at literary journals in their spare time would never miss someone with talent, I'm sure." He rolled his eyes at her.

"Sarcasm doesn't help, George," she felt tears coming.

"And hypocrisy doesn't help either, Andie!"

"I'm not a hypocrite! I tried for a long time and then I realised it was just never going to happen," her voice cracked but she ploughed on. "I'm not sure Caroline even had a chance to try for that long, she was too busy supporting Lawrence while he ponced about being fabulous."

"Oh come on," George turned as though to storm into his room but seemed to change his mind. He stormed back towards her instead. "Get over yourself," he hissed. "People work for years, decades even, to get an ounce of recognition and they do it because they feel like they have something that needs to be said. You didn't give up because you decided you weren't good enough. No one ever feels good enough. You gave up because you got tired of trying. It was laziness, Andie, pure and simple. And you know what? I bet it was for Caroline as well. You do her a disservice by thinking Lawrence somehow manipulated her into giving up. She gave up because she couldn't stand the fight anymore. So go ahead and hate Lawrence for having the gall to work hard, really hard, for years, but just be honest while you do it." His footsteps echoed across the kitchen tiles. Andie's hands shook as she leant against the wall. The kettle clicked off with a loud snap. Food, wine and regret was swirling in her stomach and she decided to forgo the tea. She brushed her teeth and crawled into bed, feeling the fresh cotton against her skin, willing sleep to come so she could forget George's words.

***

The next day Andie strode into the library with a sheen of sweat on her skin, thankful that the building was at least 10 degrees cooler than outside. On the top floor she found the A3 sized, hard-cover books detailing every Australian art period from early-Aboriginal cave drawings right up to the early 2000s. She sat down on the floor, not caring that she looked like a child. She pulled several books at random off the shelf and began looking through them. They dug painfully into the flesh of her thighs but she remained where she was.

She flicked through the pages. Endless works of art, some beautiful, some not, some which immediately caught her eye, some she was happy to pass by. These, even the ones which had no appeal for her, were the cream of the crop. To make it into an internationally published book about a certain period required a level of talent and recognition which was beyond just about everyone. For every one of these artists there was a hundred, a thousand even, whose work was never seen by anyone but friends and family. She forced herself to continue turning pages, to continue being overwhelmed. She felt tears of frustration coming to her eyes. This immense body of work – sometimes outstanding and sometimes ordinary, but even the ordinary ones had a voice, an ability to speak to a certain number of people – was forever growing larger. Was it really so difficult to understand why Caroline had chosen not to compete for a place in these books?

She stopped suddenly, her breath caught in her throat. It was a painting of Lawrence's, the painting from the kitchen. Her eyes bore into it, wanting to see more, wanting to feel the presence that she had felt in their house, but it refused to come. On the page it was flat, almost colourless. The power and vulnerability of the figures were reduced to a slightly uncomfortable, awkward moment. Her eyes skimmed the several paragraphs written about the painting, unable to stop and read any of it. She turned the page and saw a rough pencil sketch, vaguely reminiscent of the previous painting. The caption claimed it was the first in a series of sketches Lawrence had made before starting the major work.

She closed the book and breathed out. She pushed the book off her lap and onto the floor and stood up quickly. The books lay in a discarded pile behind her. She descended the stairs, almost tripping, and stomped the forty-minute walk to her house in twenty five minutes. She arrived breathless and hot but with her mind clear, her misgivings crystallised, and she knew what she had to do. She sat on the front step of the house, the concrete rough under her legs, and called Caroline.

"Andie, hello. How are you?" Her voice was crisp but gentle.

"Hi Caroline. I was just wondering if – would it be possible for us to do the next interview this afternoon? Or tomorrow, if that suits you better." Andie crossed her fingers.

"I'm home at the moment, Lawrence is at his exhibition. I'll have to leave here about six but you're welcome to come over now if you'd like."

"Thank you." Andie was embarrassed by the crack in her voice. "I'll see you soon."

Caroline opened the door with a thin but warm smile. It shook slightly at the expression on Andie's face. "What is it?"

"I think I know what's been bothering me." Caroline stepped to the side, gesturing for Andie to come in to the house. Andie walked down the now familiar hallway, into the kitchen. She stared at the painting hanging on the main wall. She felt her breathing slow. "How long did it take Lawrence to paint this?"

Caroline's eyebrows raised slightly and she turned away to start making a pot of tea. "Probably twelve months in total, from when he first had the idea. There's a lot of planning that has to be done before a painting of that size. Especially when you don't have the money to be wasting canvases. Or paint. Why?"

"This incredible work didn't happen overnight. Twelve months, Caroline! Don't tell me you wouldn't have been able

A Perilous Margin

to turn your 'mediocre' works into something great in twelve months!"

"But I never believed that it could be done," Caroline's voice was gentle. It infuriated Andie. "The work that Lawrence put into this, that he puts into all his work, it needs such a strong foundation of self-belief. I've never been like that."

"But that's the problem!" Andie's voice was loud. "Why not? You *are* just as talented. Did he ever tell you that? Did anyone? I understand that mediocrity exists, but I don't think genius just appears. It has to be worked for and so many women just don't put in the work. Men get these incredibly supportive women in their lives, they get to devote all their time to creating art and producing works of genius, while their talented partners lose all belief in themselves!" A pot of tea stood between the two women, untouched. Caroline took a step backwards and lent against the stove, facing Andie with her arms crossed. She didn't respond. Andie took a deep breath.

"Artists are the people who comment on what is happening in life, right now. They give a voice to an age, and women aren't truly part of that voice. Artists are the people who shape our impressions of the world and our impressions are shallower because of these women!"

"There are plenty of talented, creative women working hard. And they have supportive partners."

"Did Lawrence support you?"

"You want to blame Lawrence but if you blame anyone it

should be me. I lacked the confidence and it shouldn't be up to him to spoonfeed me inspiration. He always told me I could do whatever I wanted. He never stopped me." An edge had come in to Caroline's voice.

"That's not the same thing. It has to be more than words. Someone to make money if you need time out; someone to make sure there's food in the house; to keep things marginally clean; to make the boring everyday decisions that have to be made. Did he do that for you?"

"He didn't have to. I did that for him."

"Would he have done it?"

Caroline looked at Andie for a long time as though at a puzzle. "No. He wouldn't have. But," her eyes were shining, "he never expected me to do all that for him. It wasn't on his mind that it needed to be done. We could both have followed our hearts and lived like students forever, or I could have put my work towards living, while he created. I did it because I wanted it done. He would have been just as happy if I hadn't done it."

"But you couldn't just let everything else go?"

"No. I guess there is a grain of domesticity in me after all. Not necessarily that I have to be doing those things, but that they need to be done by someone. He wasn't going to do them, not out of spite or malice, it just wasn't on his mind. But it was on my mind, so here we are. I wanted us to be a family, a strong family, and that was part of it." Caroline wiped the corner of her eye surreptitiously.

"So what, men can be purely creative but women have to

be domestically and financially cared for? Virginia will be so pleased that she continues to be right, a hundred years later." She tried to make it sound light, but the bitterness was heavy. Caroline shrugged.

"A room of one's own and five-hundred a year, isn't that what she said? Though I suppose it would be more like thirty-thousand a year now. I don't know anymore, Andie. I know that things happened in my life that I didn't choose, but that seemed natural at the time. But I also know that I did choose Lawrence, I chose to put him first, to put us first. And I'm glad I did. My life, despite your obvious distaste for it, has actually been a good one. I hope that your hard work pays off." Andie knew what was coming and held her breath. "I don't think we should continue these interviews anymore. I'll show you out." And with that, Caroline walked out of the kitchen and back to the front door. She touched Andie's forearm gently at the front step. "Good luck, really." And her smile was genuine.

***

Andie awoke to a tap on her bedroom door. The sun had risen and warmed her room, and she knew it must be close to midday. She had been in bed for almost twelve hours. Her body ached. She grunted audibly enough for the door-knocker to hear her. "You alive, Andie?" She grunted again. George opened the door a fraction and stuck his head in. "Delivery just came for you."

"What?" She was out of bed and pushing past George before he had time to answer. A box of flowers with a white card. She opened the card while George, who had evidently also been disturbed from bed by the delivery, leaned on the counter and yawned loudly.

"Whosifrom?"

"Caroline." She stuck the card back into the box and slid down to sit on the cold floor.

"You okay?" George asked, sliding down to sit beside her.

"I think I'm having a crisis of faith."

"Faith in what?"

"In women." She stared at the oven door, greased to dark orange, but she knew George was watching her. "You were right. She just chose to stop. It wasn't Lawrence, it was her. She was scared. She was too lazy to fight for it." She could not bring herself to meet his eyes, but she needed to keep talking. "While I was growing up, I was determined to believe that women had the same ambition and drive as men, and that society just refused to allow them an adequate place. Celine seemed to be proof of that. But maybe she was the exception and most women are actually willingly stepping aside, choosing not to compete, choosing to remove themselves from the conversation. Why are so few women prepared to value their intellectual contributions over their – reproductive ones? I'm so tired of people needing to be convinced that women are ambitious. There should be so much evidence that it's beyond doubt by now. We've been allowed in universities for a hundred years, where did all those graduates go?"

"Hang on, hang on, I know I gave you a hard time the

other night. But I didn't mean all women are lazy, just you and Caroline!" He gave her a friendly dig in the ribs but she could not bring herself to smile. "Look, you're just blind. They're all online, these women you're railing against. It's the only slightly even playing-field there is. Google any topic you want and you'll find evidence that women both have opinions about it and are expressing those opinions publicly, where they don't have to compete so much. Not all women slink off the face of the earth when they get married, and not all women who don't get married contribute anything very useful to the world, anyway. I think you're looking around for someone to blame and deciding it's entirely the fault of the sisterhood."

"Isn't that what you were saying?"

"No! Jesus, Andie. You're looking at an individual, Caroline, and somehow projecting her motivations onto all women. You can't do that. I mean, Charlotte gave up too. Were her motivations the same?"

"No, she just lost interest, apparently."

"And Caroline wanted to be with Lawrence?" He asked.

"And be well-fed," Andie said, trying to force a smile. George laughed. "The problem is," she continued, "that the lives of women who just lost interest, or decided to prioritise other things, look the same as women who weren't really given a chance. Maybe it just looks like there's a lack of opportunity and support, but really a lot of women don't even want it."

"Not all men get to do what they want to, either, you

know. You can't look at Lawrence and say, well he got to do what he wants, it must be because he's a man."

"I know that. But walk into any gallery, go to any music festival or any cinema, or look at any literary prize list and there are just so many men. It's depressing." After a few moments Andie looked up at him, shaking her head slightly. "The world's just a bit fucked really, isn't it?"

"That's the spirit," he said, but he was looking at her closely, seriously.

"What?" She asked.

"Can I ask you something?"

"Okay," she said, hesitantly.

"Your mother left to follow her dreams."

"That's not a question."

"Don't you think that maybe you're now trying to figure out why other women stay?"

She flapped her hand dismissively. "Of course I want to know why they stay! But more than that, I want to know why staying in a relationship so often seems to mean forgoing creative ambition. My mother had to *leave,* George, not just the family but the country! That's how stifling we were –" her voice cracked and she looked away, trying to hide her sudden tears.

"Oh come on," George said, though his voice was gentle. "Look, you know that I love your family, and Joey, but I can't really see him being the supportive type. Not really. Looking after the kids and house, sure, but the extra things – creating space, that constant unquestioning encouragement

A Perilous Margin

and belief – I can't imagine him doing that." He looked apologetic as he said it, as though she might be offended but Andie nodded, feeling the tears start to come.

"That's what he told her," she said. "The family had to come first. So instead, she put us last."

George put his arm around her shoulders and she leant into him, closing her eyes, willing the tears away. "Not all men are like that," he said quietly. "I meant what I said the other night. You were so talented. You probably still are, you just don't try anymore."

She looked at him, feeling the ambition she had ignored for so long, the absolute need to write that she had pretended wasn't real, begin raising its head.

***

Hollow-eyed students were rushing through the campus to hand in final assignments, the sun glared off faces which had seen nothing but computer screens for weeks. Shining out of the desperation were the students who had already finished. Their skin glowed with the promise of the approaching summer and long holiday. Their laughter sat over the campus, calling to those students still hauling themselves towards the end. The student bar was overflowing, alcohol fresh on the morning air, precious student allowances being stretched to cover just one more discounted burrito.

The tutorial room in which Andie was sitting replicated the atmosphere of the campus: most of the students had completed their presentations, today they were here to listen to the last two. Andie was holding her notes in one hand, rereading them although she knew them back to front. The general chatter, even louder than usual, was not enough to distract her. Time seemed extra fluid when she was stressed and, within moments, Marco had invited her to the front to deliver her presentation.

"For my assignment," she began wishing her voice would stop trembling. She saw Manuel's look of surprise at her obvious nerves. "I interviewed Lawrence McGovernor and his wife Caroline." This seemed to catch the attention of the seven students in the room. They knew the name, and she was the only one to interview two people. She continued speaking into the silence. "Lawrence McGovernor is one of Australia's most successful painters. He met his wife Caroline here at Sydney University in the seventies. Caroline was also studying visual arts and won an award here for one of her sculptures. I began by looking at the relationship between art and institutions, using Lawrence's several decades of exhibiting as a basis. Once I had spoken to Caroline, however, I began to think about how marriage was a non-artistic world for her, but not for him. I ended up combining both topics to look at why Lawrence was able to continue creating art while married when Caroline couldn't, but also why institutions seemed much more willing to exhibit Lawrence's work than Caroline's even after purchasing some of her sculptures. I looked at the way that institutional bias influenced Caroline's marriage and contributed to it becoming a non-artistic world for her but not for Lawrence." She saw Manuel roll his eyes slightly and, remembering his contribution to the women and art tutorial, tried to ignore him. There were five women in the room and two men, plus Marco, and she decided to direct her presentation to the women. She immediately felt her nerves subside somewhat.

Andie knew what she had to do when she returned home. Her room was cold: the temperature always dropped once the sun sank and the evening star appeared. She sat on the floor, a piece of paper clasped in her shaking hand. The words on the paper shimmered in front of her. I wrote this, she thought to herself. It had been years since she had read her own work. She had filed it away when she left Leon, keeping it carefully enclosed in a non-transparent folder. Since then it had lain in her bottom drawer, kept company by old bills, swimming goggles, foreign coins.

Now it was in front of her and the effect was surprising. She had hidden it away in a state of dejection, self-hatred, complete and utter frustration at her lack of talent. And now, re-reading it, the words appeared smooth, glassy almost, beautiful. It was not perfect, and certainly not ready for publication, but it was the beginning of something. She had written this particular one, she remembered, over a weekend when Leon was away. It was near the end of their relationship and he had gone away to a dental conference. He had told her to think about what it was she wanted while he was away. And, in defiance, she had spent the weekend writing. One weekend and she had expected to achieve her best, something worthy of the greats if she was going to be great.

Her knees creaked as she stood, taping the paper beside the printed photos of Lawrence and Caroline's works. She stood, staring at the three pieces of paper. As a final year project, Caroline's sculpture would have taken the best part of six months. Lawrence had been in his thirties when he had completed his, and had taken close to a year to finish it. And now hers, Andie's, sitting there unobtrusively beside two great works, holding its own despite how young she had been and how quickly she had thrown it aside. Her hands spasmed as she removed the hairband from her ponytail and ran her fingers through the tangled mess. She heard George's keys jangle as he opened the front door. He appeared in her doorway, his bag pulling his shoulder down. His hair was plastered against his face. "Fucking Sydney and its four fucking seasons in a day."

"Buy an umbrella, George, it's not that hard," She smiled and handed him a towel.

"Did you have any more interviews today?"

"No, I did my presentation actually. So it's all over."

"No more dinner invitations either, then?"

"I can only hope!" She took the slightly damp towel back from him and hung it over the back of a chair. She could feel him studying her.

"Did you get what you wanted?" He asked, stepping closer and brushing the hair off her shoulder.

"I guess so." She didn't move away. "I got an unjust and often depressing world, but perhaps that is what I was meant to get. Messy ideas flowing from messy choices." She could not meet his eyes. He nodded slowly, stepped closer and hugged her. His skin was cold but his body radiated heat.

"Is that one of your stories?" he said, and when she looked at him she saw him staring at the paper taped to the wall.

"Yes. I'm thinking of continuing with it. Fixing it up."

He looked down at her and smiled. She could feel his breath on her cheek. "A bit of hard work can go a long way, as my father used to say," he murmured. With a sigh, he stepped away, letting her go. She felt a pull of disappointment.

"You're actually really lucky, you know," he said without looking at her.

"What do you mean?"

"You know there is something that you want to do. And you're decent at it. Your secret passion is doable, and it's only secret because you keep it like that."

"And what's your secret passion?"

"That's just it, I don't have one. You talk about how you wish you were better, or more recognised. More successful. But just having something that calls to you, you're lucky. We pretend, for some reason, that everyone has that. But some of us don't. I don't."

"That's not true! You're on your way to being some hotshot political analyst, I know you are."

"Perhaps. Maybe I'll spend my life commenting on changes that other people are making, but I will never actually make any of my own. That's for you, and your kind to do. While me and my kind mercilessly tear you down." He grinned at her, but it was not a happy smile.

"You just wait. I can see great things in store for you."

He shrugged. He was not asking for pity, or a morale boost. "We can't all be great."

TWENTY-EIGHT

"Just relax, it'll be fine," Caroline said but Lawrence snarled and turned away. It was the worst thing to say to someone who was panicked. His shirt, she saw before he put on his suit jacket, was already stained with sweat. Once he was at the gallery his public persona would emerge, and he would be the charming artist everyone knew. These last few hours though had been Caroline's alone to deal with. Her tension was not helped by her dress which was different to her usual style. She had bought it on a rare whim. A pale mauve, more formal than she had worn to an exhibition opening in years, and too young. The silken material grabbed at the swell of flesh over her hips and she felt her arms wobble. She also had to wear heels with it, low ones but still, she was unused to it and she felt the muscles over her knees tremble from the permanent contraction.

The sunlight in the kitchen was just beginning to fade after the hot day. It was the first day that truly felt like summer. It smelt of Christmas, of the beach. But it had been overshadowed by the sour mood which had attached itself to Lawrence the night before. For a few days he had been on a high, happy and enthusiastic and laughing. The night before had been the brick wall of reality, however, and over dinner he had visibly changed, the smile leaving in place a scowl, his shoulders slumping. And now, the sun was setting and they were running late. He was expected to be late, of course, he had that reputation by now. But Caroline, a punctual person, became edgy as the clock moved further past the time they were supposed to be there.

His jacket snapped through his fingers as he adjusted it and she could hear his huff of annoyance as he left the kitchen. The front door was thrown against the wall and the screech of the fly-screen told her that he had left the house. She drank the last of her white wine and snatched the keys from the hook. Tonight, she did not want to be responsible for looking after his moods. She felt as though she needed all her energy for herself. She knew that Andie planned to attend and was worried that she would throw herself at the younger woman's feet, begging forgiveness. Even if she controlled herself, Andie had the look of someone who could read every impulse. Would it show on her face that she had lied during their last conversation? That the peace she had claimed to have reached was still taunting her, just out of reach?

Lawrence was already in the passenger seat of the waiting taxi, his phone held up to his face as he furiously jabbed at the screen with his finger. She slammed the car door shut. The taxi driver was quiet as they took their seats and stayed silent as he carefully moved the car into reverse and began the drive into the city. Looking at the back of Lawrence's head, resolutely bowed towards his phone, caused a new wave of frustration within Caroline. She forced herself to stare out of the window at the cars snaking themselves along the road in the growing darkness.

When they arrived at the gallery Lawrence opened his

A Perilous Margin

door immediately. The driver looked out after him, then glanced back at Caroline. "He is a busy man, is he?" She smiled thinly in agreement and handed over some cash, enough for the fare and a generous tip. Sometimes, when Lawrence was being a bastard, being kind gave her an extra thrill of superiority.

The taxi had dropped them just around the corner, and Lawrence was now skulking in the shadows, glancing up at the gallery from time to time. They were supposed to arrive together in a show of marital support. Caroline took his arm silently and they walked in together.

A burst of sound greeted them and smiling faces swam in front of Caroline's eyes. The happiness was so extreme she could not help but think it must be fake. Lawrence's arm relaxed around her for a moment before he let her go and continued walking alone. Sylvia was at his side in an instant, her already long frame elongated further by her black dress. She threw a quick smile over her shoulder at Caroline before ushering Lawrence into the crowd. Caroline turned and made for the drinks table. She could hear Lawrence's voice booming over the wave of people surrounding him. His mood had soared and now he was in full flight. She took a glass of champagne and moved towards the back of the main space, smiling at various greetings but not stopping to talk.

The room was dimmed more than strictly necessary, although the contrast with the spotlights which shone on the paintings did create a powerful atmosphere. Caroline had seen many of the paintings before, in passing, but had yet to stop and try to appreciate them. As always, the idea of strangers seeing her studying her husband's paintings was disconcerting, and she barely allowed her eyes to flick to the sides. Her legs felt gummy in self-consciousness as she walked.

A group of three young, twenty-somethings passed her on their way out for a smoke, their cigarettes already dangling from their lips. A woman had emerged from behind the make-shift bar to begin collecting glasses. Her fringe obscured her eyebrows and fluttered over her eyelids, her voice, as she excused herself with a laugh, was rough. Her sheer black blouse was catching the eye of everyone she squeezed by, a relaxed hand on an elbow here and there to make room for herself. Caroline had always wanted to operate with such assured sex appeal. The time to learn that, she reminded herself, was long gone.

Penny was standing in a corner with a small man whose rosy face gleamed with sweat. The man was talking animatedly, though Penny looked bored and her gaze was roaming the room. She spotted Caroline and waved her over. The man paused politely and looked enquiringly at Caroline as she approached. "Good turn out," Penny said, obviously aware that she was cutting off the man's story. He blinked quickly, then turned and left. The two women stood side by side, gazing around at the room. Some familiar faces, now lined with decades, were around, but most seemed unfamiliar. A face flickered in and out of Caroline's line of vision and she grabbed Penny's arm.

"Wha –?" Penny almost said before she, too, saw the familiar face. Her hair had greyed at the sides, a natural colour that few women, including Caroline, would allow to grow, but it had the tell-tale curls around her ears. She now wore glasses, thick black frames sitting in squares around her eyes, and she was smiling, something that used to be a rarity. Even in the darkness of the room, she was easily recognisable. "Bridget!" Penny called loudly, causing several people to look up, including Lawrence, who had been standing with his back to the entrance. It took Caroline a moment to decide she no longer wanted to be there. She didn't want to see Lawrence's surprised delight or, even worse, his lack of surprise. Had he known she was coming? While Penny was distracted, Caroline escaped to a side room. She stood, trying to catch her breath, staring at a painting without really seeing it.

A hand came from behind her to clasp her elbow. She saw a flash of powder-blue nails before she turned and Lucy's face appeared, beaming brightly. "Caroline!" Caroline felt herself freeze as Lucy hugged her. "I'm so glad to see you! Isn't this just fantastic?" Her enthusiasm was loud.

"Hi, Lucy, I'm glad you could come."

"Oh I wouldn't have missed it for the world! When Lawrence gave me the invitation I just couldn't resist, you know? I brought a friend actually," Lucy peered around then shrugged, "I guess she's in the loo or something. She isn't a big art fan, actually," she rolled her eyes. "But I promised to introduce her to Lawrence anyway. You know, he's been such a help to me lately! I don't know how I would have passed my last project if it wasn't for his guidance." Lucy grinned widely as Caroline was pulled from her polite nodding with a snap.

"You've been meeting with Lawrence?"

"Of course, he's just been fantastic. I thought you must have said something to him, after all? Seeing his works in progress was just so inspiring, and to go from that to here, with actual finished products! It's like a miracle! Oh there's my friend now, I'd better go save her. It was nice to see you, Caroline!" And with another arm squeeze, Lucy left. Caroline remained where she was, feeling like she was swaying slightly. Realising through her daze that she probably looked strange she took a step forward and stumbled on her heel. A hand caught her elbow in support, the nails short and chipped, and she looked up into Andie's familiar wide face.

"Oh, Andie."

"Hang on there, I've got you," Andie said, gesturing to the strap which had slid off the back of Caroline's heel and was causing her shoe to flap against the floor. Caroline held firmly to the young woman's arm and adjusted her shoe.

As she straightened she managed to say, "Thank you," although she heard her voice waver.

"Are you okay?" Andie asked, her eyes wide in concern as Caroline stumbled again. Caroline shuffled slowly over to the wall and leant against it. She closed her eyes but she could feel Andie's presence with her. "Would you like some water? Or should I find Lawrence?"

"No," Caroline reached out and grasped Andie's hand tightly. "Don't find Lawrence."

"Okay, okay I'll just stay here." Caroline gripped Andie's hand, and felt the young woman's palm begin to sweat. She could not bear to open her eyes, to see the concern, or the impatience to get away.

"Stability," Caroline heard herself say, "is not as stable as it sounds." She placed a hand over her heart and could feel it racing. She opened her eyes and saw Andie looking at her in concern. "If I had trusted myself, I could have done more." She spoke slowly, willing Andie to understand. "Do you see? It wasn't supporting him that was the problem, it was trusting myself to – be okay. To be okay even if I wasn't extraordinary." Andie had stopped nodding but Caroline felt herself regain some composure, and suddenly wanted to be away. She squeezed Andie's hand briefly before letting it go. "Anyway, it is what it is. I'm glad you could come," she smiled at the face still creased in concern and looked around. She saw an emergency exit door propped open and left Andie standing by the wall.

A young man in a black uniform was leaning against a fence, smoking. He straightened quickly at her arrival. There was an awkward pause as they waited to see what the other would do. After a few moments, he held out the pack of cigarettes. She took one and he held his lighter up for her. She smiled and walked a few steps away from the gallery.

She heard the door screech as he went back into the gallery. She breathed deeply and felt her heartrate retreat back to normalcy. The smoke created a cloud around her face. It had been a long time since she last smoked. The lights from the city multiplied in front of her as her eyes adjusted to the darkness. She could still hear the exhibition. She wondered who Bridget was talking to. She made the cigarette last as long as she could. Just as she was stubbing it out and looking for a bin, Penny appeared. She looked at the now dead cigarette in Caroline's hands but didn't mention it. "The speeches are starting," she said.

They returned to the largest of the exhibition rooms, Caroline's stomach tensed with nerves. A woman, Sylvia's boss, whose name Caroline could not remember, was giving a speech. Bridget was standing at the front of the crowd.

"I didn't know she was coming," Caroline said, her voice low, for Penny's ears only, as an explanation for her behaviour.

"Neither did I," Penny said, standing close to Caroline so she could feel her friend's warmth.

The woman speaking seemed unused to the microphone and kept spitting into it with bursts of sound. It was a relief when Lawrence took the stage. His voice was loud but its depth allowed it to carry over the room gently. He gave thanks to the gallery for their help, he made self-deprecating jokes about being a temperamental artist which the audience laughed at. He thanked everyone for coming. Caroline saw his gaze linger on Bridget at the front but then

A Perilous Margin

he turned, his eyes searching for Caroline's. "And a special thank you to my wife, who has always been my biggest supporter." He gave a wave and stepped away from the microphone.

Her gaze followed Lawrence as he moved from the stage to join Bridget. Penny's hand moved to clasp Caroline firmly around the waist, not in restraint but in comfort. They stood together, studying the pair. The spotlight from the stage was on them, and under the harsh lighting, Caroline realised with surprise that Bridget was middle-aged. Of course she was, because they all were, but seeing the woman who had been the pinnacle of youthful beauty looking suddenly old almost made her laugh. Her face had wrinkles and was no longer luminous, her neck had folds of skin, bags hung from her eyes. Not only did she look old, she looked like it had been a tough couple of decades. And Caroline really did laugh then. She had made it, just like that. She had kept Lawrence for all these years and now the idea that Bridget, with her grey hair and thickened waist, could be some kind of threat was absurd. She turned to Penny, who looked surprised by her laughter.

"We're getting old, aren't we Penny?"

Penny glanced back at Bridget and seemed to realise what Caroline had seen. She smiled. "Yeah, Car, I guess we are. She more than the rest of us!"

They laughed, not entirely with amusement. I have survived, Caroline thought to herself, and the relief was almost physical. She turned her back so she could no longer see Lawrence and Bridget and instead her eyes found Sylvia, and a thought occurred to her. She squeezed Penny's hand and felt her friend return the action. That small sign of support gave her the courage to follow through on her thought. She approached Sylvia, with no regrets about her own aging and stooped frame, feeling them as proof of her endurance. She held out a hand. "Congratulations, Sylvia," she said. "It's a wonderful opening."

"Caroline, how good to see you again. Thank you, as you know Lawrence has been working very hard with us."

"Mmm," Caroline said, not really listening. "Sylvia, I believe some of my old work is still here."

"Oh, yes it is."

"I'd like to arrange to buy it back. You understand, I'm sure."

"Of course, although to be honest I'm not sure you will find much interest in it. Not that it isn't very good, it is of course that's why the gallery bought it. But it is a bit out of date now." The woman's smile was slick, fully aware of the insults she was giving.

Caroline ignored her. "Well, this is not the only gallery in Sydney. I work at Peacock's in Pyrmont, I'm sure they will be interested. I'll arrange the transfer later this week," and Caroline left, a surge of energy she had not felt for years coursing through her.

It was only later, sitting in a taxi alone while Lawrence continued on at the gallery, that Caroline felt her amusement, her energy, deflate. She had avoided the genetic lottery which had claimed her mother and Grace, her approaching sixtieth birthday meant she had already outlived both of them. And Lucy and those other young women with whom Lawrence had never done anything but flirt, were so clearly not a threat. Maybe they never had been after Bridget, who she, Caroline, had also outlasted. Caroline knew she would start again, building her work and forcing the world to take notice, but she couldn't help feeling the thirty years of unnecessary anxiety sitting behind her. Perhaps it was meant to be like this, perhaps she had to be certain before she could be confident in herself, confident in her talent and, most importantly, confident in her ability to say something worth listening to.

EPILOGUE

New Year's Day 2014

Andie's tea shimmers on the coffee table as George's foot thumps the floor, keeping time with Charlotte's viola. Andie and Joey sing along quietly: it is Scarborough Fair by Simon and Garfunkel, one of the songs Celine used to sing to them.

"Sshhh," George says suddenly and leans forward to turn up the radio which is playing from the laptop on the coffee table. The announcer is speaking and they all pause to listen, Andie unable to meet anyone's gaze.

"The first piece which is going to be read is by a talented young writer from Sydney," the announcer says, his voice gravelly. "This is her first time as a finalist in a competition and we are honoured to have her work included today. This is A Night Time's Creeping by Andrea Hawken, read by Samuel Jones."

The room is still, no one seems to be breathing. The actor's voice is smooth and not what she is expecting but she forces herself not to focus on the strangeness. Hearing her words coming from the radio and seeing her family listen to them makes her want to squirm but she keeps still, worried that a rustle from her clothes will drown out the words. The three minutes feel endless and then are suddenly over. George let's out a great whoop and shouts "Go Andie!" and everyone else claps and cheers, ignoring the announcer's final words of the segment.

A Perilous Margin

Joey shuts the laptop and stands up. "I think we need to celebrate that," he says gruffly and disappears into the kitchen. They can hear the clink of bottles as he rummages in the fridge. Andie meets Charlotte's eye and is relieved at the understanding in her sister's expression.

"He's proud, he might just show it oddly," Charlotte says and reaches over to squeeze her hand. "Well done, Andie, it was fantastic."

Andie exhales. In the thrill of the moment it is all she needs. George picks up the printout of the story which Andie had banned anyone from reading until they had heard it. He settles into the armchair, holding the paper tightly. Charlotte has picked up her viola again and Fi joins in this time on her violin. They have moved on from Scarborough Fair to The Only Living Boy in New York.

Andie looks around at the room, at her family. The energy they had before the broadcast seems to have disappeared, they are all quiet now. She feels like she has absorbed their energy and it is now charging around in her blood stream, exhilarating and exhausting her. Pete wanders over from where he had been leaning against the door and sits down beside her in Joey's now vacant seat. He smiles at her.

"How are you feeling?"

She feels like she could cry with relief but holds it in. "How do you do this so often?" She tries to make it sound like a joke but knows her desperation comes through.

"What, bare my soul?"

"Yes!"

He looks over to Charlotte who is showing something on the sheet music to Fi, then turns back to Andie. "It helps to have someone who thinks you're pretty great, no matter what." His gaze flicks to George who is holding her story so close to his face it looks like he could go cross-eyed. Pete leans over to her and whispers, "I don't think he's going anywhere."

THE END

About the Author

Alison Theresa grew up in Canberra, Australia. She graduated from University of Sydney and now lives and works in London. This is her first novel.